All at once a formation of jets swooped toward them, partnered by the huge roar of the engines.

Little Jake laughed and pointed at the planes. "Daddy. Daddy!"

Celia shook her head. How many times had she lived through this scene? Ships launched and docked, planes took off and landed…her life with Mack seemed to be a never-ending parade of hellos and goodbyes.

The squadron flew in, the band played and the families cheered as pilots and crew hopped down to the tarmac.

"Mack!" He heard her voice, then saw her wave. A big grin broke out on his face and he jogged in their direction.

"Jakester!" Lifting the boy out of Celia's arms, Mack gave him a big hug, then turned to his wife. "Hi, gorgeous. How are you?"

"Much better now." She put her arms around his neck and stood on tiptoe. "Welcome home."

"Not quite home yet." Mack bent his head and kissed her, searching for the real welcome in Celia's soft mouth.

Her lips warmed, responding with the passion he knew she could give. "That's right," Mack murmured. "Now I'm home."

Dear Reader,

When people ask "Where do you get your ideas?" I have a number of different answers, depending on the story. For *The Scrapbook,* I have to say that parts of my life have served as inspiration. My husband graduated from the U.S. Naval Academy, and I was a Navy wife for twenty years. We lived in many of the settings that appear in this story, including California, Florida and Virginia. Here and there, an experience similar to mine may have crept into the book.

But this story really belongs to Celia and Mack Butler, newlyweds who set out together on the great adventure of Navy life. Maintaining romance within a lifelong relationship is challenging enough. A military career, with its frequent separations and the constant call of duty, presents unique problems but also offers remarkable rewards. As Celia and Mack discover their individual strengths, they also learn to depend on each other for comfort, support and, best of all, unending love.

I am thrilled to be part of Harlequin's Everlasting Love series. I hope you enjoy *The Scrapbook,* along with the other offerings from this new line of romantic stories.

All the best,

Lynnette Kent

The Scrapbook

Lynnette Kent

TORONTO • NEW YORK • LONDON
AMSTERDAM • PARIS • SYDNEY • HAMBURG
STOCKHOLM • ATHENS • TOKYO • MILAN • MADRID
PRAGUE • WARSAW • BUDAPEST • AUCKLAND

ISBN-13: 978-0-373-65411-6
ISBN-10:   0-373-65411-1

THE SCRAPBOOK

This edition published by arrangement with Harlequin Books S.A.

® and TM are trademarks of the publisher. Trademarks indicated with ® are registered in the United States Patent and Trademark Office, the Canadian Trade Marks Office and in other countries.

www.eHarlequin.com

Printed in U.S.A.

ABOUT THE AUTHOR

Lynnette Kent began writing her first romance in the fourth grade, about a ship's stowaway who falls in love with her captain, Christopher Columbus. Years of scribbling later, her husband suggested she write "one of those Harlequin romances" she loved to read. With his patience and her two daughters' support, Lynnette realized her dream of being a published novelist. She now lives in North Carolina, where she divides her time between books—writing and reading—and the horses she adores. Feel free to contact Lynnette via her Web site, www.lynnette-kent.com, or with a letter to PMB 304, Westwood Shopping Center, Fayetteville, NC 28314.

Books by Lynette Kent

HARLEQUIN SUPERROMANCE

★Home to Loveless County
★★The Brennan Brothers
†At the Carolina Diner

To my own Navy brats, Elizabeth and Rebecca, who endured the many moves with style and good humor, and who are now beginning their own life journeys.

Bon voyage!

Prologue

After searching the backyard and most of the house, Jake Butler finally found his girlfriend, Avery, in the family room. She looked up as he came in.

"I got tired of all the noise out by the pool," she said with her shy smile. "I needed some quiet."

He grinned as he sat down beside her on the couch. "I asked my mom why we had to invite so many people to Dad's retirement party. She said they'd made a thousand friends in his years with the Navy. I think they're all here tonight."

Avery pointed to the big album on her lap. "I found this on the coffee table. I hope it's okay if I look at it."

"Sure." Jake reached over and opened the cover. "That's the scrapbook mom's been keeping ever since she and Dad got married. Just about everything that's ever happened to our family is in there."

He turned to the first page. "See, it all started with their wedding…"

Chapter 1

Our Wedding Day
May 22, 1985
We posed for this picture at the top of the Naval Academy
Chapel steps, and a second one, with a kiss, underneath
the arch of swords. Then one more at the bottom of the
steps, with Mack's friends in a double row behind us,
swords still raised—six handsome men wearing brilliant
white.

In Celia's opinion, her new husband outshone them all. The high-collared dress uniform dramatized Mack's dark brown hair, bright blue eyes and tanned skin. Standing next to her groom, she felt like a sparrow perched beside an eagle. A pregnant sparrow.

Not obviously, thank goodness. She was only three months along, so the princess lines of her gown camouflaged her slight belly bump. The baby would stay a secret for a little while longer…a secret from everyone but the groom. If she hadn't told him, her dream wedding might have remained only that—a wistful dream.

She'd broken the news six weeks ago, while they'd waited for pizza during their usual Saturday night date. Mack had stared at her as if she'd sprouted two heads. "You're…pregnant?"

Celia nodded. "The baby's due in November. Around Thanksgiving."

"But…" He raked a hand through his hair, and the diamond in his USNA class ring flashed fire under the restaurant lights. "Are you sure…?"

Why wouldn't he hope she was mistaken? She had, herself, until the third test—like the first two—came up positive. "Yes, I'm sure."

Mack looked at his hands, pressed flat on the tabletop. His cheeks flushed red under his tan. "But…how could this happen? I mean, we used—"

"Shh!" She glanced at the crowded tables around them. "I don't know how it happened. I guess something went wrong."

He snorted and shook his head. "You can say that again."

Aggravation was not the reaction she'd hoped for. "Forget I said anything." She surged out of her chair. "I'm sorry I bothered you. Have a nice life."

"Celia—" Mack grabbed for her hand.

She jerked away, feeling her clammy skin slide against

his. With her arms wrapped across her churning stomach, she stumbled across the room, reaching the exit just as the door opened from outside. The newcomer barreled in, stepping on Celia's foot and knocking her sideways in the process. She knew an instant of fear before her knees buckled and the world mercifully went black.

Mack arrived in time to keep the unconscious Celia from hitting the floor. She wilted against him, practically weightless.

"I called 9-1-1." Timmy, the owner of the place, used two fingers to brush a honey-gold curl out of Celia's pale face. "Should be here in five minutes."

"She's already coming around," Mack said. Her forehead creased, and she lifted a defensive hand to ward off…what?

Timmy clicked his tongue. "You oughta get her checked out. I don't want to get sued."

"You won't get sued." Looking down again, he saw her long, dark lashes flutter. "Celia? Celia, it's okay. I've got you."

At the sound of his voice, she opened her brown eyes wide. Panic flooded into her face, and her body stiffened in his hold.

"Shh, shh." Mack rested her weight on his knee and cupped her cheek with his free hand. "Relax, honey. I'm going to take care of you. I'll take care of everything. I promise."

"P-put me down," she whispered. "I want to go h-home."

He couldn't let her go, not until they'd had a chance to talk. "Let's get you checked out by a doctor first. The ambulance is right outside." Red lights flashed through the narrow windows on either side of the door.

"No." She clutched at the front of his shirt. "Please, Mack, no…"

Despite her protests, the EMTs strapped Celia to a gurney and locked her inside the back of their truck. Mack paid for the pizza they hadn't touched, took the pie with him and drove to the hospital, cursing himself and praying for a chance to make things right.

He just hadn't gotten around to considering the specifics of getting married, that was all. Only six weeks from finishing his last year at the Academy, he was thinking about taking exams, about interviews for flight school, about graduation. He'd assumed his future would include Celia, of course. But the first months of aviation training were tough. He'd intended to get firmly settled into his career as a Navy pilot before asking her to be his wife.

Tonight, making wedding plans had moved to the top of his priority list. For one thing, if the Academy found out he'd gotten a girl pregnant before graduation, he'd be out in the street on his butt in a matter of minutes. *Kiss that carrier command goodbye, Butler.*

As an officer and a gentleman, he owed Celia every possible consideration. More important, his Irish Catholic mother would flay him alive if he fathered a child and didn't marry the mother.

What tortured him, though, was remembering the hurt in Celia's sweet brown eyes when she'd thought he didn't care about the baby. *Their* baby. For a moment, she'd believed that he would leave her to take on this responsibility alone. He must not have done a good job of convincing her he loved her, if she could reach such a conclusion so quickly.

He intended to correct that mistake right away.

Even in a small town like Annapolis, Saturday night meant chaos in the emergency room. The waiting area was standing room only, and several patients had been stashed on gurneys in a hallway. One of them was Celia.

"Mack." She started to sit up as he took her hand. "I don't need this. Please, just take me home."

He eased her back to the pillow. "I need to know you're okay. It won't take long once we've got somebody's attention."

"That could take all night." She rolled her head from side to side. "I don't want to stay here all night."

"You won't." Mack hitched a hip onto the gurney beside hers. "Meanwhile, we can plan our wedding."

Celia stared at him, her mouth open. "Wedding? What are you talking about?"

Mack slipped his class ring onto her middle finger, where it hung loosely. "Will you marry me, Celia Monroe?"

She pulled her finger out of the ring and her hand away from his. "No. I will not." People in the hallway glanced at them, and she lowered her voice. "I am not going to marry you just because I'm pregnant."

He stared at her from under lowered eyebrows. "There's no chance you're having an abortion. None at all."

"Of course not!"

"What are your other options?"

"I…" She looked at the wall beside her. "We'll be fine. You don't have to worry."

Mack pressed his point home. "Then why tell me? Why did I need to know, if you didn't want to get married?"

Celia turned her whole body away from him, curling up into a ball. Her shoulders shook with the force of her sobs. She flinched when Mack laid his hand on her shoulder.

He maintained the contact. "Celia, honey, I am not going to desert you and our baby. We're going to get married right after graduation. You'll go with me to Norfolk, and then to Pensacola when I start flight school. That's all there is to it." Leaning close, he kissed her cheek, then drew back a little and pulled her around to face him. "I love you." He held her gaze with his own. "And I want to take care of you. I want us to take care of each other."

Celia couldn't look away. Mack's eyes were Chesapeake-blue, as mesmerizing as the bay on a summer afternoon. Like his Irish ancestors, he could talk the sun out of the sky when he put his mind to it. Six months ago, he'd talked her out of her virginity and now…now he wanted to marry her. How was she supposed to say no when this was what she'd longed for since their very first kiss?

"Yes, Mack" she said softly. "I will marry you."

Celia and Mack
Dancing at their Wedding Reception
Lucky for us, the weather was gorgeous—sunny, warm

but not hot. We left the chapel and drove across the Severn River to a state park, where the caterer had put white cloths over the picnic tables and benches. We ate strawberries, drank champagne and danced barefoot on the grass.

"If you'd given me more time," Grace Monroe said, "we could have thrown a really wonderful reception."

Celia put an arm around her mother's shoulders. "What could be better than a brilliant day with the sparkling river nearby, green grass and cold, crisp champagne?"

Grace looked at her daughter's bare feet. "You'll have grass stains on your hem. And none of our friends were able to attend on such short notice. I would have thought you'd know it takes at least six months to plan a proper wedding."

"You've done it beautifully in only four weeks." She gave her mom a squeeze. "I'm going to rescue Mack. His eyes are starting to glaze over."

She went to stand beside her husband—her husband!—as he listened to her father replay an Army-Navy football game. "The punt went deep, I ran back, and back some more…then that ball socked me in the gut. I grabbed it, started zigzagging my way…" He turned his head to look at Celia. "Hey, darlin'. Did you want something?"

"A dance." She propped her hands on her hips and looked from her dad to Mack. "Which of you handsome men will do me the honor?"

"Age before beauty." Dan Monroe took her arm and at the same time put a palm on Mack's chest to push him back a step. "You'll get to dance with her the rest of her life, son. This one's mine."

Mack laughed. "Whatever you say, sir." But he gave Celia a wink before turning toward the bar.

As they swayed to a slow tune from the forties, Celia couldn't help staring at Mack over her dad's shoulder.

"Can't take your eyes of him, can you, darlin'?"

Her cheeks heated up. "Um…no. I do love him, Daddy."

"Glad to hear that." He drew back far enough to see her face. "You're taking on a big job, being a Navy wife."

"I remember. You were gone a lot."

"And I was just an engineer, not bucking for command like Mack. That kind of ambition is more than a career, Celia. It's an obsession."

She patted her dad on the shoulder. "We'll be fine. I promise."

"Anything we can do to help, you let us know. I've got plenty of time now that I'm retired. Your mother and I will be more than willing to take care of our grand-children, no matter where you are. Just don't wait too long to get started, okay? We aren't getting any younger."

With a secret smile, Celia turned her head away and danced a little closer. *If you only knew, Daddy. If you only knew.*

Mack bolted down one glass of champagne while standing at the bar, then took another before he turned around.

"How're you holding up?" Doug Lennox clapped him on the back. "Got the wedding night jitters yet?"

"Nah." Mack hadn't told Doug, his best friend and

best man, about the baby. Loose lips sink ships, as the saying went. Talking too much could damage his career. "I wouldn't mind getting on the road, though. This standing around…"

"Yeah, it's kinda a waste of time. And how do they expect a man to drink champagne at noon? Where's the beer?"

"No beer," Mack said mournfully. "I asked."

They commiserated in silence for a minute. "I'm sorry your family couldn't be here," Doug said. "I know they would have liked to see you get married."

"Yeah." Mack shrugged. "My mom doesn't travel much, since the Parkinson's diagnosis. She wasn't feeling well enough to come down for graduation, and my step-father stayed home with her. My brothers couldn't take time off in the middle of the week."

"That's tough."

"As soon as I can take some leave, Celia and I will go up to Boston."

"Maybe that's better. You'll have more time to visit with them." Doug ran a finger underneath the high collar of his uniform jacket. "You can drink all the beer you want and you won't have to stand around for hours in this monkey suit."

Chuckling, Mack nodded. "You could be right about that!"

Despite the absence of his family, Celia had done her best to make the day special, without much help or input from him, thanks to finals and the red tape involved with graduation. At such short notice, they'd been damn lucky to get a Thursday morning wedding slot in the chapel, and then only because some poor guy's girlfriend had run away with his brother just three weeks before the ceremony. Celia had had barely enough time to issue invitations by telephone.

Mack watched her laugh at something her father said. She looked beautiful today…had he told her that? She'd pinned her dark gold curls up under a veil, and the white dress showed off her pretty shoulders and graceful neck. No, she wasn't very tall, but he remembered thinking, at the Delaware-Navy football game where he'd seen her for the first time, that she was perfectly built—round in all the right places, with slender legs and a sweet, kissable mouth. Speaking of which…

He crossed the grassy dance floor and tapped on his father-in-law's shoulder. "May I cut in, sir?"

Commander Monroe stepped back and Celia turned to Mack with her arms raised, her smile wide. "What took you so long?"

He bent his head close to hers. "Can we leave now?"

"Well…"

"Because…" He kissed her neck, just a swift peck. "I'm tired—" another kiss "—of waiting for—" one more "—you." Then he took her mouth with his.

When they came up for air, she sighed his name.

"In two hours," he whispered, "we could be in a cool, comfortable bedroom. Alone. Naked." He felt her shiver. "I promise, I'll make you very happy."

Celia drew back. "What," she asked, "are we waiting for?"

★ ★ ★

Mack and Celia
in a horsedrawn carriage in front of
the Williamsburg Inn
After the wedding, we drove south to Williamsburg,
Virginia.
We played croquet on the lawn—Mack won, of course—
and then enjoyed drinks on the stone terrace overlooking
the golf course. After dark, we ate in the elegant dining
room and danced to live music. Virginia is definitely the
place for lovers. Pure magic!

Her parents had made the reservation for them as a wedding gift.

"Oh, Mack, isn't this lovely?" Celia pivoted in the center of the room as he tipped the porter. "Eighteenth century furniture and all these gorgeous fabrics. I feel as if we've stepped back two hundred years."

He came up behind her and slipped his arms around her waist. "It's very nice," he agreed, then pressed a kiss on the curve of her shoulder. "Nice and private." His mouth traveled to her ear, where his warm breath set off a shiver along her spine.

"And just what's on your mind, Ensign Butler?" Celia smiled as his warm hand slipped under her tank top to stroke her ribs and stomach.

"Well, Mrs. Butler, I'm thinking how soft you are." His fingers drifted to the hollow between her breasts. "How sweet you smell." He nosed her hair, took a deep breath.

"White Shoulders," she told him breathlessly.

"Mmm." He kissed a path from the nape of her neck to her upper arm. "Not white. Cream, fresh cream. With freckles sprinkled like cinnamon sugar." He slipped her skirt over her hips, let the soft fabric swirl to the floor.

"It's…been a long time." Celia could feel her bones melting.

"Four weeks, four days." In one move, Mack turned her to face him and lifted her tank top over her head. He stared at her body for a long moment. "God, I've missed you."

Celia grabbed at his shoulders to keep herself standing. "Oh, Mack. I love you so much."

His kiss kept her from saying anything else. A minute later she'd unbuttoned his shirt and gotten her hands on his bare skin. The strong, smooth play of muscles across his back and shoulders left her breathless. His mouth on her breasts had her gasping.

As they stretched out together on the bed, Celia stopped worrying for the first time in more than a month. What they found together, with wandering hands and mouths, with sighs and moans of pleasure, would keep Mack happy. Her friends had never, in all their frank confessions, described this kind of endless, spellbinding desire, this brilliant cataclysm of release.

She fell asleep smiling, desperately in love with her husband, certain that the passion between them would lock their hearts together, forever.

As long as we both shall live.

Mack woke up slowly, disoriented by the strange pattern of light on the ceiling, an unfamiliar scent in the air. Then he recognized the weight on his chest as Celia's hand and arm, the tickle under his nose as her feathery curls. In the next second he acknowledged the satisfied softness of his muscles.

Married, he remembered. *For better or worse. Till death us do part.* The last piece fell into place—*a baby.* On the way. Panic surged over him, and he squeezed his eyes shut.

What did he know about being a husband, let alone a father?

His dad, the S.O.B., had decided four sons was one too many, and had walked out on the family just after Mack was born, leaving the five of them to fend for themselves. There'd been male teachers and coaches along the way—Maeve Butler had seen to that—but not until Mack was in high school had she found a man she'd trusted enough to marry.

Their father's desertion was probably why his older brothers were still single, Mack thought. And maybe why he'd put off thinking about getting married. Could he trust himself to do right by Celia and their child, or would he turn out to be an irresponsible jerk?

Like father, like son?

Chapter 2

Mack and Celia in the doorway of Unit #133,
Beach Haven Apartments, Norfolk, Virginia
June 3, 1985
Our first home! Thanks to the Navy's housing office, we
found this cute little apartment in Norfolk, just twenty
minutes from where Mack works. Only three rooms—
kitchen, living room and bedroom, plus the bath—but
that's all we need.

I can't wait to decorate!

Mack pulled into the space marked 133 and cut the
engine. "Man, what a day." He groaned and let his
head fall back against the seat. "I'm trashed."

"You worked every bit as hard as the movers did."

Celia had been doing her best to ignore her own backache and headache. She didn't want to take any kind of medicine, for the baby's sake. "And then drove for five hours. You need a shower and a good night's sleep."

"On the floor." He shook his head as he got out of the car. "I still think we should stay in a motel tonight."

"But this is our home. Why stay anywhere else?"

"Because there's no furniture? No dishes to eat off or pans to cook with?" He fished through his pockets, pulling out change, car keys, receipts. "Because I don't have the door key? Did I give it to you?"

"I don't think so." Celia felt around in her purse. "I don't have any keys."

"Maybe I left it in the car." Mack leaned through the door to search the center console, the glove compartment, the side pockets. "Where the hell did I put the key? Look in your purse again."

Kneeling, Celia emptied the contents of her bag onto the square of grass outside their only window. "No key."

Mack swore. "I've already lost the damn key. Great." He raked a hand through his hair. "Just terrific. Get back in the car, Celia. We're going to a motel."

"Did you put the key in your suitcase?" She went to the trunk of the Corvette. "Or your shaving kit?"

He glared at her across the bright red length of the car. "Let's get a room," he said, his voice leashed like a growling dog, "and I'll search every nook and cranny. Tomorrow. In daylight."

Celia shut the trunk lid slowly, carefully. She didn't want to argue with Mack. But she was tired of motel rooms and restaurant food. She wanted to be *home*. "We could check with the management. They probably have a master key."

"Fine." He put up his hands in surrender. "Let's go find the night manager. We wouldn't want to miss this opportunity to sleep on the floor."

After she gathered the contents of her purse, they walked in silence toward the office. A full moon rode high in the sky, turning the asphalt parking lot to silver and the concrete sidewalks to shimmering white.

"Virginia smells good," Celia commented. "Honeysuckle maybe."

Mack grunted in response.

"And it's not too hot. We could probably do without air-conditioning, sleep with the window open."

"Assuming we can get inside at all."

She hooked her hands through his elbow. "We will."

He stopped and looked down at her. "Are you always this obnoxiously optimistic?" The twinkle reappeared in his eyes.

Celia grinned up at him. "Pretty much all the time. Think you can stand it?"

He gave an exaggerated sigh. "It'll be a real struggle."

They found the night manager, a college kid, asleep on the office couch and none too happy about being awakened. He wanted to charge them twenty dollars for a lost key, but Mack convinced him they would find the key when the movers arrived in the morning. Grumbling, the kid stomped ahead of them to unit 133, wrenched the door open and stomped away again without waiting for a thank-you or offering to help in any way.

"Nice guy." Mack carried Celia's two giant suitcases into the bedroom. "Welcome to Norfolk and all that stuff."

"We don't have to see him again." She opened the red suitcase and took out the sheets, blankets and towels she'd packed, then turned to face the room. "Now, where should the bed go?"

"Does it matter tonight?" He set his own bag against a wall. "We can figure that out tomorrow when the actual furniture arrives."

"Or we can go ahead and decide right now." When he returned with the box of cleaning supplies they'd brought from her place in Annapolis, she was moving his duffel bag to a different wall.

"Hey, that's heavy." Mack rushed over to grab the handle. "You shouldn't be lifting that kind of weight." For the first time, he noticed how tired she looked. She squinted in the low light from the overhead bulb and kept one hand pressed against her lower back. *Oh, hell.* "Why don't you sit down and let me finish?"

She smiled at him, *dammit.* "I'm fine."

"Or better yet, go take a shower. A bath." In ten days of marriage, he'd come to realize how much his new wife enjoyed her baths.

"I will. I just want to make the bed. So move your suitcase over there."

Mack rolled his eyes and complied. Celia shook out a blanket and let it float to the floor, where it lay almost perfectly smooth. She followed with a quilt, and then pale blue sheets that made Mack's muscles ache with the anticipation of lying down. In another moment, she pulled pillows out of that heavy red suitcase he'd cursed when he lifted it into the car. Cased in pale blue, they soon rested on the makeshift bed. He wasn't sure he'd ever seen a more inviting place to sleep.

"Now I'll take a shower," Celia said, gathering her robe out of the suitcase. "A quick one. Then it'll be your turn."

Though her baths could last for hours, this time she kept her word and was finished before he got the car locked and the door closed behind him. When he peeked through the open bathroom door, he found a dry towel hanging on the rack and his shaving kit on the back of the toilet.

"Go ahead," she called from the bedroom. "I'm brushing my hair."

The thought of Celia, fresh and clean, stroking a brush through her soft curls, drove the fatigue from Mack's muscles. He took a navy shower, five minutes tops, and shaved for good measure. A pair of clean boxer shorts hung on the doorknob when he finished. He took the hint and pulled them on, then switched off the bathroom light.

Moonlight filtered through the darkness of the three inadequate rooms he'd chosen as a home for his family. To his left, the empty kitchen and living room remained cave-like. On the right, though, silver glazed the walls and floor. Across from the doorway, Celia lay on the makeshift bed, her bare shoulders gleaming.

"Come to bed," she said, in the tone that never failed to turn him on.

"Yes, ma'am." He knelt on the floor and pulled back

the top sheet to find his wife clad in only a pair of pink lace panties.

"Nice," he said hoarsely.

"Not for much longer," she said ruefully, putting a hand on her belly. "I'm getting fat."

Mack swallowed hard. He wasn't ready to think about that. "Not to me." Lying down, he gathered her into his arms. "I looked in my shaving kit. I still don't know where I put that stupid key."

Celia reached up and fingered the chain around her neck. "Jewelry box." On the chain hung the missing key. "I recall you saying you'd put it there so we'd be able to find it."

He groaned. "Yeah, I did, didn't I?" How irresponsible could he be, forgetting something so simple? "Guess I'd better put it on my key ring, so I'll know next time."

"We'll get copies made," Celia promised. "I'll have one, and we'll put one in the car and two in the house." She stroked her hand across his chest and ribs, over his hip, then reached between their bodies.

"Right now," she whispered, "we've got better things to do." A breeze drifted through the window on a beam of light. "Make love to me, Mack. Please."

"My pleasure." In a second the pink lace vanished, and he was, indeed, home.

Mack and Celia with
the Butler Family…
Maeve and her husband, William,
plus Ty, James and Colin

Boston, Massachusetts
July 4, 1985
We went to the Boston Pops concert and a simply mi-
raculous fireworks display. William gave each of us a tiny
U.S. flag to wave in time with the music.

As soon as Mack stopped the car in front of the white-shingled house, people started streaming through the door onto the porch. Celia wiped her palms on her skirt as he came around to help her out of the low seat.

"Don't look so scared," he told her, grinning. "They don't bite." His hand on her back propelled her down the sidewalk to meet his family.

Amid the handshakes and the backslapping, Celia could see that Mack's brothers were all as tall—and nearly as handsome—as Mack himself. She smiled up at them and tried to attach names to faces—James, Tyrone, Colin. Mr. Randolph, Mack's stepfather, wanted her to call him William. She was so busy concentrating, she didn't realize she'd been propelled forward until she stood before the person she was most afraid of—Mack's mother.

Maeve Randolph was willow-slim and beautiful, with a cap of black hair and bright blue eyes…Mack's eyes. "I'm so glad to meet you." She didn't bother with a handshake but simply folded Celia into a hug. "You've made my son very happy."

Drawing back, she looked Celia up and down. "And he'll be even happier soon, I see. Mack didn't tell us you were expecting."

"We just found out." Mack put an arm around each of them.

Maeve glanced up at her son with smiling, knowing eyes. "And when is the baby due?"

"Early in the New Year," he said, a little too loudly, a little too quickly. Mack had persuaded Celia that a small lie about the due date would forestall difficult questions. "Good thing we'll be in Pensacola, instead of the ice and snow up here, right? Now, where's this fine lunch spread I was promised?"

Celia wasn't surprised at the abrupt shift of subject. When she and Mack were alone together, he rarely mentioned the baby unless she did. She'd bought a couple of books on pregnancy and infants, but she'd never seen him pick one up to read. Soon she'd have to make an appointment with the obstetrical clinic at the naval hospital and start seeing a doctor. There would be tests, an ultrasound examination. Would Mack go with her? Would they shop for baby gear together, or should she plan to go by herself?

Tears welled up at the thought, just as Mack's stepfather started to give thanks for the meal. Celia squeezed her eyes shut, thankful for the excuse to hide her fears.

"We thank you, as well, for our new daughter, Mack's wife, Celia," William prayed. "A pretty girl is always welcome here."

From the opposite end of the table came a sniff of disapproval. Celia peeked through her lowered lashes and saw her new stepfather-in-law, with his eyes squeezed shut, grinning at Maeve's protest.

"Bless the grandchild she's carrying. Bless our Mack

as he begins his career in the Navy. Keep us all safe as we do our work, and grant us love at home. Amen."

Five men at the table made for a lively meal. Having grown up an only child, Celia enjoyed watching Mack spar with his brothers and his stepdad. Maeve stood her ground in the midst of the masculine tide, putting one son in his place with a quick quip, challenging her husband with the lift of an arched black brow. But as Mack and Ty squabbled over the last piece of blueberry pie, Celia, sitting closest to her mother-in-law, noticed fatigue in the curve of Maeve's shoulders, and the tired lines around her eyes.

She put her hand on the older woman's arm and felt the tremor running underneath the soft lavender sweater. "Mack and I will clean up," she said. "It's the least we can do."

"I have an even better idea." Mack got to his feet and began stacking dishes. "You two and William can go sit on the porch. The fabulous Butler boys know their way around a kitchen. Right?" He looked sternly at his brothers, who groaned and sighed. "Right?"

Pretending to complain, Mack's brothers followed his example, while William wrapped an arm around Maeve's waist and guided her to the swing on the front porch. Celia settled on a chair nearby and didn't refuse the lap blanket William offered, after spreading one over his wife's knees.

He sat down beside Maeve and stretched his arm along the back of the swing. "I don't imagine you see this kind of chilly gray weather on the Fourth of July down in Maryland and Virginia."

"More like ninety degrees, sunny and humid." Celia fingered the fringe on her blanket. "This is a lovely break from the southern summer."

"We were so sorry we couldn't see you and Mack get married," Maeve said. "I loved the pictures you sent."

"I'm sorry, too." An awkward pause lengthened while she tried to frame an explanation for the rush. "I know Mack missed having his family there, but when a spot came open at the chapel, we felt we should go ahead, since his friends would all be scattered after graduation…." She realized she was babbling, and let her words trail off.

"Perfectly understandable." William waved away her discomfort. "Especially since you're giving us a grandchild."

"Do you hope for a boy or a girl?" Maeve combed the fringe of the afghan over her knees with trembling fingers. "They can tell pretty early these days."

"I think a boy would be nice, the first time."

William laughed. "You're already thinking about the next time?"

Celia felt her cheeks heat with a blush. "Well…"

Maeve cast a reproving look at her husband. "The more babies, the better, I always say. I never regretted having four boys, not for a second."

"And Mack's bound to be a good father," William said. "He's nothing like his own dad."

That earned him another harsh glance from his wife. "I suppose Mack's told you about Charlie Butler."

"Just that he wasn't around while Mack was growing up." Celia hadn't pressed him for details, and Mack hadn't volunteered any.

"Abandoned his wife and kids," William corrected. "Left for work one morning and never came back, the bastard."

"We survived," Maeve said, with a proud lift of her chin. "More than survived. I gave my boys a good up-bringing, without any man's help."

"Because you're a remarkable woman." William sat back against the swing, letting his anger leak away. "But you didn't deserve to work so hard all your life." Taking Maeve's hand, he smoothed his fingers over her blue-veined skin. "I only wish I'd met you sooner, so I could have made things easier."

The love and concern in his face left Celia blinking back tears. His wife stroked his jawline with her free hand.

"You're here now," she said softly. "That's what matters."

Mack stepped through the screen door. "KP completed," he announced. "Time to take Celia on a tour of the old neighborhood, show her all the important landmarks of my childhood."

"Like the window in Mr. Donahue's house you broke when you were learning to pitch?" James followed him onto the porch.

"And the tree you fell out of, after betting me you could climb all the way to the top branch?" Colin leaned against the door frame.

"How about that spot out by the river where you used to take your girlfriends to neck?" Ty came around from the back of the house, carrying a garbage can. "It's collection day tomorrow, right, Mom?"

Mack shook his head. "Leave me some dignity if you don't mind, guys." He held out at hand to Celia. "So what do you want to see first—the tree I fell out of or the window I broke?"

She winked at him. "I want to see the place you took your girlfriends."

Mack's face turned a beet red as the rest of the Butler brothers roared with laughter.

The Early Birds
Mack and Mom in the garden
July 1985
Maeve gave me one of her peony blossoms that morning, and I've kept it all these years, pressed between the pages of Mack's heavy dictionary. The faded pink is sweet, but you can see the original color in this picture—a deep, vibrant rose. Gorgeous, like Maeve's whole garden!

The aroma of brewing coffee signaled that Maeve had gotten up, but Mack couldn't find her inside the house. A glance through the living room window revealed his mother seated on a small stool, weeding her front garden.

He came down the front steps with a mug in each hand. They didn't speak until they'd both downed the first few gulps.

"Mmm." His mom lifted her face to the breeze. "The only thing missing in this perfect morning was coffee. Thank you."

"You're welcome." As he had when he'd been a young boy, Mack sat cross-legged on the sidewalk running between the flower beds. "Your peonies are pretty this year."

"We had a very rainy spring. And so much snow last winter! I was afraid they might have rotted."

"Nothing in your garden would dare rot." He noted the tidiness of the beds. "James and Ty and Colin help you keep up with the work?"

She nodded. "And William provides a steady flow of advice from his chair on the porch."

They shared a grin. "William always has advice," Mack murmured.

"I like your Celia," Maeve said after a moment. "She's very sweet."

"She is." He sipped his coffee.

"Very pretty."

"Mmm-hmm."

"You're going to be a wonderful father."

He didn't say anything. After a minute she looked over. "You don't think so?"

"I'm a little short on experience."

"Most first-time fathers are." She glanced up again. "That's not what you mean, though. Is it?"

Mack hid behind a sip of coffee and a shrug. "Could be I take after Charlie Butler."

His mother's gaze hardened. "Absolutely not," she said firmly. "Even if you resemble him the most of all my sons."

A chill went down his back. He hadn't known—there had never been any pictures. "That must have made it hard on you, all these years."

"Never." Maeve gripped his arm until he felt the tips of her nails in his skin. "You were always an individual, separate from me and Charlie and your three brothers.

You always understood right and wrong, always recognized your responsibilities. I never worried about what choices you would make."

"You're a little biased, Mom, when it comes to your sons."

"I trust you, Mackenzie Butler," she said fiercely. "You should trust yourself."

Covering her hand with his palm, he squeezed gently. "I'll work on it."

Maeve held on another moment. "Love makes you strong, Mack. Strong enough to become the person you want to be." Her blue eyes shone with tears. "If you don't trust yourself, trust Celia and the love you share. That's what will see you through."

Before Mack could reply, the porch door opened and Celia stepped outside, camera in hand. "Smile, you two. What a great picture!"

They posed again, standing up. After William made breakfast for the four of them, it was time to head back to Norfolk. The Navy wanted Mack back on the job Monday morning.

"Take care of that wife of yours," William ordered as they put the luggage in the trunk. "She's a treasure."

"I don't need you to tell me that," Mack said irritably.

"Touchy, touchy." The older man punched him lightly in the arm. "You'll do fine. Just keep your priorities straight."

"What does that mean?"

"Your wife comes first, always, followed by the kids." William shut the trunk lid. "As long as you remember that principle, everything else will fall into place."

Mack thought about what he'd heard concerning Navy flight school—the intense competition, the long hours of study he would have to put in. He looked into the future, to years of overseas deployments, with months at a time spent a world apart from Celia and their child.

"Terrific," he muttered to himself, watching Celia hug Maeve in a tearful goodbye. "Married barely six weeks and I've already screwed up!"

Chapter 3

Mack's First Flight
December 1, 1985
Whiting Field, Milton, Florida
Such a small plane! Not at all military looking, with its
red nose and tail and white body. Mack assured me he'd
be as safe as if he flew in a big jetliner, but I didn't believe
him!

Mack hardly slept the night before he was scheduled to take the controls on the training flight. Even after he finally gave up studying and climbed into bed, around 2:00 a.m., his mind was still racing. Celia pretended to be asleep, but she was aware of his restlessness and the tension in his body. She drove him to work at 7:00 a.m. as usual and put on her best smile when he leaned through the window of the car to kiss her goodbye.

"Have fun," she said. "I know it'll go great!"

"Yeah. I can't wait. I've wanted to fly since I saw the Blue Angels for the first time, when I was seven." He grinned, but then he swallowed hard. "I'll see you this afternoon."

Celia watched as he squared his shoulders under the khaki uniform shirt and approached the hangar door with those long strides she loved. Now she only had ten hours to occupy until she could be with Mack again.

The baby inside her kicked almost constantly during the drive back to the entrance of the naval base. Against her impulses, Celia kept both hands on the steering wheel. "Sorry, Junior, but I'm afraid this snazzy car will head off on its own if I don't hold tight. Your daddy sure loves his Corvette."

A small foot pushed against her womb as if trying to break through. "I know, I know. We need a car that will hold you and your car seat, your stroller and diaper bag and all that stuff. I hate to bother your daddy, though, because he's studying so hard and he wants so much to get the best grades." The higher Mack ranked in the class, the more likely he would get his first choice of planes to fly—jets, of course.

Once back in civilian territory, Celia drove toward the big city of Pensacola. She'd agreed to meet several wives of Mack's classmates for breakfast at a diner with a bay view.

"We have to stick together," Ariel Hayden declared as they waited for their food. "Our men will be gone most of the time. We'll be each other's support systems."

"Damn straight." Jan Anderson blew a cloud of cigarette smoke across the table. "I had to have my mother as my Lamaze coach for the first two kids."

Celia pretended to look around the restaurant, turning her head away to avoid inhaling the fumes.

"You're expecting again?" Ariel asked.

"No, not yet." Jan winked. "But not for lack of trying."

"Are you doing Lamaze, Celia?" Roberta Willis sat on her right, fanning the air in front of them to deflect the smoke. "Is Mack going to be your coach?"

"I've gone to the first two classes." She took a sip of water. "Umm…Mack and I are practicing at home."

Ariel nodded. "Yeah, I know that routine. He sends you to class while he's studying, right? And if you're lucky, he'll take a few minutes to practice before he drops into a dead sleep."

Celia hated to confirm the accuracy of that assessment. "Well…"

"As long as he's there when the baby comes, everything will be fine." Roberta patted Celia's hand. "And you're so close to delivery, you know that'll happen while he's still in school here. How long do you have left?"

"About four weeks," she said, keeping to the fiction she and Mack had agreed upon.

"Have you got the nursery all fixed up?"

She wished she could lie. "Not yet."

"There's one of those baby superstores right down the road," Jan said. "We could run by, pick up a few things."

Celia thought of her checkbook balance. "That's okay—"

"Good idea." Ariel sliced at her pancakes with enthusiasm. "My in-laws are visiting and they've got the kids. I don't plan to go home until I absolutely can't avoid it one minute longer!"

On the drive to the superstore, Celia swore to herself that she wouldn't get carried away. She wanted to do her baby shopping with Mack. The fact that she couldn't get him away from the books and out of the house meant they hadn't even chosen a crib yet. They'd get to it in the next few weeks.

Anyway, the Corvette wouldn't hold much more than a baby outfit and a blanket or two. She simply couldn't carry anything else.

But Jan owned one of the new minivans. Ariel drove a pickup truck. And Roberta's daddy was an oil company executive in Texas, so she knew how to spend money.

By noon, the three of them had assembled the new crib and rearranged Celia's bedroom to accommodate it. Roberta stowed the green crib sheets, striped baby towels and blankets in the drawers of the matching changing table, which fit snugly into the empty space by the bathroom at the end of the tiny hallway.

"This will be perfect." Ariel stood in the bedroom, admiring the crib she'd just made up. "The natural wood looks great with your bed and dresser."

"It really does." Celia nodded, ignoring the huge ball of dread in her chest.

"When the store delivers the rocking chair, have them put it in that corner." Jan had moved the sofa to a different wall. More frightening still, she'd disconnected

Mack's stereo equipment and transferred the complicated system to the dining nook.

"Is that couch part of Mack's bachelor haul?" Roberta shook her head. "Leave it to a guy to pick brown plaid."

"We bought it after we got married." Celia felt compelled to defend Mack's choice, though she didn't like the sofa much, either. "We got a good deal. And—and brown's a fairly neutral color."

Jan, Ariel and Roberta nodded in commiseration. "Right."

"Sure."

"I know how that goes."

After all their help, Celia felt compelled to offer her friends lunch, and they accepted. She served up the pasta she'd planned for dinner that night, with garlic toast, and Mack's favorite mint chocolate chip ice cream for dessert. By the time they left, her refrigerator was empty and her house completely transformed from the one Mack had left that morning. She couldn't think of her credit card balance without feeling sick to her stomach.

But she loved washing the towels and sheets and blankets in the sweet-smelling baby detergent she'd bought on her last grocery run. And she lay on her left side on the bed for a long time, weaving dreams around the crib. Her baby would sleep here, right beside her. She could wake up in the night and watch him breathe. Or watch *her* breathe...though Celia felt sure she was carrying a boy. She and Mack hadn't talked about names yet, but she'd already christened the baby Mack, Jr. in her mind.

Afternoon traffic heading to the naval air station was

heavy and slow, and though she'd left home early, she arrived at the hangar later than Mack's usual quitting time. When he hadn't emerged after half an hour, Celia got out of the Corvette and approached the huge dark doorway, a host of butterflies migrating in her throat and stomach. She'd never been inside and wasn't sure she was allowed this close. Maybe the interior was classified or something?

But where was Mack?

"They had weather delays this morning," an older man said over his shoulder as he worked on the wheel of the airplane parked inside the hangar. "Got a late start. He should be coming down any minute." He nodded toward the door opposite the one Celia had entered. "Out there."

She couldn't believe what he was saying. "I can watch?"

He shrugged. "Sure. His first time up, he won't be at the controls for landing, anyway."

She heard the plane before she saw it, which gave her a chance to get her camera out of its bag. Not as small as she'd expected, the TC3 glinted in the sunlight as it approached the runway. Celia snapped several shots of the plane in the air and a couple as it taxied to the hangar.

Still wearing his flight helmet, Mack climbed down several rungs of the ladder from the cockpit, then turned and hopped to the ground. In the next second, he took off the big helmet, and Celia could see his wide grin, the sparks of delight in his eyes. He caught sight of her and the smile widened as he hurried in her direction, his sage-green flight suit flapping in the afternoon breeze.

The man he'd flown with caught up with him. Celia

took a couple of pictures as the two men conferred, and another when the senior officer patted Mack on the back before walking away. And she still had her camera ready when Mack pumped his fist over his head in a gesture of triumph.

Before she could say a word of greeting, he caught her in his arms and whirled her around. "Man, what a rush! I took the controls and it was like I didn't need the ground anymore—I could go anywhere, do anything." With his arm around her waist, he walked her toward the hangar. "We're going out to dinner, sweetheart, somewhere nice. Pizza or burgers won't cover this."

They ended up at a seafood restaurant on the ocean. With the new credit card balance branded on her brain, Celia kept her eye on the prices and ordered carefully. Mack ate surf and turf while taking her through his day minute by minute, explaining every detail of his preflight check, his flying time and his observation of the landing process. Celia didn't follow word for word, but she basked in his pleasure. She loved seeing him get exactly what he wanted.

After a walk on the beach, with more flight talk, they took the short drive home almost in silence. Mack seemed to have finally wound down, and he yawned a couple of times. But Celia's tension ratcheted upward with each passing mile. She should have told him over dinner, warned him about what she'd done. They hadn't had a serious argument since the night he proposed. How mad would he be?

Always the gentleman, Mack opened the door and

ushered her into the apartment ahead of him. One step over the threshold, though, he stopped dead.

"Holy hell," he said loudly. "What happened here?" The door snapped shut at his back. "Did you move this stuff yourself?"

Celia faced him from across the room. "No. Jan and Ariel and—and Roberta were here."

His jaw dropped when he caught sight of his stereo equipment over by the dining table. "You unhooked the sound system? Man, that'll take days to get straightened out again." Hands propped on his hips, he glared at her. "What's going on?"

"I bought some things. For the baby."

He didn't say anything for a moment. "What kind of things?"

"A rocking chair. It'll go in that corner, which is why Jan moved the couch and the stereo."

Mack's eyes narrowed. His mouth became a thin, straight line.

"There's a—a crib, too." Celia went into the bedroom, waiting for a breathless minute until he came to stand in the doorway, giving the crib a long stare.

"And a changing table, some blankets and towels and sheets." She chattered on nervously. "I know it was too much, but Jan and Ariel and Roberta were there, and we do need a few things to…to care for the baby properly. I could probably get a sales job during the Christmas rush… Even if I worked for just four weeks, that would pay most of it off…."

Leaving Celia still talking, Mack went back into the

hallway to look at the "changing table." For changing diapers, he gathered, opening the drawers to find three baby-size blankets striped in green and white, three fitted sheets, all green, and three towels with the same stripe as the blankets. The fabrics seemed too light to be much use—they felt like clouds against his fingertips. How fragile a baby must be, to need such delicate treatment!

He squeezed his eyes shut. God, he was tired. The physical stress of flight school, the late-night studying and the exhilaration of his first flight had drained every ounce of his energy...and allowed him to push all thoughts of the baby aside.

So Celia had done what was needed without him. What kind of husband would allow his wife to bear this burden alone?

When he returned to the bedroom, Celia stood silent and motionless by the crib, her eyes wide and worried, her lower lip trembling.

Self-contempt burned in Mack's gut. Moving carefully, he sat on the corner of the bed nearest the crib and reached for Celia's hand. "Come here, honey."

Her fingers were cold. He wrapped his palms around both of her fists. "I've been stupid and selfish."

Those big brown eyes filled with tears. "Don't say that. You've got an important job to do."

"Yeah...being a husband and a father. It's time I started living up to the requirements."

She shook her head. "No requirements, Mack. Just what you want to give."

He gathered her close, folding his arms around her

and resting his head against her big round belly. Immediately, the baby kicked at his cheek. Celia chuckled. Mack yawned until his jaw cracked.

"You should come to bed." She slipped from his hold and went to turn down the bedcovers. "You must be exhausted."

"I need to do some studying first."

"Oh, Mack. Can't you take off just tonight?"

"Nope. I have to read a couple of chapters before I go in tomorrow." He rubbed his eyes until he saw stars, then jerked to his feet. "You get to bed. I'll be in later." Fumbling a kiss onto her head somewhere, he went into the rearranged living room and pulled out his manuals.

When he woke up on the couch the next morning with the training guide lying across his face, Mack faced the fact that he'd failed his wife *and* endangered the only career he'd ever wanted.

Mackenzie Callaghan Butler, Jr.
Two hours old, with his mom
December 10, 1985
Such thick, dark hair, just like his dad! We didn't know then that those dark blue eyes would turn brown. But we always knew he'd be handsome. Through all the moves, I kept his baby identification bracelet safe. Isn't it amazing, how small his wrist was?

Mack had lost all feeling in his fingers, which were trapped in Celia's grip. "Breathe, honey. C'mon. Breathe."

The doctor tapped him on the shoulder. "Ensign Butler, could we talk for a minute?"

"No," Celia wailed. "You can't leave!"

He pried his hand free. "I'll be right back, honey. I promise. One minute."

In the hallway, Mack faced the obstetrician. "It's not going too good, is it?"

Dr. Cameron shook his head. "The baby's not making progress through the birth canal. I don't see any reason to let this go on—six hours of hard pushing is enough, even without signs of fetal distress. I want to do a C-section."

"Will Celia be okay?"

"She's a healthy girl. I think we'll have a screaming baby and a much more comfortable mom in about thirty minutes."

"No. No, no, no." When they told her, Celia jerked her head from side to side. "I can do this. I really can." Her ponytail dripped sweat; her face was swollen and flushed bright red. "Just give me a few more minutes…." She drew a breath and began to bear down. "I can do it…." Her hand groped for Mack's, took hold. He winced.

A nurse came in ten minutes later. "OR's ready." She packed up Celia's IV, detached the fetal monitor and went to the head of the bed. "Let's get you a baby."

"No, no." Celia cried all the way down the hall. "I want to do it myself!"

"You've done it," Mack said, stroking her forehead with a piece of gauze as they prepared her for the anesthetic. "You've done it for eighteen hours. Let's just get the baby, honey. Doesn't matter how."

"Mack, I wanted…" She relaxed suddenly. "Oh, my God. That's wonderful."

He looked up at the anesthesiologist, then at Celia. "What? What's going on?"

"I can't feel anything below my arms." Celia sighed. "Oh, how lovely." The nurse rolled her to her back and Celia smiled up at him. "Maybe you're right about this."

"Here we go," Dr. Cameron said. "We'll have a baby in a few minutes, Mrs. Butler."

Mack turned his back to Celia's feet and kept his eyes on her face, which shone with joy. "I can't wait," she exclaimed.

"Me, neither." Mack was surprised to realize it was the truth.

When he glanced over his shoulder a moment later, his heart stopped in his chest.

"Mack, what's wrong?" Celia had read his expression. "What is it?" She couldn't see over the screen they'd placed just above her shoulders.

"I—" Mack croaked. "I don't…"

The doctor had drawn a limp, messy creature out of the opening he'd made in the drapes placed over Celia's body. Mack could make out dark hair, but the baby looked anything but human.

"Mack?" Celia's voice rose to a hysterical pitch.

Gowned and masked, several people huddled around…it. Silence blanketed the operating room. Was this what death sounded like?

He heard a slap, like a snapped rubber band. In the next instant, a baby cried. *Their* baby.

"Oh, oh, Mack!"

He couldn't talk for the tears in his throat.

"Well, Ensign, Mrs. Butler, looks like you've got yourself a boy here." Dr. Cameron broke away from the huddle and came toward Mack, carrying a bundle of blanket about the size of a small puppy. "He's nice and big." The doctor grinned as the baby continued to cry. "With a good pair of lungs." He held out the bundle. "Congratulations."

Mack stared at the baby. He was supposed to…to hold it? What if he dropped it, before Celia even had a chance to see it…him? Mack stepped back. "Celia, here's your baby, honey."

For a second she looked up at him, hurt flaring in her eyes. Then she turned her gaze to the infant. "Oh, baby. So sweet. Just perfect." Tears ran down her cheeks. "I want to hold him."

Dr. Cameron turned back to Mack and this time forced the baby into his arms. "You'll be able to hold him real soon. Let me finish up here and we'll send you back to your room. When you've had a nap, you'll get to hold your son."

Mack stared down into a face the likes of which he'd never seen before. Tiny, wrinkled, pink, with that shock of brown-black hair. "A boy. Look, Celia, a boy!" Bending over, he showed her their son. "What's his name?"

She smiled sleepily. "Mack, Jr., of course. He looks…" she yawned "…just like his dad."

Chapter 4

Ensign and Mrs. Mack Butler and son
Christmas Day 1985
Grandmother and Granddad Monroe came to visit and
caught the three of us at our least photogenic—Mack after
an all-night study session, Mack, Jr. in one of his after-
noon colic attacks, and me still in my nightgown, with
scraggly hair and no clue what to do with my miserable
son. The tree was really pretty.

Christmas dinner was delicious, because her
mother took over the kitchen. Her dad held a
wailing Mack, Jr. for a little while so Celia could
shower, put on some decent clothes and brush her
hair. Otherwise, she'd have eaten in her wrinkled

nightgown with the milk stains on it. The baby wouldn't nurse when he got colicky, and she'd leaked all afternoon.

Now she ate with her son draped over her shoulder, finally asleep.

"Are you sure you don't want to put him down?" Her mother glanced at Celia's full plate, when everyone else had gone on to second helpings. "The poor little boy has got to be exhausted. We can pull the bassinet into the dining room and pick him up as soon as he stirs."

"I'm okay, Mom." She should have thought to put him over her right shoulder. Since she was left-handed, holding even an infant's nine pounds on that side made eating awkward.

Dan Monroe cleared his throat. "So, Mack, when's your first solo flight?"

Mack looked up from his plate. "Early in January, sir. I've done my training runs, but with the holiday, the schedule's pretty light. That's okay, though." He yawned before he could get his hand to his face. "I've still got tons of stuff to learn. The little guy there makes concentrating a challenge sometimes." He gave a tired grin and forked up a mouthful of mashed potatoes.

Dan Monroe's face stiffened. Grace raised one eyebrow, a sure sign of disapproval. Celia rushed into speech. "This dinner is terrific, Mom. I haven't cooked much this month—poor Mack's been surviving on sandwiches and carrot sticks."

"Babies do take up a lot of time," her mother said. "I

remember how terrified I was the first day your father went to work and left me home alone with you."

Celia laughed quietly. "I know what you mean. Mack picked us up at the hospital and drove us home, then had to leave right away. I had no idea what I was doing, and I couldn't stand up straight after the surgery. Poor baby cried until we both fell asleep in the rocking chair about three in the afternoon." She rubbed Mack, Jr.'s back with gentle fingers. Looking at her parents' faces, she realized that her story had not improved their moods. "We survived," she said lamely, "though Mack had to make his own dinner that night."

"And there wasn't much to work with," Mack added. "I had bacon and eggs four nights running that first week."

"Maybe you should have taken some leave," Dan Monroe growled. "Most guys do when a new kid comes."

Mack straightened up in his chair and squared his shoulders. His blue eyes flashed like steel striking stone. "Taking leave in the middle of flight training would send a signal to the brass that I'm not committed to the program. The slightest doubt about my willingness to work could cost me the command I'm shooting for." His tone softened. "You know how it is, sir. The needs of the Navy…"

Celia's dad didn't bend. "In my book, the needs of your family come first."

"But you retired as a commander, sir. I intend to make captain. Maybe even admiral, if my luck holds."

Celia gasped and heard her mother do the same. Her dad's jaw dropped. "I beg your pardon?"

Mack held up his hands in a gesture of surrender. "I

apologize, Commander. That was absolutely uncalled for. I'm exhausted, or I would never have said something so rude. You served long and honorably and I respect your career, sir." He blew out a breath. "But I want those captain's stripes, sir. I want a carrier command. Every step I take in the Navy is aimed toward that end. Celia understands, I think." He looked at her, his eyes questioning.

Celia wanted there to be no doubt about her loyalties. "Of course I do. Mack's career benefits the whole family. And the whole family will always be behind him one hundred percent."

Her dad's frown didn't lighten, and the tension at the table didn't ease. Lucky for her, Mack, Jr. chose that moment to wake up with a wail.

"Poor baby." She scooted her chair back and got to her feet. "I'm going to try to feed him. Y'all be nice to each other while I'm gone."

By the time she got her son to sleep, lying in the crib, her parents had cleaned up the kitchen and gone back to their hotel. Mack sat on the sofa with his papers and books spread around him, studying hard. She cut herself a piece of pumpkin pie, added whipped cream and went back to the living to sit in the rocking chair.

"Your parents said good-night. They're coming over tomorrow morning to take us to breakfast." Mack didn't look up from his work.

"That will be nice." She leaned her head back and closed her eyes, enjoying the quiet, the sweet taste of the pie and the fresh piney scent of the Christmas tree. These days, if the baby was asleep, she usually was, too. Unfortunately, he only slept for two hours at a time. What she wouldn't give for six straight hours in bed....

When she opened her eyes, she found Mack gazing at her. She straightened up in the chair. "Is something wrong?"

He shook his head. "I thought your dad was going to slug me at dinner."

Celia had tried not to think about that confrontation. "You made him seem—I don't know—lazy because he'd only made commander."

"I didn't intend to. I was just trying to point out that people with different goals have different standards of behavior."

"That wasn't respectful."

"He's the one who criticized me for going to work!" Mack slammed his book closed. "I'm doing my best to take care of my wife and baby and make sure I can keep my career going. But somehow I'm the bad guy?"

The pumpkin pie now tasted like dirt. Celia closed her eyes in a futile effort to keep the tears from escaping. "Sorry," she said as she stood up. "I'm really tired tonight. I think I'll go to bed while Mack, Jr. is still asleep."

"Celia." Mack followed her into the bedroom. "Celia, I didn't mean—"

She held up a hand. "I know what you didn't mean. Just let it drop, Mack. I'll be okay."

She curled up on the bed with her face toward the baby's crib and her back to him. Mack leaned against the door frame and rubbed his eyes with his fingers.

The real problem was that Dan Monroe was right. The demands of flight school and the demands of a new baby, plus the needs of a wife who'd had major surgery, were more than Mack could manage.

"All I want for Christmas is a good night's sleep," he muttered, unzipping his jeans. Wearing his boxers and T-shirt, he switched off the lamp and eased under the covers.

Silence. Darkness. Mack blew out a long breath and closed his eyes for a few seconds. He only realized he'd fallen asleep when he woke up again.

The baby was crying. Celia sat on the side of the bed with her arm through the rails of the crib, gently rubbing his back.

Mack rolled over. "Is he hungry?"

"I fed him. I changed him. I rocked him. He just doesn't want to go back to sleep." Her head drooped. Tears thickened her voice. "But I'm so tired."

A glance at his watch showed Mack he'd slept for six hours. Not what he'd hoped, but more than usual. He swung his legs to the floor. "I'll get him."

Celia popped off the bed. "No, that's okay. I'll—"

He stretched out a hand and gave her a gentle push on the shoulder that sent her back to the mattress. "You get some sleep. I'm off until Monday, so I can spend a little while managing the baby." Reaching into the crib, Mack rolled the screaming little guy over, slipped his hands beneath the tiny head and butt and picked up his son.

"See you in a few hours," he told Celia, then shut the bedroom door before she could escape.

There was not, he quickly discovered, a lot to do with a two-week-old kid. The pacifier only worked for a minute, tops, and only if held by the grown-up. A bottle of water lasted just as long as the first taste. If it wasn't Mom's milk, Mack, Jr. wasn't interested. The rocking chair kept the peace, but while Mack got drowsy, Mack, Jr. didn't even blink. The baby carrier looked like a good option, but the minute he lost body contact, the little guy scrunched up his face and started to wail.

"Okay, okay." Mack put the kid on his shoulder again. "Sorry." With the baby gnawing on his own fist, they sneaked back into the bedroom for Mack's jeans and shoes. He pulled on his pants one-handed. In the diaper bag, he found a tiny knitted suit, complete with feet, hand covers and a hood, that he'd seen Celia use when she took the baby outdoors.

"You and me, son, are going for a walk."

He would never tell anyone how long it took him to figure out that stupid little outfit. What did he know? Boys didn't play with dolls, and he'd been the youngest in his family.

By the time the sun was up, father and son were ready to move out. Mack took a blanket along just in case, but the day was mild, with a softness in the air that felt more like spring than the dead of winter. He was fine in his shirtsleeves. M.J. would be okay.

They walked around the parking lot, and Mack talked about the different cars they saw. He described the Corvette and explained how they'd traded it in for a blue Malibu, so there'd be room for a car seat.

"Yeah, I was bummed out for a while. I loved that car." He stared down into the intense, dark blue eyes of the baby reclining in the crook of his arm. "But a man's got to do what a man's got to do."

Across from their apartment complex was a neighborhood of single-family houses, where Christmas decorations adorned every possible surface. As Mack walked through, kids appeared in the yards to play with their new toys—bikes, skateboards and skates, basketballs, robots and air guns and airplanes. The breeze smelled of bacon, sausage and coffee, and Mack's stomach rumbled in response. M.J. whimpered.

"Yeah, it's been awhile. I bet you're getting ready for another meal. Someday, though…" He executed an about-face and headed for the main street. "Someday you're gonna be just like these kids—going outside to play. Will you play baseball, like your old man? I was good, you know. Good enough to play for Navy. Maybe you'll go for soccer, like your uncle James. Or basketball, like Granddad Randolph. Man, is he gonna make a fuss over you!"

M.J. became less and less interested in conversation as they got closer to home. When Mack opened the apartment door, the baby let fly with a piercing shriek.

Celia hurried out of the bedroom. "Oh, my. That sounds awful." She took the baby and sat down in the rocker, adjusting her shirt at the same time. In just a few seconds, the screaming stopped.

"Whew." Mack dropped down on the couch. "Too bad I don't have the right equipment."

"Did you have a terrible time? You were gone almost three hours." The shine was back in her hair, Mack was glad to see, and in her eyes. She'd ironed her shirt and put on makeup. So now he knew the secret to getting *his* Celia back.

He stretched his arms high over his head. "Not a bad time at all. I took M.J. on a tour of the neighborhood."

"M.J.? Where did that come from?"

"Mack, Jr. is a mouthful. I shortened it to M.J."

She gazed at the baby as he nursed. "Hmm. M.J. works." Her smile, when she looked up again, was sweet and all for him. "You're a good dad, Mackenzie Butler."

"Not so far." Mack got down on his knees by the rocking chair and put a hand on his son's back. Then he claimed his wife's mouth for a long, warm kiss. "But I'll do better from now on, Mrs. Butler. I promise you that."

Mack, Jr.'s first steps
Kingsville, Texas
November 24, 1986
Mack was lucky to be home that day and I was lucky to have the camera close by to catch our little boy walking from the couch to his dad sitting on the floor. Having gotten the hang of the process, M.J. hasn't stopped since. My baby is growing up!

M.J. walked before his first birthday, and Mack made his first carrier landing a few months later, on Valentine's Day. To keep from thinking about what could happen— a tiny plane at full speed landing on a hundred-foot runway in the middle of the ocean, with only a hook and a wire to stop it—Celia cleaned the house like a madwoman, went to the commissary for groceries and set about making a romantic dinner for two. M.J. "helped," of course. He'd probably still be awake for hours after Mack got home. At least this house had two bedrooms, and M.J. slept through most nights. She and Mack would have time alone.

Unless his plane crashed. But she wouldn't think about that.

The florist's van didn't stop at her door during the day, and the mail contained only bills. She'd hoped Mack would remember Valentine's day, but didn't expect it and didn't remind him. So she really shouldn't feel disappointed if he forgot.

Late in the afternoon, she left the beef bourguignon simmering, put M.J. in the car seat and went to get Mack at the naval air station. The flat, open Texas countryside still amazed her—miles and miles of plowed fields with nothing on the horizon, no trees for shade, no hills or dips in the road. Mack said he appreciated having nothing to run into as he learned to fly jets.

At the airfield, the lack of activity indicated that the pilots hadn't returned from their ocean flight. Celia took M.J. out of the car and let him run across the open ground. He seemed so grown up to her now, so different from the helpless infant of a year ago. Far from being helpless, these days he was likely to attempt whatever stunt came into his mischievous little head. She hoped keeping up with a fifteen-month-old would help her get rid of the extra pounds she hadn't been able to drop since M.J.'s birth.

Celia heard the jets before she saw them, a roaring in the distance. M.J. stopped and turned to look up at the sky.

"Da. Da. Da."

She stared at her son. "Daddy? Are you saying Daddy?"

M.J. kept his eyes on the approaching planes. "Da. Da."

Swooping him up, she hugged the baby close and watched the five Skyhawk jets soar overhead, with a noise like the end of the world. They disappeared into the empty blue sky, then returned one at a time to make a smooth descent and park in a straight line beside the hangar.

She and M.J. were waiting nearby when Mack hopped out of his plane. Celia primed M.J. "Is that Daddy? Your daddy?"

Right on cue, as Mack got close, M.J. said, "Da. Da. Da. Da."

Mack took a step back. "He's talking? He called me Daddy?" He shifted the toddler from Celia's hold and lifted him high above his head, to M.J.'s delight. "That's right. Daddy. You got it, son. And your daddy is the heat, let me tell you."

Bringing M.J. down to his shoulder, he put the other arm around Celia and started toward the car. "I was so good, man, you wouldn't believe it. I set that baby down, full throttle, vrrrooom…!" M.J. laughed at the rumbling voice. "The hook caught—wham! I'm jerked against the belts until I think my brains are coming out my nose."

"Mack!"

He chuckled. "That's just what it felt like. Didn't actually happen. The air boss comes over the radio, says, 'You can throttle down now, son. You're not gonna make the ship go any faster.'" Mack grinned. "So I cut back, followed the instructions to get back in line. Next thing

I know, I'm hooked to the catapult, checking all the readings, getting the go-ahead. Throttle up. Whoosh! I'm launched, pressed back against the seat with a hundred g's and all I see in front of me is sky. It's like being God."

Smiling, Celia handed him the car keys. "I guess you had a good time?"

"Oh, yeah."

Back at the house, the luscious smell of the stew warmed the chilly evening. Mack played with M.J. until Celia had dinner ready. She thought about slipping into something nice, but Mack seemed comfortable in his jeans. So she brushed her hair, freshened her makeup and touched White Shoulders to her wrists and throat. That should do it.

"Ready to eat?" She picked M.J. up off the floor, wiped his hands and face and then set him in his high chair. Mack came into the dining room behind them.

"Wow—candles and flowers and wine. What's the occasion?"

Celia pretended to be busy carrying in the big pot of stew, and didn't answer.

After a minute, he remembered. The grin he'd been wearing since she'd picked him up at the hangar faded. "Damn, honey. I'm sorry. I was so focused on this landing today…"

Seeing his obvious remorse, she banished her hurt feelings. "I know. Don't worry about it. If you'll feed M.J. his dinner tonight, that'll be more than enough for me."

Mack lifted an eyebrow and sent her a sexy glance. "That's enough?"

She smiled back. "Until the baby's asleep, anyway."

Mack recounted his day second by second while they ate, and he cleaned up the kitchen afterward. Celia gave a yawning, fussy M.J. his bath, read him *Goodnight, Moon* and rocked him into dreamland.

"Alone at last," she said, watching from the kitchen doorway as Mack wiped down the counter. "He was one tired little boy. How about dessert?" She took the chocolate mousse from the refrigerator. "And we have champagne."

"You thought of everything." Mack put his arms around her from behind as she spooned up the mousse. "I feel like a jerk."

"But you're my jerk." She reached back and patted him on the cheek. "Bring me some flowers when I'm not expecting it. That'll be even better."

They took their bowls and the champagne into bedroom. Celia went to the bathroom to put on her peach satin gown and came back to find Mack bare-chested, already under the covers.

"I thought you were taking a bath," he said as she slipped in beside him. "You don't seem to do that much anymore."

"No time." She savored a spoonful of the mousse. "Two hours in the bathtub would give M.J. the opportunity to destroy the house or run away. Or both. And at night, I'd rather fall asleep in bed." She gave him a slow smile. "Beside you."

He leaned over for a kiss. "Nice."

With her third glass of champagne, Celia found the

courage to bring up the question she'd been thinking about for several months now.

"Mack?"

"Mmm?" He lay on his side, his head propped up on one palm as he trailed the fingers of his other hand along her arm.

"Have you thought about…more babies?"

His hand stilled and his shocked blue eyes came to her face. "More? As in, making another baby?"

She laughed. "Exactly."

"Man. That's…coming out of left field." He rolled to his back and put his elbow over his face. "Are *you* thinking about it?"

Her soft hand settled on his chest, stroking his breastbone and setting off fires down below. "Well, M.J.'s getting to be a real kid. Especially now that he's talking. And…a little girl might be nice."

The idea of another baby—another pregnancy, another delivery that put Celia at risk—terrified Mack. How would he cope with yet another infant who cried all the time, kept them awake all night long? What did he know about girls, anyway?

"I miss having a baby," Celia whispered. She kissed Mack's shoulder, his collarbone, the pulse point under his jaw.

Despite the drumming in his blood, Mack could hear the longing in her voice. He knew that as an only child, she'd always wished for brothers and sisters. She wanted them now for M.J.

If that's what he could do to make her happy…

He tangled his fingers in her hair and brought her mouth up to his. "Girls are definitely nice," he said, and took a nip of her lower lip. "I can see the appeal of having a little princess running around the place. As long as she looks like you."

"No guarantees," Celia gasped, when he let her up for air.

Mack grinned. "I'm a naval aviator. I'll take my chances."

Chapter 5

Lieutenant Junior Grade Mack Butler
receives his Wings of Gold from Mrs. Butler
October 10, 1987
That was such a wonderful day! Mack got the award for
having the top grade in his class, plus awards for his bombing
and strafing expertise. I got to pin on his pilot's wings,
though I could barely reach his chest with my big eight-
months-pregnant belly between us. The command gave each
wife a rose and a certificate for putting up with flight school.
Well-deserved, if I do say so myself! Best of all, Maeve and
William came down to Texas for the occasion, so they got
to meet M.J. and my parents. And they stayed long enough
to be there when Courtney was born. I've got my little girl!

"Not again. Please, God, not again."

It was seven o'clock on a cold January morning. Mack had left for his cross-country flight three hours ago. Mack, Jr. and baby Courtney were still fast asleep.

Celia sat on the edge of the bathtub staring at the indicator wand. Even when she squinted her eyes, the results didn't change.

Pregnant. Just three months after Courtney's birth—another C-section, another long recovery—she was expecting again. Why? How?

Well, she knew how. She remembered the squadron Christmas party, and the open bar Mack had visited frequently during the evening. She remembered driving the babysitter home herself, and returning to find Mack trying to cope with a starving Courtney. Once the baby went back to sleep, they'd both realized that the six-week mark had passed. They were free to make love. Celia recalled taking full advantage of that opportunity.

And now look what had happened.

After the kids were up and fed, she called her friend Sharyn, a pilot's wife who worked as a nurse at the naval hospital. "I thought I couldn't get pregnant while I was nursing the baby."

"That's usually true, yes. But we recommend using some kind of birth control, to be safe."

"Now you tell me." M.J. ran through the house holding a toy airplane over his head, making engine sounds at the top of his voice. Courtney wanted to nurse for the third time since waking at seven-thirty. "I thought two kids, a boy and a girl, would be enough."

"God must have special plans for that third baby," Sharyn said. "You never know when you might be carrying the one who cures cancer or world hunger."

"Just what I need—more responsibility."

"You'll be okay, Celia. And you'll love this one just like the others."

"You should know. You've already got four." She hung up the phone and switched Courtney to the other breast. The real question wouldn't be answered until Mack came back in another few days.

Would *he* love this one, too? How would *he* feel about three babies in three years?

Weather delays kept him away from home for an extra couple of days, so by the time she picked him up at the airfield, he'd been gone almost a week. She parked as close as she could to the hangar, but he had to race through a downpour to reach the car.

"Man, what lousy weather!" He brought raindrops and cold air and vitality into the car. Leaning over to kiss her, he asked, "How's it going?"

"Good. Great." Celia backed out of the parking place. "M.J. fell asleep on the drive. He'll wake up when we get home, and be raring to go."

Mack groaned. "And I'm beat. Teaching takes more energy than being the student—you've got to think three or four steps ahead of them just in case something goes wrong."

"Sort of like taking care of a two-year-old—anticipate the danger before he can get to it."

"Except we're moving at three hundred miles an

hour or more." Mack stretched and yawned. "Man, what a day."

Feeling as though she'd been put in her place, Celia set her jaw and nodded. "What a week."

Over a dinner of meat loaf and mashed potatoes, accompanied by M.J.'s constant chatter and bubbles and burps from Courtney, Mack told her about the restaurants he'd visited in San Diego. "Great seafood. Steaks as big as the plate. I'll take you to some of these places when we're out there."

She stared at him, mouth open. "We're going to San Diego? On vacation?"

"I've been talking to the detailer—the guy who assigns everybody to their billets. He says San Diego would be a good choice for our next station. Lots of ships deploy out of there, which would give me a chance to hook up with some of the officers who are heading for the top."

"What will that accomplish?" California? She'd been hoping for Virginia, near their families.

"I'll get along faster with sponsors in high places." When she frowned at him, he shrugged. "Politics is everything. I'll succeed better if I have higher-ups on my side."

"Wh-when will this happen? Should I start packing?"

"We'll be here for another year yet, at least. They always plan these moves a long time in advance. Don't worry."

Oh, sure. Why should she worry, just because she had a third baby on the way? "I'm going to get the kids to bed. Can you read M.J. his story?"

She thought she saw Mack hesitate, but that might have been her imagination. "Sure. Be glad to."

Peace settled over the house about nine o'clock. With both children asleep and Mack reading aviation journals in bed, Celia decided that she'd earned a long, soaking bath, her first in a couple of years. She moved all the toys and the baby soaps into a laundry hamper, took the inflatable child seat out of the tub and searched in the back of the linen closet for some bubble bath. While the water ran she rummaged around for a couple of thick Christmas candles in the box of decorations stashed under the dining table.

At last, sinking into the warm, scented water, soothed by the flickering light, Celia tried to relax. But all she could think was, *Three babies. If I gain another ten pounds, I'll be as big as a house.*

Before even fifteen minutes had passed, she washed, rinsed off in the shower and drained the tub. Luckily, the mirror over the sink only showed her body from the shoulders up. Her hair was still blond, thanks to the Texas sun, and she kept a light tan most of the year. Her face was a little full, maybe, but not as full as her hips. Even her newest nightgown tended to pull across her butt. Had Mack noticed?

As she came into the bedroom, he looked up from his magazine. "That didn't last long."

"I just wanted to be clean," she told him. "I don't have time to waste on soaking."

"Hmm." He'd gone back to his reading, having barely listened to what she said.

With her legs under the covers, Celia sat back against her pillow and waited for her husband to realize she was upset. He kept his eyes on the journal. The rustle of a turning page was the only sound in the house.

"I'm pregnant," she said at last, loudly and harshly.

"Mmm." Mack flipped the page. He read for a moment more, lifted his head, then jerked around to meet her gaze. "You're *what?*"

"Pregnant." Now that she had his attention, she scooted all the way under the blanket and closed her eyes.

"No way." She heard the magazine hit the wall and flutter to the floor. "You just had a baby."

"Well, now I'm having another one."

"When?"

"September sometime."

Mack slid down in the bed so they lay side by side for a while without talking. "What do you think?" At least he didn't ask, "Are you sure?" this time.

"I can't think."

"Do you feel okay?"

The question brought tears to her eyes. "I don't know. I'm too busy to find out." A sob escaped before she could catch it back.

"Aw, Celia." Mack rolled over and pulled her into his arms. "It's gonna be okay, babe. You're a great mom, for one or two or three kids. We'll have a fantastic time, two girls and a boy or two boys and a girl."

"In San Diego?" Until they'd moved here, Texas had seemed like the edge of the known world. California might as well be a different planet.

"Wherever the Navy sends us. We're a family and we'll face whatever comes together."

On that promise, Celia could finally relax. She cuddled closer into her husband's embrace. In just a few minutes, she'd fallen asleep.

Mack stayed awake for a long time. "Make this the last one," he whispered into his wife's soft curls. "Please, Celia. Let's stop at three."

June 3, 1989
Dear Mack, This is our first night on the road. The kids rode pretty well, though I'm already tired of the silly song tape. M.J. likes to count the trucks with me. He counts up to twenty by himself. Courtney sleeps in the morning and afternoon and whines from eleven to two. Ella's quiet except when she's hungry. She loves the car seat mobile you bought. Looking forward to arriving…storing up hugs and kisses.
Much love, Celia

Mack looked at the front of the postcard again—a line of cars with their rear wheels in the air, headlights buried in the ground. "Cadillac Ranch in Amarillo, Texas." They must be desperate for entertainment in Amarillo, he thought.

"Buy a girl a drink, sailor?" Lieutenant Commander Peyton Abbott slid onto the stool next to his at the officers club bar.

"Yes, ma'am." He signaled the bartender.

"Double whiskey and ginger," she said, then swiveled until her crossed knees brushed Mack's hip. "Don't be so formal. You can call me Peyton. Off duty, at least."

"Yes, ma'am." He took a swig of his beer. Lieutenant Commander Abbott was an engineering officer stationed aboard the aircraft carrier *Midway,* the ship he'd be flying from and landing on come August. One of the first women to graduate from the Academy, she was climbing the command ladder at top speed. There had been a husband, he'd heard, but more recently the tall, slender woman with short black hair and sexy green eyes had earned a reputation for enjoying shore liberty in the best Navy tradition.

She reached over and picked up Celia's postcard. "A waste of good automobiles," she said, flicking the Cadillacs with one fingertip. Before he could retrieve the card, she'd glanced over Celia's note. "From your wife?"

"Yes." He barely cut off the "ma'am."

"She's driving from Texas, is that right? With your children?"

Mack nodded. "The Navy in its wisdom refused to change the day I had to report for duty. But they scheduled the pick up and delivery of my household goods a month later. So Celia stayed in Texas to handle the move. When she does get here, she'll probably be close to crazy."

"You think she's not strong enough to endure the trip?"

"Not at all. Celia's a wonder when it comes to managing the kids—has 'em all dressed and ready for church on Sundays, with time to spare. She cooks, cleans, tells stories…" He wouldn't voice his next thought, which had to do with the willing lover he found in his bed every night.

"A paragon, then." Peyton sipped her drink, holding his eyes with her own.

"Pretty close." Mack grinned. "As long as you don't expect her to iron the uniform. The number of shirts I've replaced due to scorch marks…"

"A small price to pay."

"You got that right." He polished off his beer, signaled for a second.

"Getting married early in your career has worked out pretty well, it seems." She shook her head. "Not me. I wanted the career too much. You know…join the Navy and see the world. My husband just couldn't compete."

"This wasn't exactly what I planned, either. But I'm heading in the direction I intended. Pretty soon, I'll be landing that Hornet on the carrier with my eyes closed." He imitated the descent and approach of a jet with one flattened hand.

His companion laughed. "No doubt you'll get plenty of practice during five months at sea. And plenty of chances to pick up bargains in Hong Kong, the Philippines and Hawaii. I know some of the best jewelry dealers on the Pacific Rim. Does your Celia like pearls?"

"Sure. But—"

Peyton put her hand over his. "I know just the place to buy her a necklace she'll die for. I'll take you there."

With his face heating up, Mack slid his hand away to reach for his beer. "Sounds terrific. Thanks." She knew the rules as well as he did—no fraternization between ranks. He must have misinterpreted the gesture. Or just be missing Celia's warmth a little too much.

Peyton ordered a second drink, and Mack ended up with a third beer to keep her company. He walked her to the parking lot and made sure her car started before heading to his own, a small, cheap import with four wheels, one engine and no air-conditioning. Just before he opened the door, the Lieutenant Commander's yellow Camaro pulled up.

She rolled down the window. "I live about five minutes away. How about some coffee at my place?"

Not a hard question to answer, even after three beers. "Thanks, but the furniture is supposed to arrive early tomorrow morning. I think I'd better get some sleep first."

She shrugged. "Suit yourself."

Mack wasn't sure whether he read irritation or challenge in those green eyes. Whichever, he hoped she'd sleep it off along with the two stiff drinks. Making an enemy of a superior officer would not do his fitness report any good. He'd have to walk a tightrope between appeasing Peyton Abbott and encouraging her…even if that meant staying away from the bar at the O Club.

His phone call to the household goods office the next morning produced bad news—no furniture delivery that day. On Friday, the moving van was reported still in transit, and delivery would not be made over the weekend. Celia and the kids were due to arrive on Sunday…to an empty house. At least he would be there to greet them.

Wrong. Friday afternoon, his squadron was detailed for an unscheduled training flight, San Diego to Bremerton, Washington, and back again on Monday. He tried to call Celia, but got no answer in the motel room, that evening or the next morning.

All he could do was leave a note, then hope his family would somehow find their own way to their new—empty—home.

The House that Mack Bought
Mack, Jr., Courtney and Ella outside the new house in
San Diego. The color—robin's-egg blue—was a surprise.
There wasn't much grass or a tree over ten feet tall. But
anywhere Mack is…that's home!

Celia stopped the car under the carport of the bright blue house, propped her chin on her hands, frozen around the steering wheel, and simply stared. All three kids were asleep in the back seat, and she hesitated to wake them up. After eight days of driving, and twenty-four hours of togetherness each day, she needed a minute alone.

But where was Mack? The empty driveway said *some-where else.* He hadn't called last night—the night before they were scheduled to arrive—but she didn't want to think about that, or how she'd cried herself to sleep. What she did want to do was find a bathroom. That meant waking the kids. So which was it—a little peace and quiet, or relief for her poor bladder?

Before she could decide, a bright red sports car pulled up at the curb beside the bare front yard. The woman who emerged might have been a movie star. Her sun-bleached blond hair, fabulous tan, big black sunglasses and blazing white pantsuit screamed Hollywood.

She swaggered up the driveway and leaned down by Celia's open window, with a smile full of teeth as white as the suit. "I'm Mindy Cohen, the real estate agent Mack's been working with."

Celia opened the car door and brought her rumpled, sweaty, exhausted self into the light. "It's good to meet you."

Another flash of the smile. "Mack managed to call me for a second yesterday and ask me to meet you here at the house."

"Where is he?" The kids were waking up. Her chance to go to the bathroom had vanished, but the urgency had intensified.

"His squadron was detailed to a training mission in Washington state. Strictly incommunicado."

"Oh." For the second time in twenty-four hours, Celia wanted to give in to tears.

"I have the house key, though." Mindy followed her around the car as she went to get Ella. "I can let you inside. Unfortunately, the furniture didn't make it here before the weekend."

"Oh." The kids were quiet, staring at the neighborhood around them, the low, flat-roofed houses in vibrant colors, the sandy yards and strange trees, the harsh blue sky and white sun. "Well, then…let's go inside."

Mindy marched to the front door, pausing to search through a thick ring of keys for the right one. Celia stood by the car with her legs crossed, practicing the Kegel exercises she'd been told would strengthen her bladder control. She should have started before today.

"There we go!" The real estate agent pushed the door open. "Welcome home."

Celia herded the kids into the dim interior, which smelled of fresh paint and closed windows. The narrow hallway led straight to a living room with a wall of windows looking out over a terraced backyard. And a pool.

Damn. "No, don't," she yelled, as Mindy started to open the sliding glass door to the back. "Let's leave that closed and locked for now. The kids don't know how to swim."

Mindy's blue eyes went round. "Oh! Okay."

Turning to her left, Celia found a dark passage that surely would lead to a bathroom. "I'll be right back."

She did cry, closed up in the tiny bathroom with brown tiles and pink walls. Only for a couple of minutes, though. Then she splashed her face with water, wiped her hands on the back of her jeans and returned to her role as Navy wife.

"This is great," she said, moving Mindy relentlessly toward the front door. "I don't think we'll need a motel room. We'll stay here tonight—it'll be like camping out. I think we can find the grocery store. We're fine, really. Thanks for all your help." With the agent outside, Celia shut the front door firmly and locked it, for good measure.

Then she picked up one-year-old Ella, who wanted to nurse, and looked at M.J. and Courtney with a determined smile. "Now, let's go look at your rooms. Daddy says there's a pink one and a blue one. Who wants pink?"

"Yuck," M.J. moaned.

"Me, me!" Courtney jumped up and down.

At least some parts of life remained predictable.

★ ★ ★

At 6:00 a.m. Monday morning, Mack completed his landing check with the concentration of a man possessed, then jumped down from the cockpit and raced to his car. Twenty long minutes later, he turned the corner of Bougainvillea Drive to see a dirty moving van parked in front of his blue house.

Mack swore under his breath. He'd hoped to have a few minutes alone with Celia first.

But as he climbed out of the Civic, he saw three men leaning against the truck bumper, arms folded over their chests. He joined them at the curb. "I'm Lieutenant Butler. What's going on?"

The shortest of the three shrugged. "Note on the door says nobody will be home till 9:00 a.m. So we're sittin' on our butts doin' nothin'."

"Well, I'm here now, so let's get this show on the road."

Back at the house, he found the note in Celia's handwriting taped to the door. She must've taken the kids to a motel for the night. All to the good—he could get some of the furniture in place before they arrived.

But once he'd unlocked the door and walked into the living room, he found his three children and his wife sleeping like puppies on the floor. The kids looked sweet, peaceful, with their rosy cheeks and tousled hair, their soft feet and innocent snores.

Celia lay just a little apart from the children, half on and half off the sheet she'd spread on the new carpet. Mack swallowed hard, looking at her smooth, tanned legs, her gently rounded arms, her blond curls shining in the early light. She wore a cotton gown he didn't remember, but he'd never forget the swell of her breasts under the light fabric…or the sweetness of her smile when she stirred, opened her eyes and saw him.

"Morning," she whispered.

Mack went down on his knees at her side. "Morning, yourself." Braced on his hands, he leaned down and set his mouth on hers, felt the immediate welcome that Celia always gave. "Oh, yeah," he groaned, kissing her eyelids, her temples, grazing his lips across her cheekbone before returning to her lips. "Welcome home."

She put her arms around him and pulled him closer, opening her mouth and deepening the kiss.

"We're comin' in," the truck driver called as the front door squeaked. "Where you want this bed frame?"

Mack, Jr. sat up like a marionette whose strings were pulled, looked around and squealed, "Daddy!" He launched himself across Celia, into Mack's arms. Courtney and Ella joined him almost immediately.

"Scoot into the kitchen," Mack told his wife, who was on her feet with her nightie clutched against her chest. "I'll bring in your bag and you can get dressed."

Looking anything but pleased, Celia disappeared. Mack scrambled to his feet with kids clinging to his body, and went to greet the movers.

"Back here with that bed. The room next to the bathroom."

"Thought nobody was here," the driver grumbled. "Coulda been halfway through the job by now."

Under his uniform shirt, Mack squared his shoulders.

"You could have been finished and on your way home if you'd shown up Friday like you were supposed to."

He didn't hear another complaint for the rest of the morning. At noon, he signed off on the paperwork, gave the driver fifty dollars to split with his two helpers, and went back inside to his family.

Between unpacking boxes and keeping the kids occupied, Mack couldn't grab more than a second or two alone with his wife all day long. Not until after nine, when Courtney finally surrendered to sleep, did Celia actually stop moving. He found her in the kitchen, staring with a confused expression at an assortment of small appliances and cooking utensils.

"I don't know where I got all this stuff," she said. "And I don't know where in the world I'm going to put it."

Mack grabbed her hand. "Worry about that tomorrow." He tugged her toward the family room.

"But—"

"None of that junk will walk off in the middle of the night." He dropped down on the couch and pulled her with him. "Talk to me. What do you think of the house?"

She looked around. "It's fine. Except…"

"Except?"

Behind their heads, the wall of windows looked over the pool. Celia nodded in that direction. "That terrifies me. Do you know how hard it will be to keep M.J. and Courtney out of there?"

"I know. But the price was fantastic, the location works and we have enough space. I thought we could handle it."

She slumped against the couch. "I'll be the one handling it, Mack. You'll be at work, or on a ship somewhere."

"But when I'm home, I'll teach them to swim, so they'll be safe." He refused to be daunted, not this first night after so many weeks apart. "And there's another benefit you're ignoring."

Celia lifted an eyebrow. "What's that?"

He got up again and drew her with him. "Come with me." Opening the sliding glass door onto the pool deck, he stepped out into the warm night air. "Notice that we have a high privacy fence all the way around the yard."

"And?"

"Check out the temperature of the water." He leaned down and dipped a hand into the pool. Celia did the same. "Nice, isn't it?"

She nodded. "Cool. Refreshing after the hot day."

"Right." With a quick move, Mack pulled his T-shirt over his head. "So let's go for a swim."

Celia took a step back. "I don't think—"

"Don't think." He stepped up close to her and started on the buttons of her blouse. "Just imagine…you and me, alone together in that cool, silky water."

"Mack…" The quiver in her voice told him she was interested.

He slipped the blouse off her shoulders. "Nobody can see what we're up to. Nobody knows what we're doing. It's just you…" he eased her shorts down over her hips "…and me." His own shorts dropped to the deck. "Skinny-dipping in the dark."

She hesitated a moment, her lips parted. Then, with

a skip and a couple of quick steps, she dived into the pool. Coming up on the far side, she tossed her underwear up on the deck.

"Well, sailor?" Celia stretched her arms along the edge of the pool, lifting her bare breasts just above the waterline. "What are you waiting for?"

Chapter 6

The Butler Family
Mack, Celia, M.J., Courtney and Ella
riding a camel at the San Diego Zoo
July 1989
Talk about a bumpy ride! Mack says his F/A-18 Hornet
has camels beat by a mile.

The California summer flew by. Before Celia had
gotten all their boxes unpacked, August was just
around the corner. August, and Mack's first overseas
deployment.

He took leave the third week of July, spending most
of his waking moments with M.J., Courtney and Ella.
Then there were the business details to attend to,

securing a power of attorney for Celia and establishing family records at the naval hospital.

They made the day a family outing and took the kids to the nearby San Diego Zoo. The pink flamingos at the entrance kept them mesmerized for half an hour.

"Why are they pink?" Mack, Jr. swung back and forth on the rail.

"Says on the sign it's because they eat shrimp," Mack answered. "Most flamingos are white."

M.J. looked at Celia. "Really, Mommy?"

Celia laughed. "That's what it says, honey." She saw the indignant expression on Mack's face. "Which way shall we go? To see snakes or monkeys or lions and bears?"

"Lions and bears!" M.J. scanned the signs and dashed in that direction. "I want to see the lions." Almost immediately, he vanished into the crowd."

"Mack…"

"I'll get him." With Ella sitting on his shoulders, Mack strode in the direction M.J. had taken.

"Monkeys, Mommy. Me want monkeys." Courtney pulled on Celia's skirt. "Monkeys."

Celia put her daughter in the stroller. "We'll see the monkeys, Courtney. We have to get M.J. back first."

The little girl strained against the stroller belt as Celia tried to buckle it. "Monkeys. Me see monkeys."

Biting her lower lip, Celia got the catch closed. "Sit back, sweetie. We're going to see the monkeys." She pushed the stroller in the direction Mack had taken, with Courtney working up a full-fledged tantrum. The first set of steps, going down, didn't pose a problem.

Going up the second set—backward, pulling the stroller up each bump while being jostled or sworn at by other walkers—left Celia sweaty and irritable.

At the top of the path, they came upon Mack crouched down in front of M.J.

"You don't ever run off on your own," he said sternly. "Your mom has two little girls to take care of. She can't go chasing after you. How am I supposed to go away and do my job if I have to worry all the time about whether you're getting lost or giving your mom a hard time?"

Mack, Jr. hung his head.

"I have to be able to depend on you as the man of the house." Mack winced as Ella scraped her nails across his ear. "Are you going to make me proud of you?"

Celia winced in turn. "I'm sure he will," she said, stepping behind M.J. and putting a hand on his shoulder. "Mack was a big help on our trip from Texas."

Her son gazed up at her with an expression of intense gratitude. Her husband, on the other hand, sent her an angry glare as he straightened up to his full height.

"There's the lion enclosure," Celia told M.J. "Let's go see." They walked sedately to the exhibit, with M.J. staying close to the stroller but on the opposite side from his dad. When they reached the lions, he went to stand at the rail, almost timidly. Celia released Courtney from the stroller and walked her up to stand with her brother. After a minute, Mack and Ella joined them.

"You thought I was being too hard on him." He said it without looking her way.

"He's not even four years old, Mack. He's not ready

to be the man of the house." She reached up and took Ella by the waist. "Let me hold her for a while. She's driving you crazy."

"I'm fine." He kept hold of the baby's knees.

"Mack, your scalp is red where she's been yanking your hair." Celia tugged gently and he released Ella. "I don't mind holding her. Lord knows, I do it enough."

"Yeah, that's pretty obvious." He shoved his hands into the pockets of his shorts.

"What is that supposed to mean?"

He shrugged one shoulder.

"Mack?"

"I could disappear for good and the kids would barely notice. They look to you for discipline, for comfort, for entertainment."

She stared at him, speechless. What did he expect? He'd been out of their lives for more than a month.

"If I go in to Ella in the middle of the night, she doesn't settle until she sees you. I might as well not bother."

"She's just been weaned, Mack. She wakes up and thinks she should nurse." Celia tried for humor. "You can't do that for her, you know."

He didn't smile. "Courtney looks to you for confirmation on everything I say. M.J.—well, he barely tolerates me."

At that moment, their son turned around. "They're asleep," he said in a stage whisper. "Let's see something else."

Mack stepped up to the rail. "Courtney, we're going to the tigers." He took her hand.

"Monkeys." She stomped her foot. "Want monkeys."

He swung her into his arms. "Monkeys it is, princess. Let's find those silly guys."

And so the afternoon went, seesawing between M.J. and Courtney, with Mack and Celia trying to create some kind of balance. By the time they reached the car again, she was exhausted.

The lucky children fell asleep before they'd left the boundaries of Balboa Park. Since this was Friday, rush hour had commenced and traffic heading north on I-5 had come to a standstill.

Celia didn't know how to bridge the uneasy silence in the front seat of the car. "The children love you," she said finally.

Again, Mack shrugged that one shoulder.

"But you're not the person who's with them every day, every night. You can't expect—"

"Until two months ago, I was there for almost every day of their lives. Doesn't that count for something?"

"I said they love you."

"But they mind you."

"There's not that much minding involved, Mack. Our children are not badly behaved."

"And what would you have done if I hadn't been there today? Would you have found M.J. before some pervert grabbed him? Before he got hopelessly lost?"

"I would have been in real trouble," she told him earnestly. "M.J. could have gotten hurt before I found him. Of course we needed you today—we always need you." Tears stung her eyes. "I don't know what we'll do when you're gone for five months."

Mack felt a surge of relief…followed by a tide of guilt. He hadn't intended to make Celia cry.

"You'll do great." He reached over and grabbed her hand. "There's lots of support in the squadron, too. Before you know it, December will come and I'll be under your feet again."

She smiled, like sunshine through a rain shower, and glanced back at the kids. The traffic picked up and Mack put both hands on the steering wheel. He wasn't sure he'd made anything better—a crack had opened and not quite closed again. He had roughly five days to make sure it did.

Saturday they stayed around the house, with Mack trying to foresee any maintenance problems that might come up while he was gone. He spent time in the pool with M.J., who was becoming a good little swimmer, and Courtney, who was terrified of the water. Given that Celia would be here by herself with three kids, maybe that wasn't such a bad thing.

Celia disappeared in the afternoon to get her hair done. The air wing—all the pilots and flight officers who would be leaving on the carrier with Mack—was hosting a "dining out" that evening at the Miramar Officers' Club. For the first time since his graduation from the Academy he'd be wearing the formal uniform, with its short white jacket, gold cummerbund, bow tie, tucked shirt and satin-striped pants. Mack hadn't seen Celia's dress yet. All she'd said after shopping for two days was "blue."

The kids were napping—a minor miracle—and he was clipping the oleander hedge on the side of the house when she returned. Tires squealed as Celia stopped in the driveway, followed by the slap of the screen door.

Mack waited for her to come out and show him her hair. After ten minutes, he went looking for his wife.

He found her in the tiny bathroom off their bedroom, her face streaked with tears. Her hair…

"Damn, Celia. What'd they do to you?"

Her blond curls had been straightened to lanky shreds. Half of those shreds were piled on top of her head in a stiff, chaotic mess, with the rest of the lifeless strands hanging around her shoulders.

Hairpins exploded all over the bathroom floor as Celia clawed at the mess. "I can't believe I threw away thirty dollars on this disaster," she said, her voice close to a growl. "I should have walked out without paying!"

"Why didn't you?"

"Because the CO's wife was in there, that's why!" She threw him a dirty look as she turned on the shower full blast. "I was afraid to make a scene in case she told her husband and ruined your career."

"Oh, Celia." He worked hard not to laugh. "I'll be okay." Watching her jerk off her clothes gave him an idea. Stepping close, he smoothed a hand down her bare arm. "Why don't I join you? I could wash—"

Her glare made him back away again. "Are you crazy? I've got two hours to pull myself together for this dinner of yours. I don't know if that's long enough. Go away!" She pushed him back into the bedroom and shut the door in his face.

After checking to see that the kids were still asleep,

Mack went back to his hedge. When he came in the house thirty minutes later, he found his uniform plus a change of skivvies and socks hanging in the hall bathroom. The bedroom door was locked.

He wondered whether Celia would ever come out again.

Lieutenant and Mrs. Mackenzie Butler
CVW 11 Dining Out
August 4, 1989
Mack's dress uniform from the Academy still fits him,
which drives me crazy!

Stepping into the officers club, Celia knew her eyes were still puffy. Her hair wasn't special, just the usual shoulder-length fall, but anything was better than the bimbo disaster the salon had given her. She'd put on some extra makeup, which made her feel like a little girl playing dress-up.

And her dress… She straightened her shoulders and pulled in her stomach muscles. In the store, the simple blue sheath had seemed sophisticated, elegant. She wore the pearl earrings Mack had given her for a wedding gift, and silver sandals to match the clutch purse she carried.

But when she caught sight of herself in one of the mirrors in the O Club dining room, she saw a short, chubby blonde standing by Mack's side. Still the sparrow trying to keep up with an eagle.

The other women in the room noticed Mack. Celia watched their eyes slide over him and then come back for a longer look. And those women were gorgeous—tanned, fit, dressed with California flair. Celia didn't miss their manicured nails—hands and feet—and their perfect hair.

She sucked in her stomach again. Mack and two of his fellow officers had been talking about planes for fifteen minutes now. Their wives spoke to each other, complaining about their jobs. Celia sipped her wine, freshened her interested smile and wondered about the children. Had they eaten the dinner she'd left? Would the babysitter, their minister's twelve-year-old daughter, rock Ella to sleep? What if Courtney decided to whine all evening? Maybe she should call—

Suddenly, one of the wives turned on her. "What do you do, Celia?"

The question was so unexpected, she couldn't think. "What do I *do*?"

Julia Van Dorn rolled her eyes. "You know. Where do you work?"

"Oh. I don't. That is, I stay home with the children."

Julia's perfect eyebrows rose almost to her feathery red bangs. "You don't have a job?"

"I didn't say that. I said I stay home with my kids."

"You have a home business?" On Julia's other side, Ava Cunningham nodded. "That's great. Avon? Mary Kay? Tupperware?"

Celia tried again. "My work is my kids."

They both gazed at her. "You and Mack are surviving on just his Navy pay?" Julia scanned Celia's dress. "That's…"

"Amazing," Ava finished for her. "I need my income just to buy clothes and fix up the house." She pretended to shudder. "I couldn't possibly stay home with the kids all day. I'd go insane."

"Me, too." Julia finished her drink. "I'm there from 6:00 p.m. until 6:00 the next morning. I have to have time for myself."

Ava toasted her with a martini glass. "Damn right. If Chet's going flying off somewhere, I don't plan to spend all my time just babysitting until he gets back."

Celia felt heat rise over her throat, into her cheeks. "I like my kids. We have fun together. Most days," she added, chuckling. "They all have their bad moods at different times."

Ava stared at her as if Celia were an alien species. "Didn't you ever want to do anything with yourself?"

"I am," she said through gritted teeth. "But I also earned a degree in elementary education. When the children are older, I'll see about teaching school."

Julia grinned at Ava. "If she survives."

"Excuse me, I need to check in with the babysitter." As she turned away, Celia saw Julia and Ava shaking their heads, in pity, maybe, or just in contempt.

Stacy, the twelve-year-old, answered the phone promptly and sounded calm. Ella had gone to sleep, M.J. and Courtney were watching a game show. The door to the pool hadn't been touched. Everything was *fine*.

Celia went to the ladies' room and shut herself into a stall, then stood there with her hands clenched around the silver clutch, breathing hard.

Mack would leave on Monday. She'd be alone, with only these *piranhas* to talk to. Her neighbors never came out of their houses except to go to work and come home again. How would she survive?

She managed not to cry again. At the mirror over the sink, she added more lipstick and powder, combed her hair, practiced her smile. Weak, but at this point, she was beyond caring. Taking a deep breath, she opened the door to the hallway.

Mack was leaning against the wall right outside. "Celia! Are you okay? You disappeared…and dinner's being served."

"I—" Another deep breath. "I called home to check on the kids. We should go sit down."

She walked past him, but he caught her arm and pulled her around to face him. "What's wrong?"

"Nothing." An automatic response. He didn't need her worries as he got ready for his big cruise.

He studied her face. "Doesn't look like nothing." With a hand at the small of her back, he walked her toward the dining room.

But Mack paused at the door, looking across the sea of tables, each table seating eight people in fancy dress, all of them chattering and, of course, drinking. He'd waited for Celia at their table for a good ten minutes. They were relegated to the back of the room, as befitted the most junior officers present. All six chairs around them were taken by single guys.

There would be speeches after dinner, toasts to the ship and to the pilots, inspirational words from the commander of the air group and the commanding officer of the carrier. Then dancing. And more drinking.

Meanwhile, the minutes of his last few days at home slipped away. He'd been getting more protective of those minutes recently. He did his job, but left work as soon as possible to get home to the kids. And Celia.

Five months without her would be a long time.

"Tell you what," he said, turning away from the dining room. "Let's blow this off."

She clutched his arm. "Mack! We can't do that!"

"Sure we can." He guided her before him toward the front door of the club.

"B-but you paid fifty dollars for the tickets."

"And we were here. I talked to the CAG—the commander of the air group—and the squadron leader, shook hands with the ship's captain. I did my duty. I don't have to stick around for plastic chicken and long-winded speeches."

She halted just over the threshold. "You want to go home?"

Mack grinned. "Not a chance. We're all dressed up. Why shouldn't we go somewhere special? Just the two of us?"

Celia's face shone like a kid's on Christmas morning. "Oh, Mack. Could we?"

He should have thought of this before. "Remember, I told you I'd take you to those San Diego restaurants? Tonight's the night." Holding her hand, he pulled her across the parking lot.

"I sure wish we still had the Corvette." He opened the passenger door of the Malibu. "That was a car built for special occasions."

"You can have one again someday. When there are no more kids to tote around."

"Yeah, I guess."

"So where are we going?"

"You'll see, sweet Celia. You'll see."

He took her to the nicest restaurant he'd heard about in San Diego—the Harbor View, on top of a tall building right beside San Diego Bay. They ate lobster and drank champagne while watching the sunset over the Pacific Ocean and the lights of the jets landing at the nearby airport.

"Takes some getting used to, having a passenger jet fly right by the window." He'd switched to coffee for the drive home. Celia was finishing up the champagne.

"They make me want to fly away." Celia stared with a dreamy gaze at the night outside the windows.

"Where would you go?" Strange that he couldn't predict what she'd say. They'd been married four years now. Somehow, there never seemed to be time for talking.

"Hawaii," she said without hesitation. "I've always wanted to see Hawaii."

"Surfing lessons?"

"Definitely." She nodded. "And I want to see a volcano. A pineapple plantation." She fought back a yawn. "And snorkel for whales."

"Snorkel for whales?" Mack sent the waiter away with his credit card. "That's a new one."

"Well, you do snorkel. And there are whales."

"Probably not in the same place."

"Oh." She didn't catch the yawn this time. "I guess that's something else for the future."

"Maybe." He signed the credit slip, then stood to help

Celia out of her chair. In the process, he managed to kiss her shoulder, just where her neck began. "You never know."

They kissed again as they rode the elevator. In the Malibu, with its bench seat Celia slid right next to him, putting her hand on his thigh.

"You'd better stop that," Mack said hoarsely. "I still have to take the babysitter home."

"Mmm." Celia leaned her head on his shoulder and continued to stroke her fingers over the inside of his leg.

"I'll stay in the car," he announced as he pulled into their driveway. "Send Stacy out and I'll drive her home. But then…" He grabbed his wife's hand as she started to get out. "Then, lady, you're going to pay."

She sent him a sexy grin. "Oh, goody."

Stacy lived about ten minutes away, but the drive there and back barely cooled Mack down. Inside the house, the living room was dark. Only a faint light came down the hallway from the master bedroom. Out of habit, he looked in on the girls, who were sleeping like cherubs, at least for now. Both of them still tended to wake up about 3:00 a.m., crying for their mommy. Mack, Jr. was sprawled across his bed, also fast asleep. The night had cooled down nicely—no need to regret the air-conditioning system they didn't have.

And in the master bedroom, a lovely woman waited for him in bed. She'd pulled the sheet up under her arms, but her creamy shoulders were bare and Mack didn't think there would be any barriers when he reached for her.

He closed the door behind him.

"You're overdressed," Celia said softly.

Taking his time, Mack removed his uniform. His slow, deliberate movements heightened the anticipation in the room. When he finally slipped under the sheet, Celia's body met his, skin to skin. With a desert breeze blowing through the window, they knew nothing but their need for each other.

Later, as he held her, Mack realized Celia was crying. "Hey, baby, what's wrong?"

"Nothing," she sobbed, turning away from him. Her shoulders shook, and her breath rasped in her throat.

Mack held her close, her back to his front, and wondered what to do. He'd never loved her to tears before. Was that a good thing? Or was that even what had happened?

"Come on, Celia. Tell me what's going on. You've been upset all night."

She continued to cry for a while. All at once, she rolled over and threw her arm over his chest. "I miss you!"

Ah. "I'm not gone." Her cheeks smeared tears, and probably makeup, onto his bare shoulder.

"Tuesday." She sobbed. "You'll be gone."

He brought up his arm to hold her closer. "Yeah, I will."

"What will I do?"

"The same as you always do. But without me causing extra complications."

At that, she cried harder. For the first time, Mack fully faced his immediate future—a gray-walled room he would share with two other guys, instead of the cozy home Celia could create out of almost nothing.

Wardroom meals, instead of Celia's cooking. She always made an effort to prepare just what he liked. Especially hot dogs and beans, his all-time favorite dish.

Cold sheets, unwarmed by Celia's soft skin.

He took a deep breath. "You'll be so busy, with all the kids' activities you've got lined up. Between T-Ball and toddler music and story times at three different libraries, plus keeping the bills paid and doing all the maintenance around here, you'll look up in December and say, "Damn, I was supposed to pick up Mack at the docks today. I don't have time for that!"

She gave a watery chuckle. "I'm sure." Her body had started to relax.

He brushed her hair back from her drying face. "So you'll bundle the kids into the car, which you've kept in great running order, and rush down to Coronado, and I'll be standing on the pier by myself, just waiting after everybody else has gone."

"Uh-huh." Practically asleep.

"And I'll ask what's for dinner, and you'll say…"

Her soft breath had gone deep and even. Mack smiled, though his eyes burned.

"…and you'll say, 'Hot dogs and beans.'" He took a deep breath, looking over the months ahead. "I hope."

Chapter 7

Official Navy Photograph
The Aircraft Carrier USS Midway
departing for the Indian Ocean
August 1989

The launch day dawned bright and hot, like most days in San Diego in August. Mack had chosen to ride the carrier out to sea this first time, rather than fly with the squadron, and he had to be aboard the vessel by 0730. So the whole household was awake at dawn, getting dressed, sharing a breakfast of pancakes and sausage.

M.J. and Courtney fell asleep again on the drive into San Diego. Ella was happy to stare out the window, leaving a heavy silence in the car. Tears threatened every five minutes or so, but Celia was getting better at pushing them back. She could cry all afternoon and evening.

Mack drove without saying anything, but his fingers tapped the steering wheel in odd patterns, a sure sign his mind was busy.

"What are you thinking?"

He laughed a little. "I was thinking about carrier landings, actually."

Not dreading the impending separation as she was? "What about carrier landings?" Any conversation would be better than silent agony.

"Just going over the approach—you know, the angle of descent, the throttle back, release the landing gear, sight the lights…and then just as you hit the deck, you throttle up to speed and pray to God the tail hook catches before you reach the edge of the ship." He shook his head. "I've practiced as many times as anybody else. But this is for real. This is the job."

Celia cleared her throat. "What happens if the hook doesn't catch?"

"You try to gain elevation, come back for another landing. Or…"

"Or?"

"You ditch the plane, eject into the water and wait for them to pick you up. That's the easy part."

"What's the hard part?"

"Explaining to the Navy how you lost their multi-million dollar aircraft. And finding a civilian job."

"Well." She sat back against the seat. "You'll have to avoid ditching the plane."

"I plan to do just that." His tight smile belied the confidence in his words. Mack was nervous. And she couldn't do a thing to help.

Before she was ready, they were climbing the ramp for the Coronado Bay Bridge. The high arch over San Diego Bay gave a wonderful view of the island and the city, with the Pacific Ocean on one side and the mountains on the other.

Then down again onto Coronado Island, through the quaint little village to North Island Naval Base and, finally, the docks where the huge gray bulk of the USS *Midway* loomed. Thirty minutes to departure.

Mack parked the car, unloaded M.J. and picked up Courtney. He pointed to the flags at the top of the ship and described the messages they signaled. Then he walked along the side of the massive vessel, explaining how an aircraft carrier worked and what he'd be doing while he was gone.

With only fifteen minutes left, he hugged and kissed Ella. Then he looked at Celia. "Guess I'd better go aboard. Wouldn't want them leaving without me."

She couldn't speak without crying, so she nodded in response. His free arm came around her shoulders.

"Take care of yourself, Celia. I'll miss you."

"Mack," she gasped. Then he kissed her, and she fought to memorize the taste, the feel, for the days to come.

When he drew back, her tears were on his cheeks and his own eyes were wet. One more hug for Ella, a kiss for M.J. and Courtney…

Then he shouldered his duffel bag and walked away without looking back.

None of the children made a sound. Celia's tears poured unchecked, and she didn't have a hand free to wipe them away. She stared at the dull paint on the side of the *Midway,* trying to decide whether she should go now or wait until the ship sailed.

"Sucks, don't it?"

The wry voice surprised her. She hadn't known there was anyone nearby. About two yards away stood the woman who spoke—tall and on the heavy side, with short dark curls, a red nose and swollen eyes.

"Yes," Celia said. "It sucks."

"Have a tissue." Holding out a full-size box, the woman came closer. "I learned the first time to bring along supplies."

"You've done this before?"

"This is Jerry's second cruise." She hit her forehead with the heel of her hand. "I always forget to introduce myself. Bea Fiedler."

"Celia Butler."

Bea nodded. "Jerry described you after the dining out."

"That can't be good."

"Oh, sure. He said, 'Butler's got a gorgeous wife and the flight instincts of an eagle. He'll reach the top. Fast.'"

"Um…thanks."

The other woman shrugged. "Jerry's a good flight officer. Not the best, but he can see ability in other guys."

Celia wasn't sure what to say, so she looked up to the deck of the ship, where the crew was gathering at the rail. Sailors in bright white uniforms with blue scarves waved and called to the crowd on the pier. The officers wore khaki slacks and shirts, but were doing the same thing—trying to get the attention of their loved ones on shore.

M.J. grabbed her arm. "Is Daddy there? Mommy, do you see Daddy?"

"I don't think so." Celia squinted against the glare of all the white uniforms. "Everybody looks the same. No, wait. There he is. See, M.J., right in front of the flag line."

Mack, Jr. began jumping up and down, yelling and waving to his dad. Courtney joined the effort. Celia held Ella up above her head, watching as Mack caught sight of his kids and waved back.

All at once, the ship began to slide along the pier, almost without sound. Most of the crowd walked along, still waving.

But the dock ended, and the *Midway* didn't stop. Within a few minutes they could see the entire mass of the ship, her crew members lining the deck like brown and white popsicle sticks. Then the ship itself became a toy in the big tub of the Pacific Ocean. Finally, the horizon went flat. Empty.

The sun still shone brightly, but to Celia's eyes a shadow had dropped over the world. She turned blindly away from the sea.

"We should get some breakfast," Bea said, walking beside her as she herded the kids back toward the parking lot.

"That would be nice." Celia tried to pull her thoughts together. "But we ate before we came." Sort of. She hadn't managed more than a couple of bites.

Bea patted her shoulder. "Yeah, I know how that goes. I'll bet the kids are hungry, too. Aren't you?"

The kids didn't need convincing, of course. Before she could protest, Celia found herself in the Malibu, following Bea's orange VW Beetle over the Coronado Bridge, into her new life as a deployed sailor's wife.

USS **Midway** *Postcard*
August 15, 1989
Dear Celia,
Imagine me in the cockpit of the F-18 on the front of this card, soaring from the flight deck into the nighttime sky. My first night takeoff and landing went great. The stars are amazing out on the ocean. Wish you were here to enjoy them with me. Outside the plane, life aboard ship is pretty boring. Hope you and the kids are well. You're the first thing I think about when I wake up and the last thing on my mind before I go to sleep. I miss you, honey.
Love, Mack

The North Island Officers' Wives Club met for lunch on the first Monday of September. Bea convinced Celia to go, and they shopped together for clothes to wear. The teenager who looked after Bea's twin boys agreed to take on Celia's bunch with the help of her ten-year-old sister.

"All we do is show up, smile and make points," Bea explained as they approached the bridge to Coronado Island. "You have to play this side of the game if you want your husband to get promoted. The CO's wife can make or break her husband's perception of Mack."

"That's not fair."

"That's the Navy."

Celia blew out a breath and braked as the traffic ahead of her on the bridge came to a stop. "Great. I hate being perched up here in the sky. I hate this bridge, period."

When the line of cars started moving, Bea said, "I talked to Jerry last night."

"You did? How?"

"Ship-to-shore phone call."

"What did he say?"

"'Hi. Everything okay? Love you.'" She sighed. "It lasted about sixty seconds."

"After two weeks, that's better than nothing." Those two weeks seemed even longer now, knowing communication was possible.

"You'll hear from Mack soon. The new guys get their privileges last."

"I know." Celia banged the steering wheel with her fist. "Let me off of this bridge, dammit!"

Getting off the bridge meant arriving at the officers' club, where a noise like the squawking of chickens with a wolf in the henhouse met them at the door. Celia followed Bea past the bar to the dining room, filled wall-to-wall with chattering women. Tall, slim, stylish women.

Bea surveyed the crowd from the doorway. "There's the receiving line. Let's face the dragons first, then find somebody we can actually talk to."

With her knees shaking, Celia ran the gauntlet—the base commander's wife, the ship commander's wife, the executive officer's wife and the officers of the Wives

Club, all formidable women in their forties and fifties who offered cold hands and cool smiles. She was thankful for the name tags everyone wore, and only hoped she hadn't made any crucial mistakes.

"Finally." Bea took her arm as Celia turned away from the last "dragon". "I see Sissy Williams across the room. She said she'd save us a couple of seats."

Three hours later, Celia slid behind the steering wheel of the Malibu once again. With the air-conditioning running full blast against the blazing afternoon, she massaged her cheeks to release her frozen smile.

"That wasn't so bad." Bea buckled her seat belt. "The chicken salad was really good. And the cheesecake…yum."

"And did you notice how almost every woman there—except us—took one bite and sent the rest back to the kitchen?"

Her friend shrugged. "Their loss."

"And my gain." Celia sighed and put the car into gear. "The waistband on this skirt is about to cut me in half."

"Thank God for elastic." As they sat once more on the top of the bridge span, Bea reconsidered. "Although at this rate, I'll be as wide as I am tall by the time Jerry gets back. What we need to do is hit the gym."

As traffic moved and allowed them off the bridge, Celia relaxed. "I can't afford a gym membership."

"There's an exercise room at the O Club on Miramar."

Celia frowned at the thought of a treadmill workout. "A babysitter every day for three kids really adds up."

"Yeah."

"There's a walking path at Lake Miramar," Celia said, once she'd maneuvered onto Interstate 5. "We went there once with Mack. You and I could push the strollers, while M.J. rides his bike."

Bea nodded. "We can do that." Then she sighed. "Though I feel like inhaling another piece of cheesecake, just thinking about it. I hate exercise."

"Well, from now on, cheesecake is out. Sugar free pudding is in."

"Sugar free gelatin."

"Sugar free cola."

"No way. I don't give up my caffeine sugar fix for anybody, even Jerry."

"Did you notice Julia Van Dorn today? She wears a size 2, if that. How about Ava Cunningham? I think she wears a 0."

"No."

"Yes. I'm comfortable in a 14 these days. How about you?"

"Damn you." Bea threw her a wrathful glance. "Damn you!"

"The Posse"
Halloween 1989
Adam and Aaron Fiedler, 4 years old
Mack, Jr., almost 4, Courtney, 2, and Ella, 1 year
Bea and I put together cowboy outfits for all the kids, even baby Ella. They looked like a little band of Texas Rangers galloping around the neighborhood.

Soon enough, their devotion to exercise and diet began to pay off. At the October Wives Club meeting,

Celia wore a dress she hadn't been able to get into since Courtney was born. She even had a little room to spare in the waist, thanks to the sit-ups she managed in the morning before the kids woke up. At the luncheon, she ate one bite of the warm apple pie with ice cream and pushed her plate away. And she met Bea that evening for a slightly longer-than-usual walk around the lake.

The December club meeting served as a combination holiday party and homecoming planning session—the carrier would return in just a couple of weeks. The menu was heavy on vegetables and fruit, very light on calories. Everyone talked about welcoming their men home.

Wearing a brand-new dress in the size ten she'd aimed for, Celia enjoyed her lunch with the friends she had made over the last several months, wives of the younger officers on the ship, most with children around the same age as hers. They swapped babysitters and recipes, cooperated on a big Halloween party in the park for all the kids, and were crocheting blankets for babies in the naval hospital. They'd even planned a party in January to get husbands and wives together for a special night.

As dessert was served, a glance at the table behind her showed Julia Van Dorn and Ava Cunningham sitting together. Celia smiled quietly and turned back to her friends.

A few minutes later, though, Ava's voice pierced the din of conversation. "That's what Trip said. The two of them have been caught together more than once."

Julia didn't bother to whisper. "Caught? You mean…"

"He didn't go into details. But they've got to know

they're asking for trouble. Fraternization is strictly against the rules."

"He's barely a lieutenant. Not to mention married."

"That part is probably easy to forget." They cackled at each other. "Just like his dumpy little wife."

Celia avoided the gazes of the women at her table, even Bea's. There was no reason to believe Julia and Ava were talking about Mack. She wouldn't give anyone the satisfaction of seeing her upset.

Then, in the restroom, she heard two voices she didn't know. "That Peyton Abbott—I hate the thought of her living on the ship with all of those men, one of them being my husband." After a pause, the same person said, "Would you call me dumpy?"

"No, I would not. They weren't talking about your Steve. You know he's got eyes for nobody but you."

"Still, that she-wolf scares me. I heard she's got one of the new guys in tow already. I saw them myself in June, at the O Club with their heads close together. Peyton Abbott and that new hotshot F-18 pilot...what's his name? Oh, yes—Mack Butler."

The USS Midway
arriving at North Island Naval Base
after a Pacific deployment
December 1989
It's so impressive to watch the tiny tugboats guiding that
huge ship between the piers. Sailors in blue uniforms, all
spaced the same distance apart, stand at attention on the
deck. We wives are filled with pride and love as we think

about where they've been and what they've done for their country.

Mack closed his seabag and checked the zipper on his duffel one more time. As he straightened up, he caught a glimpse of himself in the mirror. Would Celia like the mustache? Did he have time to shave?

The intercom crackled. "All hands on deck. Prepare for ship's arrival at Naval Station North Island."

Too late. Buttoning his jacket, he grabbed his cap and joined the crush of people heading up the ladders to the flight deck. Most of the men he flew with had taken the planes off the ship this morning, to land at the Miramar Naval Air Station a day early. For his first big cruise, though, he had decided to ride in with the carrier and meet his family at the dock.

The decision was a good one. Bright sunlight in an empty sky glazed the ocean with blue, black and gold. On the eastern horizon, a backdrop of brown humps became the Cuyamaca Mountains, fronted by the green palms of the coastline mixed with the spikes and cubes of the city's skyline. A stiff breeze whipped his tie out of his jacket. Who knew December in San Diego would be so chilly?

"If you stare too hard you'll ruin your eyes," Jerry Fiedler said, coming up beside him. "We'll get there eventually."

Mack thought about Celia, about the feel of her in his arms, the taste of her on his mouth, and the long string of lonely nights behind him. "After 136 days, yesterday wasn't soon enough."

"Damn straight."

They stood together as the crew lined up along the edges of the deck. Red-white-and-blue bunting had been hung from the command decks in the tower, and patriotic tunes blared from the loudspeaker. Every face wore a grin.

Tugboats attached to the sides of the carrier without fuss, like efficient parasites, and the pilot came aboard to drive the ship into port.

"Not long now," Jerry said, beating a tattoo on the rail with his fingers. "Not long."

The white blur of the city became individual buildings crowded on the low hills of the shore. Moving south, past San Diego proper, the ship headed toward the piers at the naval station. The white sands of Coronado Island became visible, the flight tower of the landing strip, and then the piers themselves. Band music floated over the choppy water. People on the docks waved, jumped, yelled. Somewhere in that mob were his kids. And Celia. Finally.

The tugboat captains knew their stuff—the *Midway* slid smoothly into her berth. Then began the wild scramble to match 4,500 sailors with their families.

Mack squinted at the crowd. "Do you see them?"

Jerry shook his head. "Maybe we should just go down there. It's got to be easier."

"Whatever you say." On the dock, though, the crowd made finding anyone impossible. Mack could see over most heads, but Celia was tiny, and the kids even smaller. They should have arranged a signal—

A pretty blonde caught his eye. Her hair was as shiny as Celia's, with the same curls, but cut shorter. She wore a bright red jacket and a short blue skirt, which drew his attention to her excellent figure, her sleek legs. Celia's hips were rounder, he remembered, her sweet rear end more of a handful….

The blonde turned around then, and he could see her face, her brilliant smile, her big brown eyes. Mack swallowed hard.

Beside him, Jerry shouted, "Bea. Over here, Bea!"

All at once, there were kids clinging to Mack's knees, a baby in his arms and a woman he wasn't sure he knew gazing up at him.

"Welcome home," she said, going up on tiptoe to put her arms around his neck and give him a kiss on the cheek. "It's so good to see you."

Before he could kiss her again, or even give her the hug he'd been storing, Celia stepped back and Jerry joined them, bringing with him the originals of the pictures Mack had lived with for four months. "Mack, let me introduce you. This is Bea, and the twins, Aaron and Adam. Bea, here's Mack."

Jerry's wife glanced at Celia, then nodded to Mack. "He's as gorgeous as the pictures, isn't he? Even with the toothbrush over his mouth."

Celia laughed. "Yes, he is."

Mack rolled his eyes. "Okay, I'm shaving it off tomorrow morning. It was just an idea."

After Mack and Jerry went back to the ship to get their bags, the two families headed to their respective cars for the drive home. The pier had become much less crowded, but the highway across the bridge had turned into a parking lot.

"I guess it's a good thing carriers don't come in every day." Mack stretched his arm along the seat as they waited for a chance to move forward. "This traffic would make living on the island a lot less appealing to me."

"I never want to live somewhere that means going over a bridge like this one on a regular basis." Celia's usually soft voice was tight and hard. "I hate being stuck so high in the air."

Mack noticed she had her hands clenched together with white-knuckled pressure. He covered them with his palm. "Relax. I won't drive off the side. If I can land on a carrier, I can keep this car on the road."

Though she grinned, as he'd wanted her to, she still seemed tense. What was going on here?

The cars ahead of them inched forward, and he put both hands on the wheel. "So, is there an instruction manual somewhere that says what we're supposed to talk about all day when the only thing I can think about is getting you into bed?"

Celia heard the question and felt her heart start bouncing around in her chest. That didn't sound like Mack was in love with someone else, did it? The way he'd been staring at her since he got off the ship—as if he could eat her alive—didn't look as if he was in love with someone else.

"You should be glad M.J. is asleep," she told him. "Otherwise, he'd be asking what you meant. He's gotten very inquisitive."

"Maybe we should wake them all up, so they'll be sure to take naps this afternoon. Long, long naps."

She gave him a provocative glance. "But then they'd want to stay up late. Wouldn't that be…" she pursed her lips for a second "…too bad?"

Mack put his head back and groaned. "Oh, yeah."

Celia made hot dogs and beans for lunch, and though the kids didn't nap again, the afternoon passed quickly enough. Her parents called from Maryland and then Mack called Massachusetts to talk to his mom and stepdad. He brought out some of the gifts he'd bought—Chinese cloth dolls for the girls and a dragon puppet for M.J., a pair of gorgeous red cloisonné vases for Celia. After a couple of hours at the park with the kids, where he kept them running, swinging, biking and climbing as long as possible, Mack grilled steaks for dinner and enjoyed two slices of the German chocolate cake Celia had made.

Eventually, the kids wound down. Celia put Ella to bed while Mack read stories to M.J. and Courtney. M.J. fell asleep fast, but Courtney—always a night owl—got three extra fairy tales out of her dad before she drifted off.

As Celia waited for Mack in their bed, her nerves took over again, as they had this morning, waiting for the ship to dock. Had he been with someone else while he was gone? Would she know it, feel it in his touch? Had she forgotten how to please him? What if they didn't…*fit* anymore?

She heard him running the shower in the hall bathroom, and the sound of the sink draining, which meant he'd shaved. Then he came into the bedroom wearing a pair of dark green pajama bottoms.

"What do you think?" he asked Celia. "They're silk."

She gazed at him as he stood there bare-chested in the moonlight. "Terrific," she said. The little weight he'd lost gave his muscles more definition. He looked more than terrific. "H-how do they feel?"

His sea-blue gaze blazed with laughter and desire. "You tell me." In one smooth move, he came into the bed beside her, cupping her shoulders in his palms. She laid her hand on his chest, fingers spread wide. Her skin was cool. He was burning up.

"You're beautiful," he murmured, easing the sheet away. "Sexy as hell." He shaped her body with his palm, from breast to ankle and back again, drawing the hem of the gown up above her knees. "You've been working out."

She stretched against his touch. "Um-hmm."

"At some gym, I guess, with a good-looking young guy for a trainer." Bracing a hand on either side of her, he leaned close. "Should I be jealous?"

Celia stared into her husband's face, searching his mind and heart. Mack wasn't thinking about anyone else, she was certain, didn't love anyone but *her*.

A warm tide of relief swept over her. She looped her arms around his neck and pulled him closer. "Let's see if I can answer that question without words."

Chapter 8

Grandmom and Granddad Randolph
March 1990
They had this picture taken for their church directory and
sent us enough prints that Mack could keep a copy with
him and each of the kids could have one to hold while
they said their prayers. Maeve had gotten very fragile—
her skin was nearly transparent and her hair had gone
completely silver. But her smile remained as welcoming
as a calm summer sea.

All through the rainy California winter, Celia ignored the persistent rumors about Mack and Lieutenant Commander Peyton. Mack's love and attention were all the proof Celia needed that an affair had never happened, would never happen.

One Friday in February, though, he called to say he'd be late. He had put the Civic in for a tune-up, but it wasn't finished, so he would get a ride from one of the guys at work. Because he had to depend on someone else, he couldn't guarantee what time he'd be home.

At seven, Celia fed the kids, who were starving and whiny. She let them stay up past their bedtime so they could talk to Daddy, but they fell asleep on the couch before Mack came in. Courtney woke when Celia carried her to the pink room, and needed a story to settle down again. Having been awake since dawn, Celia was exhausted. Mother and daughter dozed off together in Courtney's little bed.

Some time later, Celia opened her eyes to a pitch-black house. Mack had come home, turned off the lights and gone to bed without waking her up.

She climbed out of Courtney's bed, praying she wouldn't disturb the little girl, then checked Ella in the crib on the other side of the room. Across the hall, Celia pulled her nightgown out of the closet by feel and changed in the bathroom.

Then she stood by her own bed, staring down at her husband sprawled in the center of the mattress. The breeze through the open window brought her the smell of alcohol on his breath.

Her chest burned with hurt and anger. She could barely breathe. The temptation to get away, to sleep on the couch, overwhelmed her. Mack could learn how it felt to wake up and not know where she was.

But why should she sacrifice her comfort? He could just roll over, the jerk, and give her room to sleep.

She shoved at his shoulder with both hands. "Slide over, Mack. Come on, move."

He snorted and mumbled, but didn't shift.

Celia braced a knee on the mattress and pushed again. "Move."

Grumbling, with a few swear words mixed in, he flopped over—in the wrong direction, taking up her side of the bed.

"Damn." She'd fought as many battles as she intended to tonight. Stomping around the bed, she settled herself without regard to whether she woke him or not. He'd grabbed both pillows. She retrieved her own by jerking it out from under his head.

Just as she got still, he said, "Celia?" His breath was strong enough to drink.

"What?"

He reached over and set his hand on her bare arm. "Sorry."

She didn't answer.

"J.T. wanted to stop by the O Club." After a minute of silence, he said, "I couldn't get him to leave."

That would be because J.T. was single, with no wife or kids to get home to.

"Finally I got a ride with Lieutenant Commander Abbott."

Celia's heart skidded in her chest. "Really?"

Mack replied with a snore.

She lay awake until after four, picturing Mack dancing with Peyton Abbott, seeing them in a shadowed corner of a gray steel corridor on the ship, imagining stolen moments on shore in Singapore....

Surely he wouldn't be so forthright if there was something to hide. If he didn't want her to know, why would he mention the woman at all?

Saturday morning, the kids got up with the sun, as usual, found cartoons on the TV and snacked from the small bowls of cereal Celia had left on the counter for them. Around eight, she started coffee and began to make pancakes. At 8:30, M.J. cried, "Here comes Daddy!" She heard the three of them hit him like a line of football players. His response came to her as a gravelly mumble.

He slouched into the kitchen, fumbled a mug out of the cabinet, sloshed coffee on the counter, then stood with his head hanging and one arm braced as he took the first couple of gulps.

Finally, he looked at her. "'Morning."

"Good morning."

"I apologized, right?"

"You did."

"I got sucked in, is all." He chugged down more coffee. "J.T. wanted a couple of drinks, which turned into I don't know how many. I stayed to drive, but ended up with a couple—more than a couple—of drinks myself."

"That's when you went home with Lieutenant Commander Abbot?" Celia nodded, flipping a burned pancake over in the pan. "I understand."

"That's not what I said." His fingers caught Celia's chin, forcing her to look at him. "She drove me here. Period."

Searching his eyes, Celia could find no hint of shame, no shadow of a lie. Her relief blossomed into a smile. "I know." Tilting her head, she kissed his fingers. "Get the kids to the table."

Mack grinned. "Aye, aye, Captain."

That should have been the end of the matter. But she couldn't help noticing the way certain wives stopped chatting when she joined their groups. Mack occasionally stopped off at the club after work, not too frequently or too noticeably, and he never again arrived home drunk. When he talked to Celia after each visit, though, Peyton Abbott's name came up more often than not.

He's being honest with me, she rationalized. *If there were something to hide, he wouldn't be so frank.* Most nights, he reached for her in bed. If he was having an affair, surely he wouldn't want her so often.

Still, the gossip didn't die. In March, Celia told Bea she wouldn't be going to any more Wives Club meetings.

"Are you running scared?" Bea knew the whole sorry story. "I've asked Jerry. He swears there's nothing going on."

Celia shook her head. "I'm tired of the game. Let them find somebody new to torture."

After the rainy months of January, February and March, April was a welcome change with its clear skies, mild temperatures and cool nights. On weekends she and Mack took the kids to the Wild Animal Park, Sea World and the zoo. They drove into the mountains for a picnic and splurged on a weekend at Disneyland. Whirling teacups, life-size cartoon characters, singing bears and flying ships filled each minute with fun.

All three kids fell asleep on the drive home and were very grumpy when woken. Mack was tired—he'd carried at least one and sometimes two kids for most of the day. Celia craved a hot shower and a few minutes by herself, which seemed unlikely, since Mack would be going to work early the next morning.

So when the phone rang she answered impatiently. "Hello? Hello?"

"I must have gotten…Celia, is that you?" Mack's stepfather asked. "You don't sound like yourself."

Neither did he. "I'm sorry I was abrupt, William. It's me. How are you?"

"Can I talk to Mack?"

That meant bad news. She called Mack to the phone, and watched his face drain of color as he listened.

"When? Is she better?" He squeezed his eyes shut. "Do you think I should…? Right. As soon as I can."

After turning to hang up the phone, he rested his head against the wall. "Mom's in the hospital with pneumonia. Not responding to treatment."

Celia put her arms around his waist, pressing her cheek against his back. "Oh, Mack."

"She might die. What will we do without her?"

"We'll pray that doesn't happen. She's a strong lady."

But their prayers were not answered as they'd hoped. Two hours after Mack's plane landed, he stood with his brothers and his dad at Maeve's bedside as she peacefully slipped away.

Celia and the kids flew to Boston three days later— the earliest she could get affordable tickets. M.J. was airsick and Courtney cried when her ears popped. Mack met them at the gate, his face pale, his eyes red.

"I'm so sorry." Celia reached up to put her arms over his shoulders. "Are you okay?"

He blinked hard and turned away to pick up Ella and take Courtney's hand. "Sure. M.J. looks a little rough around the edges, though."

Mack, Jr.'s face went from sickly pale to embarrassed red. He stared at his feet as they walked through the terminal.

"He got airsick," Celia said quietly.

Mack stopped in his tracks. "Airsick? On the plane?" He looked at M.J in horror. "You don't like to fly?"

M.J. sidled behind Celia. "It was a rough flight until we got over the Rockies," she said. "M.J. wasn't the only one. He did just fine for his first time."

Mack didn't pick up on the message she was sending with her angry glare. "I knew the first time I stepped inside a plane that was what I wanted to do with my life. I've never been airsick, even doing consecutive barrel rolls. Over and over and over…"

At the bobbing motion of his hand and his head, along with the roll of his words, Celia felt herself getting queasy. "I don't fly well, so I guess M.J. takes after me." She gave the boy a hug. "We prefer to keep our feet on the ground, don't we?" He didn't return her smile.

At the Butler-Randolph house, snow still blanketed Maeve's garden. The sole lighted lamp in the living room couldn't fight the darkness, and the cold ashes left in the grate gave the air a smoky scent. Mack's stepdad and brothers were nowhere to be seen.

Appalled by the emptiness, Celia looked at her

husband. "Is this what you think your mother would want? All of us mourning together in the dark and cold?"

He shrugged a shoulder. "Doesn't seem to make much difference."

"That's a sorry thing to say." Mack lowered his brows in a frown, but Celia turned away and marched around the room, switching on the lights. "Go get some wood," she told him. "We need a fire." He probably thought she was overstepping her bounds. What right did she have to give orders in his mother's house?

But what right did the Butler men have to sully Maeve's memory by giving up?

In a few minutes the kids were stretched out on the carpet near the blaze, occupied with the new coloring books she'd brought along. Celia cleared away the mess left by unsupervised males—newspapers, food wrappers and drink cans, magazines and dirty socks—and straightened the couch pillows. When footsteps sounded on the porch outside, the room looked more like a home. Like Maeve Randolph's home.

William stopped on the threshold and stared. "What the hell is this?"

Celia kissed his cheek, then stepped behind him to take his coat off his shoulders. "Come in and sit down, Granddad. We'll eat dinner in a little while, but you can have a chance to relax first." She gave James, Ty and Colin a meaningful glance that moved the brothers into action.

William dropped into his chair. "What are you doing, Celia? I don't…" He put a hand over his eyes. "I don't feel too good right now."

She pressed a palm on his shoulder. "I know you don't. But sitting in the dark and starving is not going to make you feel any better." Walking toward the kitchen, she beckoned for Mack to follow. "Your brothers can keep an eye on the kids while you get your dad something to drink."

At the refrigerator, she handed him beers to go around. "That's tonight's limit, by the way. Nobody's drinking themselves to sleep while my children are here."

He stared at her, his blue eyes half angry, half confused. "Who put you in charge?"

Fear fluttered in her chest, but she held her ground. "Right now, there's nobody in charge. The one thing I know is that Maeve would not approve of her family giving up on life because she passed on. Would she?"

Shifting his gaze to his shoes, Mack didn't answer.

"Would she?"

Finally, he shook his head.

"So until William is back on his feet, I guess I'll keep ordering people around. We can't leave him here alone, Mack. Not if he won't take care of himself and the house."

"You're right." He took a deep breath, then laid his hand along her jawline and gave her a brief kiss. "Thanks."

She didn't have to worry about cooking—friends had brought over plenty of food, which Maeve's men had shoved haphazardly onto refrigerator shelves. Celia warmed up lasagna and baked ham and vegetable casseroles. She toasted rolls and tossed a salad with the dressing provided, then set the table with Maeve's dishes. The pink roses around the rims made her cry, thinking of how much her mother-in-law had loved the rose bushes she'd tended. Someday maybe Celia would be able to plant a rose garden in Maeve's honor.

Dinner started out quietly, with Celia helping the children, and the men acting as if they weren't allowed to eat. Gradually, though, they relaxed, chewed, talked. Even laughed. Mack told a story about Maeve going after him with a broom when he trampled some of her flowers to retrieve a football, and Ty followed with an account of the day he'd chased a cat through the house and broken a prized Irish crystal bowl.

"Didn't sit down for two weeks," he said ruefully. "You didn't mess with Mom's treasures."

There were tears during the evening, too, as William recalled their wedding day, and Maeve's strong love for her sons.

"She would have cherished a daughter, though," he said, rubbing his eyes with his knuckles. "Somebody to share her love of lace and ribbons and pink." Then he smiled at Celia. "She did get her daughter-in-law, didn't she? You two spent hours talking about baby things."

"We did." Celia wiped tears off her cheeks. "She sent us such beautiful dresses for Ella and Courtney. I'll keep them forever."

Ty, James and Colin went to their own homes, while Celia put the children to sleep in the twin beds in Mack's old room. William retired to the guest room, unable to rest in the bed he'd shared with Maeve.

That left Mack and Celia the room with the bunk beds once shared by the older boys. While Celia changed in the bathroom, Mack pulled on a long-sleeved T-shirt and flannel pajama bottoms to stay warm during the long New England night. Sitting on the lower bunk, he braced his elbows on his knees and dropped his head in his hands.

He'd never in his life felt so exhausted, so confused. The world seemed unbalanced without his mother to keep it spinning in the right direction. Seeing William so lost, Ty and Colin and James slumped in grief.... Mack had felt himself sliding into real despair.

Then Celia had arrived.

At his thought, she opened the door and slipped inside.

"Sorry I took so long. The bathroom wasn't fit for human use." She propped her hands on her hips and surveyed the bunk beds. "I haven't slept in one of these before. Am I going to roll off the top bunk?"

"No, you aren't." He reached for her, folded her body against his and rolled back onto the bottom bunk. "You're staying right here, with me."

Her arms came around his shoulders, and she pressed his head to her breasts. He felt a soft kiss on his forehead. For the first time in four days, Mack could breathe.

"I miss her," he muttered, closing his eyes against tears.

Another kiss. "We all do."

"She was a good woman."

"And she left four good sons to continue for her."

He drew a deep breath. "Being left behind hurts."

"Yes, it does."

Mack was silent for a long time, wrestling with whys. No one, not even Celia, could give him an answer. In the quiet darkness, he remembered what Maeve had told him: *Trust Celia and the love you share. That's what will see you through.*

Now the warmth of her body reminded him that he was alive, that life would go on. He kissed her soft lips, her eyes, the hollow under her ear, and felt her shudder in response. His hands reached for smooth skin, for the curves of her hips and the lovely fullness of her breasts. Urgently, desperately, Mack made love to his wife, stifling her cries of pleasure with his mouth, finding solace for his grief in her endless generosity.

And love did, indeed, see him through.

Three miserable kiddies—
M.J., Courtney and Ella with the chicken pox
August 1990

Back in sunny southern California, they discovered that Mack's squadron had been transferred to the USS *Independence,* which meant gearing up for another Pacific deployment in August. Mack's work hours lengthened and he had weekend duty sometimes. Celia tried to avoid thinking about Peyton Abbott. Managing life with three children gave her all the challenges she could handle.

She knew she was in trouble the morning Bea called to complain. "The twins woke up yesterday with little red bumps on their faces. Then Sandra called to say her oldest had the chicken pox. We'd spent all Monday afternoon at their house."

"And we spent yesterday at yours." Celia rubbed her eyes. "I guess we'll be seeing spots in a couple of days."

Just in time to keep Celia from attending the farewell banquet for this cruise, Mack, Jr. began complaining about itches on his chest and tummy. In what seemed like minutes, he was covered with red dots. Courtney woke up scratching the next morning, and Ella was sick that afternoon.

Celia sent Mack off to the dinner by himself, and was too busy comforting miserable children to worry about LtCdr. Abbott. By the time he returned, she'd fallen asleep on Courtney's bed with the girls on either side of her.

Mack had to work the Sunday before the ship's departure. When he got home about 8:00 p.m., he found Celia crouched by the tub, where the three kids were taking a cool oatmeal bath.

He stood in the doorway, staring at the splotchy children. "I had no idea one little body could hold so many spots." As M.J. stood up to get out, Mack wrapped him in a towel and carried him to his room. "You look like a bumpy red monster," he said, patting gently. Usually, M.J. took on the role of beast at this point, growling, roaring and pretending to attack his dad.

Not tonight. "I'm not a monster!" The little boy beat his fists on Mack's shoulders. "I'm not. I'm not!"

Celia looked in. "His temperature was up before he got into the tub, so he's pretty grumpy."

"A grumpy bumpy red monster," Mack agreed, grinning.

M.J. burst into tears, tore out of his dad's hold and ran to Celia. "I'm not I'm not I'm not I'm not!"

Courtney and Ella joined in wailing. Celia tried to reassure Mack with a glance, but he was sitting on M.J.'s bed, hands clasped between his knees, staring at the floor.

She maneuvered all three children into her bedroom and put them on the big bed to dry them off and get pajamas on.

"Now," she said, pulling back the covers, "I want you three to stay right here on my bed."

"All night?" Courtney said hopefully.

"Sure." Anything for a little peace. "Daddy will read you a story—"

"Not Daddy. You!"

"You read, Mommy!"

"Mommy read!"

Celia hushed them just in time to hear the front door slam and the engine of Mack's car start up.

"Yes," she said with a sigh. "I guess I will."

Chapter 9

Mack walked into the house about 11:00 p.m. and met up with Celia as she came from the back hallway.

She stared at him with weary eyes. "I just got all three of them to sleep." She lifted her shoulders on a deep breath. "Smells like you've been to the club." Walking past him, she went into the kitchen, where she pulled out the peanut butter and jelly and bread. "Excuse me—I haven't had time to eat dinner yet."

Mack watched her make two sandwiches, put them both on a plate and pour a glass of milk. He followed when she went into the dining room. "This isn't my fault, Celia. I didn't do anything wrong."

"If you say so."

"If you say different, then tell me what the problem is."

She munched her sandwich instead of responding.

"Come on, Celia. You're not being fair."

"Fair?" Her voice had a rough edge to it unrelated to the peanut butter. "When has anything been fair?"

"What are you saying?"

"I'm saying that it wasn't exactly my preference to spend tonight nursing sick children."

"Well, yeah, but—"

"But it's my job?" She rolled her eyes. "I don't think it's particularly fair that I'll be the only parent for the next five months. That I'll make all the decisions, set the limits, choose the punishments, plus cook and clean and shop and nurse and play and drive."

Mack tried for a little humor. "You know what they say. A sailor's wife—the toughest job in the Navy."

"How condescending is that?" She got up from the table and went to stare out the window into the darkness. "I have a brain, too, you know."

"Yes, I do know." He stood behind her, cupping his hands over her shoulders. "And I really appreciate everything you do to make my job easier."

"Your job? *Your job?* You think this is about you?" Celia jerked away and stomped into the family room. "I don't care about the stupid Navy, the stupid planes and ships. This is our life, Mack. I'm trying to manage *our life!*"

"And you think I'm not?"

"You think you are?"

"Why else would I be spending the next five months on a floating tin can with a bunch of jackasses who have B.O. and bad breath?"

"Because that's exactly what you've been planning to do since you were a kid. Because being a pilot, being the eagle flying high above all those jackasses, is what you always wanted for yourself."

"It's more than that, Celia. I'm serving my country. And I'm supporting my family."

"Convenient, isn't it?"

"Hell, no, it's not convenient." He paced the length of the room and back again. "There's nothing convenient about getting woken up two or three times after midnight by crying babies, then getting up at 5:00 a.m. sharp enough to fly safely."

She sniffed. "Poor you."

"There's nothing convenient about taking ten percent off the top of the paycheck to put away for college funds. About using duct tape and baling wire to keep a miserable Honda together when other guys are driving Camaros and 'Vettes. About not even having air-conditioning in the damn car, for Pete's sake, so I show up at work already needing a shower."

He couldn't seem to stop, though he knew he should. "There's nothing convenient about always having my weekends planned for me—mow the grass, trim the trees, swim with the kids, clean the pool, go to the zoo, park, beach."

"And what would you *conveniently* do instead?"

"I could shoot baskets with some guys. Go to a ball game. Fish. Do some long-distance biking—"

"Spend the weekend with your girlfriend."

Mack was silent for a long moment. "You know that's not true."

"Then why do I keep hearing about her—and you—every time I come around a corner?"

"I don't know! Because people are evil or stupid or both?"

"So she's not there on the nights you stop off at the club for 'a few beers'?"

"Sometimes."

"But you and she don't drink together?"

"Sometimes we do. She's a senior officer—I can't tell her to piss off."

"That's why you keep her phone number in your pocket?"

"What? What are you talking about?"

Celia opened a drawer in the china cabinet and took out a small piece of paper. A napkin. "I always check your pockets before I send your uniforms to the cleaners. And this was in a pocket."

Stretching the napkin between his fingers, Mack saw the O Club insignia in the corner…and Peyton's number scribbled in blue ink across the center.

He crushed the paper in his fist. "She wrote it down and gave it to me, Celia. I put it in my pocket and forgot to throw it away. I never called her. Not once."

"You don't have to—you spend five months of the year living in the same place."

"You have no idea what it's like, living on a ship. There's no privacy, no place to go where you can't be seen and heard by somebody else. Even if I was...if I wanted...there's just no way."

"It doesn't matter." Celia dismissed the subject with a wave of her hand, a brief shrug.

"You don't trust me. That matters a lot. Especially when all I've ever done is try to live up to my responsibilities for you, for the kids."

"You have, haven't you? From the beginning, you've been determined to do the right thing."

"You have a problem with that?"

"We're another job for you, just like the Navy. Only not as much fun, probably. You do love to fly."

How could he deny the truth? But there was more than one truth here. "I love you, Celia. I love the kids."

"Good try."

"You're calling me a liar?"

They stood staring at each other across the family room, both panting, red in the face, rigid with anger and hurt. Into the silence came a child's voice.

"Mommy?" Then, louder. "Mommy? Mommy?"

"I'm coming, M.J." Celia started for the bedroom.

"We're not finished," Mack told her.

But as the remaining hours of the night passed, what talking they did solved nothing. At 4:00 a.m., Mack showered, dressed and stashed his duffel bag in the car. When he returned to the house to find Celia, she had fallen asleep in the rocking chair with Ella, who was still wide awake, on her lap. Dark-haired like her dad, with Celia's brown eyes, Ella gazed up at him somberly as she sucked on a bottle of cold grape drink.

Mack had done what he could. "Tell Mommy goodbye for me," he whispered, giving Ella a kiss on her bumpy forehead. He set his lips on Celia's hair for a moment, then straightened up and left fast. He drove through the cool California night with his eyes burning, his chest tight, his jaw clenched.

Back at the house, Celia opened her eyes as Mack left. She rocked until Ella finally fell asleep. Then she sat motionless, dry-eyed, as the sun came over the mountains and the *Independence* surged relentlessly out to sea.

Mack, Jr. on his first day of preschool
San Diego, September 1990
He's so proud of that navy-blue backpack!

Mack pinned the picture Celia had sent on the bulletin board above his desk, next to shots of the three kids at the beach, at the Wild Animal Park and in the pool. His only picture of Celia herself was one he'd taken on their honeymoon, in a garden in Williamsburg. She'd been a beautiful bride.

But was she still his wife?

Jerry Fiedler swung into the room. "Hey, Mack."

"Hey."

"Lots of mail?" Jerry flipped his cap onto his desk and dived into his rack.

"A few letters, yeah."

"Bea's nagging me about getting out again. Says she can't stand this cruise crap. Says going to the movies with Celia is all that keeps her sane."

"Maybe you should resign. Get a job with a commercial airline, R & D, something stable. Missing your kids growing up is a mistake."

"Sounds like you're thinking along those lines yourself. You've paid back your USNA obligation, haven't you? You'd make a hell of a lot more money with Delta or Eastern than sitting around out here in Mother Ocean."

Mack grunted, but didn't answer. Leaving the Navy had been on his mind constantly since they'd left port a week ago. Celia had basically commanded him to choose between his family and his career. How was he supposed to make that decision?

Jerry's snores punctuated the background noise of the ship as Mack climbed up to his own bunk with his bunch of letters. His stepdad wrote to say he was doing well enough, had been keeping up with the garden and was planning to visit Celia and the kids in October.

Celia always numbered her letters on the flap, so he'd know which one to read first. In addition to the picture of the kids, she'd sent drawings of flowers by Courtney, a handprint from Ella and a cutout coloring book picture of a plane with Mack, Jr.'s laborious signature across it. Cute kids, he had. Good kids.

Everything is fine here, Celia wrote. The kids had recovered from the chicken pox with only a few scars as mementos. Mack, Jr. had started kindergarten without any traumas or tragedies. She'd enrolled Courtney in ballet classes and took Ella to a toddler tumbling group of her own. The pool pump had stopped working; the repairman had found a drowned chipmunk in the pipe.

They'd shocked the pool with chlorine to get rid of the germs and had had no problems since. His dad would visit in October and her parents were coming for Thanksgiving. She signed *Love, Celia* with the usual row of little *X*s and *O*s, symbolizing kisses and hugs.

And that, sports fans, was all she wrote. The next letter, two days later, and the next, were pretty much the same. The kids, minor house problems and *Love, Celia XXXOOO.*

No apology, no blame. No acknowledgment of that last argument in any way at all. The whole night might never have happened.

Mack didn't know how to interpret her attitude. Should he simply take the same tack, ignore the topic in his letters? Or should he force the issue when they were both calm and able to collect their thoughts before putting them down on paper?

For lack of time, he sent his first letter back without mentioning the fight. After that, he didn't know how to bring it up, when Celia so clearly didn't intend to. Life in the middle of the ocean wasn't exactly full of excitement, so his letters didn't say much at all, really, except what movies he'd seen, which books he was reading. He signed them *Love, Mack* as he always had. What else did he have to say to make her believe he cared?

LtCdr. Abbott materialized at his door one evening, a few days before they were to dock in Singapore. "Hello, there, Lieutenant."

He got to his feet and stood at alert. "Good evening, ma'am."

"Relax." She waved him to his chair as she curled onto the end of Jerry's rack. Mack glanced over his shoulder to be sure the door stood wide open. "I haven't seen much of you this trip."

"I've been…busy."

"Have you got plans for Singapore?"

"No, ma'am. I'm on shipboard duty part of the time."

"But you'll have some liberty. Why don't we meet for dinner?"

"Thanks, but I don't think that's a good idea."

"You let a little gossip determine who your friends are?"

"I don't plan to let a little gossip derail my career, ma'am."

She sighed. "Come on, Mack. We can be friends. There doesn't have to be more than that."

"You underestimate yourself, Lieutenant Commander Abbott."

"You're saying I'm too dangerous for you to be with?"

Mack let the silence speak for him. She could take it to mean whatever she wanted.

At exactly the right moment, Jerry came into the room with his usual energy. "Oh…good evening, ma'am." He halted, but didn't quite salute. "Glad to see you. Mack, we've got a squadron briefing in ten minutes."

"Right. Thanks for stopping in, Lieutenant Commander." He got to his feet and moved to the door, ushering her with him as he went. She really didn't have much choice. "Hope to see you again sometime."

Once the LtCdr. left, with a suggestive backward

glance, Mack shook Jerry's hand. "Great idea, making up a briefing."

"I'm not," Jerry said. "Let's go. Something's up."

An hour later, Mack sat down to write another letter.

"Dear Celia, !ooks like the plans for this deployment have been changed. We're not heading for the Indian Ocean anymore. Our destination is classified, but I'm sure you'll see it in the news eventually...."

Mack Butler and Jerry Fiedler
Liberty in Singapore
September 1990

"What's Daddy and Uncle Jerry standing in front of, Mommy?"

"It looks like a temple of some kind, M.J."

"Like Adam's and Aaron's temple?"

Celia ruffled his hair. "Sort of."

"That temple has dragons on it."

"Isn't that interesting?" Mack looked thinner than she remembered. His eyes were shadowed. Had he changed so much in the three weeks since she'd seen him?

"Are there monsters in Sing-Singa..." M.J. shook his head. "Who is that big person in back of them? She has funny eyes."

"Singapore, sweetie. That's a statue, not a person. A very big, painted statue of someone called Buddha."

"I like fish," Courtney said from Celia's other side. "Can we have fish? Orange and white, like these?" Mack had sent a picture of a koi pond somewhere in Singapore.

"I don't think…" Celia stopped herself. Why not? Why couldn't they have fish? She'd be the one doing the work. "You know, Courtney, we might just see about getting some fish. Not quite so big, but little fish."

They made a family outing to a pet store that afternoon and returned with an aquarium and all the equipment. "We'll get the fish soon," she promised the kids. "First the environment has to be ready."

"Viremet," Ella said, nodding wisely.

Celia was pouring water into the tank when the phone rang. She set the sturdy plastic container on the floor and hurried to pick up. You never knew if Mack…

"Turn on the news."

"Hi, Bea." She swallowed her disappointment. "What's on the news?"

"The *Independence*. They're not going to Diego Garcia anymore. They're going to Iraq."

"The Middle East? Why would they go there?"

"The president of Iraq is threatening Kuwait. That's where a lot of U.S. oil comes from."

"But—"

"Our president wants Iraq to back down. He's sending ships into the Persian Gulf to threaten them into cooperating."

"Threaten?" Celia turned on the TV news most nights, but didn't really listen. "What does that mean?"

Bea took a deep breath. "That means U.S. planes flying over Iraq and Kuwait. That means guns on the ground pointed up at those planes. Maybe even planes fighting over Iraq, over the gulf. Battle, Celia. Jerry and Mack could be in a war."

From the other room came the sound of pouring water, then breaking glass…and a child's hysterical cry.

War. "I'll call you back, Bea. Gotta go."

Rushing to the dining room, Celia found Ella sitting on the tile floor in a puddle of water dotted with shards of glass from the broken aquarium. Courtney stood plastered against the wall on one side of the aquarium stand, hands behind her back. Mack, Jr. stood on the other side, holding the plastic pitcher.

He started talking as soon as Celia appeared. "I told her to let me do it, Mommy! I told her she wasn't big enough. And she grabbed the pitcher and made me drop it and then the aquarium fell over on Ella!"

Celia reached to pick up the screaming child. "Are you okay, baby? Did you get cut?"

"Mommy, she's bleeding!"

Ella opened her little fists, each clenched around a dagger of glass. Each dripping blood.

"Oh, God. Oh, God." In the kitchen, Celia levered the baby over the sink to run water on her hands. The blood flowed so fast she couldn't see the cuts.

"God, God, God," she muttered, pulling out dish towels to wrap around Ella's hands. "How am I going to do this? How can I drive?"

She held Ella with one arm, keeping hold of her hands through the towels, and grabbed her purse with the other. "Mack, Court, come on. Now."

In the car, she got Mack and Courtney into their car

seats, but kept Ella on the front seat, cuddled close, hands still held tight. The little girl's screams had become constant frightened sobs.

"It's okay, Ella. The clinic is just a little drive. We'll be there before you can say...Peter Rabbit."

The name got Ella's attention for a second. Then she began to cry again. M.J. and Courtney hadn't said a word. The towels around Ella's hands were beginning to turn red.

Celia parked illegally, blocking several cars, and rushed into the clinic. "Help me, please, she's cut her hands—"

The corpsman at the reception window didn't look up from his work. "Take a number, we'll get with you as soon as we can."

"I'm not taking a number. She's got to be seen now."

"Look, lady, you don't get it." He raised his face. "There's people ahead of you. Wait your turn."

"I. Need. Help. Now." She pulled the bloody towel off Ella's right hand and threw it on his desk, right under his nose. "Do you get that?"

Chapter 10

Four hours later, poor little Ella was snuggled in her crib under her favorite blanket, with one rosy cheek pillowed on her bandaged hands. The doctor had recommended antihistamine syrup to keep her drowsy and less frustrated with the wrappings. Luckily, most of the cuts were superficial—her palms had needed only a few stitches each.

Courtney and M.J. had been perfect angels during the entire ordeal, and Celia didn't have the heart to investigate the mishap any further. She made up the sofa bed, put a fairy tale videotape into the player Mack had bought just before leaving on the cruise, and kissed them both good-night.

Then she went into her room, curled up on the bed and gave in to the shakes and the tears.

She didn't realize she'd fallen asleep until the jangle of the phone woke her up. Expecting Bea, she mumbled, "Hey."

"Celia?" Mack's deep voice rolled over her like a warm ocean wave. "Are you okay?"

"Oh, Mack." She sat up, cradling the phone against her ear. "I was asleep, that's all."

"Sorry to wake you. This is the least busy time to get the phone."

"No, it's all right. I don't mind. How are you?"

"Good." He hesitated. "Good. How are the kids?"

"Fine. Well…no, really, they're fine."

"What happened?" he asked, with a laugh in his voice.

She explained, glossing over the seriousness of the aquarium disaster. "Ella was cured with a hamburger meal and an ice cream cone. There's nothing ice cream can't fix."

"I've noticed that." There was a silence, tense but not angry. "I hear our change of orders has made it to the news reports."

"You're going to Iraq?"

"That general vicinity, yeah. Just a precaution."

"What are *you* going to do there?"

"Probably just surveillance. Flyovers, reconnaissance. Nothing to worry about."

And yet you called… "I'll pass the word around."

"Great."

Another silence, filled with the crackle of ship-to-shore static. "Celia, I wanted to say—" A burst of noise in the background drowned his voice.

"Mack? I couldn't hear you."

"A bunch of guys just came in. Sorry. Listen, I've thought a lot about—" More static, more background interference. The next word she heard was a curse. "Keep it down—I'm on the phone!"

The response to his demand was even louder. Celia heard him say something that might have been "tomorrow" or "sorry," then "love." Then nothing.

She hung up quickly, in case he tried to reach her again. After an hour, hope faded away.

At least he'd called. He'd wanted to talk, cared enough to hear her voice before he went into danger. That was more encouragement than she'd had in the last month.

Or maybe he was expecting the worst, and didn't want to die without smoothing over that awful fight. Maybe he'd sent his love to the kids. She didn't doubt his devotion to Mack, Jr., Courtney and Ella. Mack might be too rigid in his expectations of M.J., somewhat uncertain about what to do with little girls, but the three of them meant the world to their dad.

If only Celia had the same confidence in his feelings for her. Was he in love with Peyton Abbott? Or just tired of having a wife? When he returned in December—if he returned—would they have a marriage left? Would he continue to stay for the children's sakes? Because she made his life easier? Because a divorce wouldn't look good on his service record? Because the sex between them was always great?

The final question didn't strike Celia until after lunch

the next day, as she rocked a drowsy Ella while the older two rested on their beds. In the middle of what usually passed for peace and quiet in her busy life, she suddenly thought, *Do I want this marriage on those terms?*

Can I live with Mack for the rest of my life, loving him with all my heart yet uncertain if he loves me the same way?

What really scared her was that she didn't know if the answer was yes. Or no.

Granddad and Grandmother Monroe with
M.J., Courtney and Ella
Thanksgiving 1990
Eighty degrees on Thanksgiving Day! We cooked a turkey on the barbecue and swam in the pool—so different from back East.

Mack called again at Thanksgiving. Celia gave each child a chance to talk to Daddy, then took the phone herself.

"How are you?" she asked him.

"Okay. Homesick." He drew an audible breath. "My orders have changed."

From his tone, the news wasn't good. "What now?"

"My squadron's been transferred back to the *Midway* when she relieves the *Independence* next month."

"That means—"

"I'll be staying here. In the Gulf."

"Mack! No!"

"Yeah."

Tears started in her eyes, cooled her cheeks, dripped off her nose and chin. "How long?"

"Not sure. Things are a little unstable over here right now."

"So I hear." From hardly noticing world events, Celia had turned into a news junkie. She couldn't go to sleep at night until she'd checked out the eleven o'clock broadcasts. "You're going to be fighting."

"I don't know. Maybe it'll be just SSDD."

"SSDD?"

"Same…ahem…stuff, different day."

"Oh." She couldn't summon a smile.

"I bought some presents in Singapore. I'll send them for Christmas."

"Don't worry about that."

"I miss you, Celia. Every day."

"Mack. Come home safe. Please."

"I'll do my best. 'Bye."

"Goodbye. I love you," she whispered, but she didn't know if he heard.

Mack, Jr., Courtney and Ella
with their new puppy, Pilot
Christmas, 1990
Since the fish didn't work out too well, we thought about different kinds of pets we might have, and finally decided on the most traditional choice. I saw this little guy at the shelter—all gray but for his white feet, the white tip on his tail and the white blaze between his eyes. He's sweet and the kids adore him. M.J. chose the name, which is perfect.

Operation Desert Storm started on January 16. Celia took the kids and the puppy to Bea's house, where they could run around in the backyard without falling into a pool while the two moms stayed glued to the television.

"I can't believe it." Bea dropped her head in her hands. "There's not supposed to be war anymore."

Celia shivered, though the house wasn't cold. "That's what they train for. They practice all the time for just this possibility."

"Who cares who controls some big sandbox on the other side of the world? I just want my husband back." Bea surged to her feet. "This is the end. I'm not doing this anymore, not putting up with this deployment crap one more time. He's out of the Navy. Or me and the kids are out of here."

"I understand." Jerry might allow Bea to change the course of his life. But Celia didn't want that kind of sacrifice for Mack. She couldn't ask him to choose between his career and his family.

Because she wasn't sure she'd like his decision.

At Bea's request, Celia returned to the Wives Club meetings, where everyone talked about the war. Some husbands had come home on the *Independence* in December, while some, like Mack and Jerry, had not. Celia managed to stay upbeat and confident, encouraging those women who were new to the service. Then she went home, hugged her children and turned on the news. Many of those winter nights found her wide-awake at 2:00 a.m., listening to the California rain, watching endless live broadcasts and wondering if Mack might be flying through those dark foreign skies.

The few letters they received were short—three or four lines to assure them he was okay, working hard, thinking of home. Celia wrote every other day, as always, and sent along the kids' projects. M.J. was getting pretty good at printing his letters, and managed to write a note all by himself every week or so.

As abruptly as it started, Desert Storm ended on the last day of February. The U.S. president claimed victory and Celia, along with Bea and the other wives, waited impatiently for news that the squadron was coming home. They'd done their job, hadn't they?

"Have you heard anything?" Bea had brought her boys over to play in the pool, but the sunny March afternoon had turned chilly, so they'd put a Disney tape in the VCR for the kids and retreated to the dining room with cups of tea.

"I haven't had any kind of letter for over two weeks." Celia held her mug with both hands. "Do you think they're okay?"

"The Navy would let us know if something had happened." She sighed. "I think."

"You hear stories…"

"I know. Sometimes men are missing, and they call them dead. Or vice versa. Sometimes they just don't know. If the plane goes down somewhere they don't want to admit…"

"I can't stand the thought of Mack as a POW. I'd rather he was dead."

"Yeah, I know what you mean."

They stared at each other with tears running down their faces. Bea reached across the table and caught her hand. "It'll be okay, Celia. We'll be okay."

She nodded. "I just keep thinking about that argument. We were in this room…"

"You know he's forgotten about that. Mack'll be so glad to see you when he comes home."

"If he comes home."

"When."

"Oh, I hope so."

From the front hallway came the distinctive clank of the mail slot opening and the rustle of letters falling through. "Mommy, the mail's here," M.J. called. The five children scrambled into the hall, racing to gather the most envelopes, to be the fastest delivering their collection of junk mail to the dining room.

"Trash, trash, bill, bill, bill, trash." Celia sighed as she sorted. "No good news today."

Ella toddled in last, unconcerned with winning any kind of race. She laid a single envelope facedown in front of Celia and then made her way back to the television.

"Another bill," Celia said. "A big one, judging by the thickness." When she looked at the front of the envelope, she gasped. "It's from Mack!"

"Excellent!" Bea pumped her arm in the air.

Celia's fingers shook as she opened the seal. The contents came out as a single packet—a plain white envelope with a flap front. She whispered the first thought that occurred to her. "A divorce notice."

Bea came around the table. "Don't be ridiculous." Grabbing the packet, she turned it over and opened the flap, then unfolded the papers within. Her jaw dropped, her eyes went round. "Oh, my God."

Celia hid her face in her hands. "What? What is it?"

Bea waited until she looked up again. "You're going to Hawaii, woman. You are going to Hawaii!"

Map of the Island of Oahu
This map shows the different roads Mack and I traveled, the beaches we visited and the places we went sightseeing. The postcards are perfect pictures, but I like the snapshots I took with Mack in them much better! The pressed flowers are an orchid and a gardenia from the leis Mack gave me in Hawaii.

Mack stood in the reception area of the airport, watching Celia's plane taxi to the gate. Inside his chest, his heart pounded in double time. He couldn't breathe, couldn't swallow past the lump in his throat. The orchids on the lei he held were going to disintegrate if he couldn't keep his hands still. Celia would find him frozen on the spot, with flakes of white orchids puddled at his feet.

He hadn't been this scared streaking through a night sky over Baghdad with Iraqi mortar shells bursting right outside his cockpit.

"Ladies and gentlemen, passengers on Flight 1564 from Los Angeles are now arriving at gate B43. Aloha and welcome."

She would be one of the first people off the plane—he'd sent a first class ticket. Mack loosened his grip on the lei, saw that he'd bent one of the orchid petals, and spent a second trying to smooth it out.

"Mack?"

He dropped the flowers. "Celia." Cupping his hands around her face, he wiped at her tears with his thumbs. "Oh, Celia." She was so beautiful, with her big brown eyes, her smooth tanned skin, that full, soft mouth….

Her taste was what he'd dreamed about all those lonely months—honey and cream, a swirl of butterscotch, the bite of fine old brandy. One kiss and he was drunk, knocked off his feet. His knees would buckle any minute.

"Mack." She pulled back, and he saw she'd blushed a dark rose. "Um…should we get my suitcase?"

"Sure." He shook his head, trying to sober up. "Sure." He'd brought something with him, right? Something to give her?

"Uh-oh." Under their feet lay a mass of crumpled orchids.

"How beautiful." Celia crouched to pick up the lei, gazing up at him. "Was this for me?"

"Yeah." He put a hand under her elbow to steady her as she stood. "I'll get you another one. They're everywhere here."

"I see that." She dropped most of the broken blossoms in a nearby trash can, but kept one and tucked it behind her ear. "So, show me Hawaii."

The practical details of securing luggage and a rental car restored Mack's sense of control. By the time they wheeled out of the airport in the convertible Mustang he'd reserved, he remembered all his plans for the week.

First things first, though. "Kids okay?"

Celia pulled her blowing hair back from her face. "They're great. Mom and Dad have made so many plans for things to do while they're in San Diego, I don't think M.J., Courtney and Ella will even notice I'm gone."

"Sure they will. Nobody's as good at anything as Mom." He didn't mean to be critical, but he saw the quick glance she gave him.

"How was your flight?"

"I slept," she said, with a guilty grin. "The whole way."

"You didn't get any of the first-class food? No free drinks?"

"I'll be sure to try out all the frills on the way back. It's just—"

He held up a hand. "You don't have to explain, honey. It's okay. Better than okay, in fact. I don't know that we'll be getting a lot of sleep while we're here."

Out of the corner of his eye, he saw her shift in the seat, crossing and recrossing her legs. Just that little hint of anticipation revved his personal engine past the red line.

This trip wasn't about sex, though. It was about romance. Mack had sworn to himself he wouldn't rush Celia into bed, even if the waiting killed him—which seemed likely, after eight months at sea.

When he stopped the car in front of the pink walls of the Royal Hawaiian Hotel, Celia gasped. "We're staying here?"

"We sure are." Mack hopped out of the Mustang and

opened the trunk for the porter. "You think you'll be comfortable enough?"

They stepped into the lobby, where Celia gave another gasp, staring at the marble floors and the rich carpets, the arches and woodwork and plants, the sheer majesty of the place.

"I've never imagined staying in a hotel like this," she whispered.

He put his hand lightly on her shoulder. "Do you want to see the room? Or we can walk out to the beach for your first look at the Hawaiian Ocean."

She searched his face, and Mack kept his need tamped down where it wouldn't show. "What do you want to do?"

"I want to hold your hand, for the first time in eight months. Anything else is up to you."

Lacing her fingers with his, Celia smiled. "Let's see this ocean."

They took off their shoes at the edge of the lawn and stepped down into the warm Hawaiian sand, then turned to walk ankle-deep in water as warm as a baby's bottle, according to Celia.

"How would you know?" Mack teased. "You didn't make bottles."

"I have friends who made bottles," she said, pretending to be miffed. "After California's freezing water, I just can't believe how warm this feels."

Two hours later, they'd admired the view of Diamond Head and the wonders of Waikiki Beach, sipped mai tais at the bar and visited a few of the hotel's gift shops.

Celia muffled a huge yawn. "It's 11:00 p.m. at home. I'm usually asleep by now."

"A nap might be a good idea." Mack turned toward the elevators. "I made late dinner reservations, just in case." In case they hadn't gotten out of bed yet.

He had a chance to study his wife as they rode up to their floor with two other couples. "You look terrific, Celia," he said, once he'd shut the door on the outside world. "Are you still walking at the park with Bea and the kids?"

"Courtney rides her tricycle now, so Ella sits in the stroller. I feel so much lighter, I'm starting to jog the whole route."

Inside their room, she turned a full circle, gazing at the sheer luxury. "This is breathtaking, Mack. And we have an ocean view!" On the lanai outside their sliding glass windows, she leaned back against the rail. "Hawaii is the most perfect place I can imagine."

Mack let himself relax. "I'm glad. You deserve perfection."

"Hardly." She chuckled. "But I'll take what I can get."

"Champagne?" He turned to the ice bucket, determined to do this right, even with desire clawing at his insides.

"Not right now, thanks. I think I'll take a bath." She pulled a robe from her suitcase and went to the bathroom door. "Pink towels, pink sheets…isn't that wonderful?"

As the water pounded in the tub, Mack dropped face-down on the huge bed. Celia's bath could last until it was time to dress for dinner. Then they'd do some dancing, maybe walk on the beach again. And he would shrivel up like a winter carrot if he had to wait until midnight to make love to his wife.

He should go for a run, work off some energy. He must have jogged a thousand miles around the deck of the *Independence* and the *Midway* in the last few months.

In the bathroom, the faucet shut off. "Mack? Can you come here a minute?"

He took a deep breath. "Sure." Swallowing hard, he turned the door handle and peered into the flower-scented steam. All he could see of Celia was her face above an ocean of bubbles. "What do you need?"

She held out a hand. "You."

After a frozen second, he pulled his shirt over his head with one swift tug. "Babe, you got me." His shorts joined his shirt on the pink tile floor. Then he stepped into the giant tub.

The water was warmer than the ocean, but not nearly as hot as his hands, sliding over Celia's slick curves. Not as hot as the kisses she gave him, the burn of her nails scraping his back. Not scalding like his blood when finally—finally—her body surrounded his and the climax rolled over them like a lava flow, molten and bright. Mack wouldn't have been surprised to see the water surrounding them boil.

Later, he brought the champagne into the bathroom and they watched through the window over the tub as darkness draped the ocean. The bubbles around them dispersed and the water cooled. With Celia sitting in front of him, her back to his chest, her head pillowed on his shoulder, Mack felt her shiver.

"We should dry off, get you warm." He checked his watch. "We've got forty minutes to dress for dinner."

A huge yawn ambushed her. "Are you hungry?"

"Aren't you?"

"Mmm." Slowly, gracefully, she pulled herself out of the tub, wrapped up in a big pink towel and wandered through the door. Mack followed, taking time to dry off and drape a towel around his waist.

In the bedroom, Celia had pulled back the covers and curled up on the rosy sheets. She held out both arms, and Mack went to sit down beside her.

"Do you really want to go out?" Her palms caressed his shoulders, stroked his biceps, his pecs, his ribs.

The fire in his belly leaped to life. "I'm at your disposal, lady."

"Oh, good." She untucked his towel, and her own. "Then come to bed."

Mack and Celia at Diamond Head
March 26, 1991
Our first full day in Hawaii.
I loved the tropical print shirts and straw hats Mack bought for us. We hiked up the trail very early in the morning to see the sunrise over Waikiki. The most amazing view—it was like watching the birth of the world!

After a gigantic breakfast, they spent the morning at the Diamond Head volcanic crater and the afternoon in the neighborhoods of Mo'ili'ili and Ka'imuki in east

Honolulu, where Celia bought souvenirs for her parents and the children. She and Mack talked about what they saw and heard and ate, what they'd learned about Hawaii. Nothing serious—past or present or future—disturbed the day.

In the small silences, Celia thought she should bring up the fight, make an apology or ask for one, somehow resolve the issue. But Mack never let those pauses get too long, and before she'd worked up the courage to talk, he would bring up a funny shipboard tale or point out some exotic sight she shouldn't miss.

And so Celia let go of her fears, forgot her anxiety. She practically forgot her own children; she would never have suspected she could go for so long without thinking of them. The world belonged to her and to Mack, and all they had to consider was which pleasure to try next. In and out of bed.

On the second day, they went to Pearl Harbor and spent hours on the *Arizona* and on the *Bowfin* submarine, followed by a late-afternoon swim on the private beach at the Royal Hawaiian and dinner at the famous Surf Restaurant. Thursday, Mack drove them to Hanauma Bay for snorkeling. They didn't see any whales. Friday took them to the north side of the island, where they toured a pineapple plantation and tried surfing on the big wave beaches. Mack could actually stand on his board. Celia used hers as a lounge chair in the sand. Over the weekend, they saw the historic sites of Honolulu, including Celia's favorite, the Foster Botanic Gardens.

Monday arrived too soon—her last full day on the

island. Her last day with Mack. He'd be flying to Japan, the *Midway*'s home port, until his squadron transferred to the *Carl Vinson* at the end of April. He'd only be gone four more weeks. To Celia, that seemed like forever.

But she refused to let sadness shadow the day. They did more shopping, more swimming, more lovemaking. And in the evening, they walked to the lawn of the hotel for a brilliant spectacle to end her vacation—the Royal Hawaiian Luau.

"Unbelievable," she said, still awestruck, when they returned to their room late that night. "The dancers, the drummers… And that magnificent food! I've never seen such a buffet in all my life." She fingered the chain of gardenia blossoms around her shoulders. "This is a beautiful lei, Mack. You didn't have to get me a special one."

"Sure I did." He folded his arms around her from behind and kissed the top of her head. "You deserve the best."

"I've got the best." Turning in his hold, she put her arms around his waist. "I love you."

"I love you, too." With one finger, he tipped her chin up for a kiss. And another…

Afterward, he pulled her close to his side and gave a big sigh. "These last eight months have been hell," he said drowsily. "I'm so glad you're back on my side." In another minute, his breathing deepened into sleep.

Just like that, they were back on the same side. No discussion, no negotiation. Maybe war did that to you—emphasized what was really important, reminded you how trivial most of your troubles were. A few nights at the club—even if Peyton Abbott was there—didn't really matter when you might not see each other again for months. Or at all.

Still, Celia couldn't relax. She lay wide-awake, stiff to the point of trembling, afraid to move in case she woke Mack up. She couldn't share what she was feeling, wouldn't burden him with a situation he couldn't change.

But she dreaded the thought of going home. Hated the prospect of night after night alone in an empty bed. Though she loved her children dearly, she didn't want to raise them without Mack. She didn't want to be their sole source of entertainment, the arbiter of their fights, the maker of peace, the only person they could turn to.

This was the job she'd signed on for, of course. She'd married Mack knowing he would be away…knowing she was pregnant and there would be children for whom she would be responsible. Six years later, it was way too late to change her mind.

So she wept silently, until her eyes burned and her lungs ached. In the morning, she managed to say goodbye to Mack without clinging too much.

A few hours later, she greeted the kids and her parents with all the love and enthusiasm she could muster, hiding from everyone how trapped she felt in her own life.

Chapter 11

Jacob Andrew Butler, One Week Old
Born October 26, 1991
It's a little hard to see the tiny baby at the center of all that medical equipment. Jake made his appearance eight weeks early and spent a month in the incubator letting his lungs develop. This was the first day his mom felt like smiling into a camera.

As Celia walked toward the front of the house, a car door slammed out on the driveway. She met Bea in the front hall. They'd long ago discarded the formality of knocking on each other's doors.

"Hey, come on in. I just made some fresh tea."

"Sounds great. Kidlets asleep? I left mine with Jerry, who's probably asleep by now, too."

"M.J.'s reading on his bed. Everybody else is napping, even Jake."

"He's so quiet, for a six-week-old. Especially a boy."

"I know. It worries me a little." Celia led the way to the kitchen and stepped on the pedal of the garbage can lid. "I wish he'd be crankier."

"What's that you're throwing away?" Bea pointed to the foil packets in Celia's hands.

"What do they look like?" She dropped all but one in the trash and held up the wrapped condom for her friend to see. "Does the word Trojan give you a hint?"

"Why would you do such a thing?"

"Well, I can't fill them with glitter and hang them on the Christmas tree, now can I?" The last packet fell into the can. "No more babies for me, remember?" Her labor with Jake had gone terribly wrong, and by the time the doctor decided on a C-section, her womb had been too damaged to be saved.

Bea shook her head. "Are you all right?"

Celia shrugged as she took down two glasses. "Sure. Four kids is more than enough to move cross-country every couple of years." And be a single parent to when their dad was six thousand miles away.

"Three's too many, as far as I'm concerned. Which is why…" The other woman took a deep breath. "Which is why Jerry's resigning his commission. We're getting out."

"Oh, Bea." Tears sprang to Celia's eyes. She turned around to find her friend's cheeks wet, as well. Arms around each other's shoulders, they cried together.

"This is silly." Celia handed Bea a clean dish towel and

got one for herself. "You're not going to another planet. We can talk on the phone all the time." She put ice in the glasses and poured the tea, then led the way into the dining room, where they sat with a plate of miniature pumpkin muffins on the table between them. "Where do you think you'll go?"

"Jerry wants to go work with his dad, in San Jose, up near San Francisco. Mr. Fiedler got in on the bottom floor with one of those new personal computer companies, and thinks the business will be really big. Since Jerry's been working with computers for years as a flight officer, the job shouldn't give him any problems."

"That sounds wonderful. You'll be able to drive into San Francisco for dinner. Or go to Napa Valley for the weekend."

"If Nana Fiedler will keep the kids." Bea stared down at her glass. "Now that it's happening, I'm not sure. I hate leaving you here by yourself."

Seeing her friend start to worry, Celia pulled herself together. "You won't be that far away. The kids and I can drive up this summer. Mack's going to fighter school in January, and then he'll leave with the *Kitty Hawk* in April. We'll come visit and stay until you're sick of us."

To her relief, Bea laughed. "That'll take quite a while." Then she sobered. "Another cruise? He hasn't been home a year yet."

"The Gulf War skewed the schedule." She got up to pour more tea. "Mack says things should slow down again."

"I've never seen anything slow about the way Mack

operates. When do *you* get a chance to choose which way to go?"

Not even to Bea had Celia confessed her reservations about the life she led. "I'm behind Mack's career choices a hundred percent."

Bea blew a raspberry. "I know that. But you deserve some equal consideration. What do you want to do? Besides take care of his children?"

"I'm fine. I'm satisfied."

"You never wanted to do anything else with your life but be married to Mack?"

"Did you?"

"I never wanted to be married to Mack." They laughed together. "Yes, I do want something else."

"What is it?"

After a moment, Bea said, "I want to write books."

"Really?" Celia sat down again. "What kind of books?"

"Romances," she said, in a low voice. "Historical romances."

"That's terrific. Have you started a story? Have you finished one?"

"I've started. I've been writing in the mornings, after Jerry goes to work and before the kids get all wound up. But I'm hoping to get a babysitter, if the money in San Jose is as good as Jerry says it will be. Then I'll write for hours." She stretched her arms over her head. "Hours and hours of time to write. Won't that be lovely?"

Celia encouraged Bea to talk about her stories and her dreams, partially to keep the conversation away from her own life. Her career was Mack's career, and she didn't expect to do anything else until he retired from the Navy. So there was no sense in thinking about what she *might* do.

For the next twenty to thirty years, at least.

Mack and Celia in front of Tiffany's Jewelers
Our Tenth Anniversary
May 1995
A long weekend, just the two of us, in New York City! Mack made all the plans in secret, so I didn't know about the trip until Mom and Dad showed up at the door on Thursday morning to take care of the kids! I kept these ticket stubs from A Chorus Line and a program from the symphony concert we attended at the Lincoln Center, plus a matchbook from the jazz club we enjoyed. In between, we walked miles and miles of sidewalks, trying to see as much of the "Big Apple" as we could!

"I still can't believe this." Saturday afternoon, Celia stepped into their hotel suite ahead of Mack and went to put her shopping bags on the sofa. "A room—no, two rooms!—at the Waldorf Astoria. It's a dream come true!" Slipping off her shoes, she sat down beside the bags. "And my feet are so tired."

Mack shut the door and came across to add the bags he'd carried to the pile. "We've walked half of Manhattan, I think. Shopping in New York is a serious undertaking."

"Shopping at FAO Schwartz is definitely serious." Celia peeked into one of the bags. "I hope M.J. likes this computer game."

"If it makes noise and has flashing pictures, he'll love it."

"I know Courtney will love the doll house. And the ballerina bear is perfect for Ella."

"Yes, and Jake will enjoy the puzzles." Mack took her hands and pulled Celia up, away from the toys. "We've bought presents for your parents, and William and the Fiedlers, and they're all going to be very pleased. So now let's get back to pleasing ourselves."

She pressed her body against his and linked her arms around his neck. "And just how should we do that?" Standing on tiptoe, she touched her mouth to his for a kiss.

"Mmm." Mack took that kiss, and several more, with great enthusiasm. Then he drew back. "That's one way, definitely. But I have a different plan in mind for right now."

"Really?"

"A plan which, I have to say, involves putting your shoes on again."

Celia winced. "More museums?"

He shook his head. "Nope."

"More food?"

"Not until our reservations for Le Cirque at eight."

"So where are we going that I have to put shoes on?"

"You'll see. But you don't have to walk. This time, we'll take a cab."

That cab deposited them on a street corner right across from Central Park. Celia gazed around as Mack leaned down to pay the driver. "Look, there's Bergdorf Goodman. And the Plaza Hotel. And FAO Schwartz again." When he straightened up, she asked, "Do we need more toys?"

"You're looking in the wrong direction." With a hand on her waist, he turned her to face the stores nearest where they stood. "I thought we ought to do some shopping here."

When she saw where he was heading, Celia stopped in her tracks. "Tiffany's?" she squeaked.

Mack grinned. "Tiffany's."

They browsed all the sparkling jewelry cases on the first floor, and visited the upper stories to marvel at china, crystal and silver. When they returned to the elevator, Mack hit the second-floor button.

"What's on the second floor?"

The door slid open, and he ushered her out with a single word. "Diamonds."

An hour later, a dazed Celia climbed into another cab for the ride back to the Waldorf. She stretched out her left arm, gazing at the ring on her third finger. "Oh, Mack. It's so beautiful." The gold band she'd worn since their wedding now nestled against a platinum-set, square-cut, one-carat diamond ring. "I'm speechless." She sniffed. "And ready to cry. This is just too much."

He put his arm around her shoulders and kissed her hair. "You're my wife, Celia. You deserve the very best I can give. These last couple of years have been tough, moving from California to Norfolk to Rhode Island, leaving your friends over and over again, putting up with too many deployments, too much schoolwork. And I can't promise it will get a lot better. But when you look at that ring, I want you to remember how much I love you."

Her tears overflowed then, and they had to ask the cab

driver for a few tissues from the box he had on the front seat. Back in the hotel suite, Celia drifted into the bedroom. Thinking she might need some time alone to recover, Mack worked on making a neater arrangement of their parcels.

Then she called out from the other room. "Mack? Can you come here a second?"

"Sure." In the bedroom, Celia had pulled the drapes closed against the afternoon sunlight. The pink-shaded bedside lamps created a soft glow in the dimness.

And his beautiful wife lay on the soft beige sheets, wearing nothing but a one-carat diamond ring. She held out that hand to him. "I love you, too, Mack Butler. Come let me show you how much."

The maître d' at Le Cirque Restaurant was not pleased to receive a call at 7:30 canceling the Butlers' 8:00 p.m. dinner reservation.

The Butler Brood
Christmas 1997
*I don't know why I dressed us all in red wool sweaters,
since we were living in Florida at the time. But see what
a cute Christmas card we made!*

"When does Dad get in?" M.J. poured himself another bowl of cereal to soak up the milk left over from the first.

"About noon, I think. Courtney, will you tie Ella's shoe, please?"

"Can I go with you, Mom?" Mack, Jr. spoke through

a mouthful of cereal flakes. "We're not doing anything in school today."

Celia looked at her son and raised a skeptical eyebrow. "The middle of November in the sixth grade, and you're not doing anything?"

"We're not, either." Courtney settled into her chair at the table. "I can go, too."

"Neither of you is going, because you both have to be at your desks in your classrooms."

"But Mom, it's no fair Jake gets to go and we don't. Daddy's been away forever."

"Y'all have gone to the landing field plenty of times. You'll be home from school at three and can spend all afternoon and evening with your dad." Unless he stayed to finish up his duties, as he had the last couple of deployments out of Norfolk. That was why, he said, he'd been promoted to squadron executive officer.

Please, Mack. Not this time. After six months of single parenting, she was never sure if the next crisis—the next argument, the next whine—would be the one that drove her over the edge.

She went to the door of the family room. "Jake, come eat breakfast. We have to take everybody to school."

Her "vacation baby," a sturdy six-year-old, nodded but didn't move. He sat eighteen inches from the TV screen, transfixed by a cooking show.

"Jake, son, you need to eat." Celia put her hands under his arms and lifted him to his feet. "M.J. and Courtney can't be late." Jake hated to be rushed. He needed three or four hours in the morning to really wake up.

But today she didn't have that kind of time. Taking his hand, she pulled him toward the kitchen. "Daddy's coming home today, Jake, and there's a lot to do."

"If I stayed home, I could help," M.J. offered.

"Me, too," his sister said. "Ellie, keep your leg still so I can tie your shoe."

"Me, three." Ella continued to swing her foot back and forth, until Courtney got fed up and slapped it, causing Ella to break into gusty sobs. "She hit me."

"Because you're not cooperating." Celia mopped up the milk M.J. had sloshed, plus the milk Jake dribbled between the cereal bowl and the edge of the table. Pilot, good dog that he was, would take care of any drips on the floor. "Be still, Ella, please. You don't want me to have to stop and tie that shoe."

Sucking her thumb, Ella allowed her sister to finish the task. Jake had finished only half of his cornflakes by the time the other kids were ready to leave.

"You can eat these in the car." Celia handed him a plastic sandwich bag of dry flakes. "Let's hit the road, guys!"

After a damp, cold winter in Norfolk and two more in Rhode Island, the mild weather in Jacksonville, Florida still surprised and delighted her. She hadn't needed more than a light sweater in the mornings, so far. By afternoon, everyone walked around in their shirtsleeves, enjoying the sunshine and the soft breeze. Florida was as green as California had been dry. Celia thought she could enjoy living here for a long time to come. If she got the chance.

The kids crawled into their usual spots in the minivan, and Courtney helped Jake buckle into his car seat.

"Thanks, sweetie." Celia smiled at her eldest daughter through the rearview mirror. Courtney had become quite the helper since starting school. Several nights a week, she volunteered to clean up after dinner while Celia took care of Jake. Even Mack couldn't be depended on for that.

"You think Dad will come to practice this afternoon?" M.J. had allowed Mack to persuade him to give baseball a try this year. "That would be so cool."

"I'll mention it when I see him." Their first stop was the elementary school, where Courtney and Ella got out. "Have a great day, girls. Love you!"

They waved and hurried up the walk, just as the warning bell rang.

"I'm gonna be late, Mom." M.J. leaned forward, as if he could make the car go faster. "Hurry."

"I think I told you that about half an hour ago when you were arguing with me about going to the airfield." Fortunately, the middle school was only a few blocks farther. Celia didn't bother to park at the curb, but simply stopped at the corner. "Here you go."

"Get Dad to pick me up, okay?"

"I'll try. Love you." She didn't get even a wave from her fast-growing son. But he made it inside the building before the bell rang.

"Whew." She relaxed back against the seat for a few seconds. "Now it's just you and me, babe."

Jake gave her his slow smile from the back seat. He never said much, though he had a pretty good vocabulary. She'd had him tested last summer, and the results had shown Jake to be working below his age group, but making progress. She might try to put him in kindergarten next fall.

"First, the cleaners," she told him. "Then the hardware store and the supermarket. Gotta have something for Daddy's welcome home lunch. And a big dinner tonight."

Her plan was to drop off the groceries, the dry cleaning and the garden supplies at home before driving to the naval air station to watch the squadron fly in. But she finished her errands at 11:15 and realized she barely had time to make the noon landing. Mayport Naval Station was all the way across the county from their neighborhood. Even if she didn't stop at the house first, she'd probably be late.

Being late meant parking a long way from the hangar. Jake couldn't be hurried, unless she carried him. And though he was small for his age, he wasn't a lightweight.

As usual, though, the planes were late, and she stood at the back of the crowd, holding Jake on one hip and hoping the ice cream in the trunk wouldn't melt too much.

All at once, a formation of jets swooped toward them, partnered by the huge roar of the engines. Jake laughed and pointed at the planes. "Daddy. Daddy!"

Celia shook her head. How many times had she lived through this scene? Ships launched and docked, planes took off and landed… Her life with Mack seemed to be a never-ending parade of hellos and goodbyes.

The squadron flew in, the band played and the families cheered as pilots and crews hopped down to the tarmac. Matt's group was one of the last to land. The crush of people had thinned, so Celia and Jake were able to move close to the rope holding back the crowd.

"Mack!" He heard her voice, then saw her wave. A big grin broke out on his face and he jogged in their direction.

"Jakester!" Lifting the boy out of Celia's arms, Mack gave him a big hug, then turned to his wife. "Hi, gorgeous. How are you?"

"Much better, now." She put her arms around his neck and stood on tiptoe. "Welcome home."

"Not quite home yet." Mack bent his head and kissed her, searching for the real welcome in Celia's soft mouth.

In the first second of contact her lips warmed, responding with the passion he knew she could give. "That's right," Mack murmured, with one more quick, gentle kiss. "Now I'm home."

Smiling and blushing, she stepped back so Mack could heft Jake in the curve of his arm. "This boy is growing," he declared, heading toward the hangar. "I bet you can see him get taller every single day."

"Just about." Celia walked beside him. "M.J. really is shooting up like a weed. He's gone through two sizes of pants and shoes since you left."

"My guess is he eats enough for at least three people, too."

"I gather you and your brothers went through the same thing?"

"We did. I think we drank half a gallon of milk a day."

Before Celia could answer, they entered the hangar, where the squadron commander immediately hailed him. "Butler!"

"Yes, sir!"

Commander Wilson smiled at Celia and gave Jake a light punch on the shoulder. "That's a good boy, there."

"Yes, sir."

With the social niceties observed, his boss got back to business. "Before you leave, Mack, we need all the flight reports filed, leave requests processed and the flight schedule for the next two weeks approved."

"Yes, sir."

Having pushed most of his own work onto Mack's desk, the commander nodded at Celia before strolling away to put an arm around his wife and walk her toward the parking lot.

Mack expected the disappointment he saw when he turned back to face Celia. "Don't worry, I anticipated this happening. I don't have much more to do—got most of it done ahead of time."

She dragged in a deep breath. "M.J. and the girls wanted to see you as soon as they got home from school. And Mack, Jr. wants you to come to ball practice. I'd planned lunch…." She pressed her hand against her lips, as if to physically stop herself from complaining.

"I'm sorry, honey. I'd intended to come straight home." He cupped a hand around her neck and pulled her close for another kiss. "But it'll be quicker if I grab something to eat here. I should be finished by three o'clock, no problem. I've got a leave request submitted, so I'll be doing us a favor by getting them into the system."

"Right." She nodded, and reached over to take Jake back. "That sounds good."

The stiff set of her shoulders, the straight line of her back, told him she wasn't appeased. "We could get some lunch," he offered, trying to compromise. "Then I'll come back to work."

"No, that's okay." The bright smile didn't reach her eyes. "Jake and I will go home and we'll see you when you get done. M.J.'s practice is at 4:30."

"I'll be there before 3:00, guaranteed."

Famous last words. Between the corrections needed on the paperwork, people to track down over lunch hour and signatures to wait for, he didn't pull into the driveway until almost four o'clock.

The kids assaulted him as soon as he opened the door. With a chorus of "Welcome home, Daddy," they wrestled him to the couch and buried him in hugs, each one trying to give him six months of news at the same time. Mack laughed and hugged back and tried to listen to everything.

Celia stood at the doorway into the dining room, smiling as she watched the frenzy. "M.J., you've got practice in fifteen minutes."

M.J. jumped to his feet. "Are you coming, Dad? Can you come, please?"

"We can all go. Just let me get out of the uniform."

"All right!" M.J. raced off to his room. Mack eased out from under Courtney, Ella and Jake and headed to the other end of the hallway. His first surprise was that Celia didn't follow him to their bedroom. His second surprise was the room itself.

"Celia?"

She did come when he called her. "What do you think?"

Standing under a new ceiling light, he pivoted in place, viewing the moss-green walls, the unfamiliar green-and-yellow-striped curtains, the modern furniture he'd never seen before. "Wow. You made some changes."

"Do you like it?"

"I—I…sure. It's a nice room." Not *their* room, where he'd been imagining them together for the last six months, on the bed they'd slept in since they got married. "Really nice." Feeling like a trespasser, he walked to the closet and opened the door.

"Wow," he said again. "Major organization." Coated wire shelves and rods had been fitted against the walls like pieces of a puzzle, with clothes hanging or folded into each space.

Celia came up behind him. "It's so much easier to keep things neat this way. The kids' clothes and toys aren't all over the place anymore."

"You did their rooms, too? Sounds expensive."

"Not too bad. Kathy Flagg and I did the installation."

He looked at her over his shoulder. "You did?"

"A couple of electric screwdrivers, a level and a measuring tape—we had a good time."

"That's great." He pulled out a shirt he did recognize, and a pair of jeans. "Why didn't you mention all this in your letters?"

She avoided his gaze. "I, um, guess I didn't think you'd be interested."

He unbuttoned his uniform shirt with fingers that shook. "Since when wouldn't I be interested in whatever you were doing at home while I was gone?"

Her hand fluttered in dismissal. "It's just a few closets, Mack."

"What else haven't you told me?"

"Nothing!" She walked to the window and stared out into the backyard. "I can't write down every minute of the day. You don't."

"You hear pretty much everything I do that's not classified."

"I can't believe your life on ship is so dull."

Mack put a hand on her shoulder and turned her to face him. "Believe it, honey. For six months I sleep, I eat, I play cards, read books. I fly. And I count the hours until I can walk across the tarmac and see your beautiful face, hold you close, feel your mouth on mine."

Now she stared at him, her eyes wide, her lips parted. "Oh, Mack. I can't believe—"

He closed his arms around her waist and pulled her hard against him. "What?"

"After more than ten years…four kids…all the separations…"

"I'm still crazy about you, Celia. I still want you." He reached up to touch the diamond on her finger. "Remember?"

Smiling, she lifted her face. "Why don't you remind me?"

"My pleasure." He stroked his lips across hers, then came back for a longer taste, settled in for a real kiss….

"Mom? Dad?" M.J.'s footsteps sounded in the hall, headed for their room. "We gotta go! Practice starts in five minutes!"

Mack groaned, pulling back. "I can't believe I'm walking away from you right now."

Celia's smile held the promise he hoped for. "Tonight," she said softly, "neither one of us will be walking away."

As usual, Mack was gone when she woke up the next morning. Celia might have thought the whole delicious night was a dream, except for the gentle aches her body always experienced after a six-month deployment. And there was tonight to look forward to.

She got the older kids off to school and was working with Jake on his verbal exercises when the phone rang. "We'll take a break, Jakey. You need a snack, don't you?"

With the phone clutched between shoulder and ear, she poured a glass of milk and spread peanut butter on graham crackers. "Hi, Mom. What's up?" They'd talked on Sunday.

"Did Mack come home?"

"He sure did. And here's a surprise—he's going to be coaching M.J.'s baseball team."

"That's nice." Her mother sounded distracted, maybe even upset.

"Is everything okay? You guys are still planning to come down for Christmas, right?" The long silence both frightened and prepared her. "Mom?"

"I'm afraid we can't come for Christmas this year. I'll be taking chemotherapy." Celia gasped as her mother finished. "I have breast cancer."

Chapter 12

Mack stayed at work later than necessary that evening, getting some of the next day's tasks finished so he would be free for baseball practice. When he walked into the kitchen just before dinner, he found Celia stirring spaghetti sauce with tears running down her face.

He stopped dead. "What's wrong?"

She jumped, dropping the spoon into the sauce. "Oh, shit. You scared me."

Celia swearing was something else new. "Sorry. What's wrong? Why the tears?" The kids were okay— he'd just sent the older three back to their homework in the living room. Jake was playing with blocks. What had happened?

She used tongs to fish out the spoon and drop it into the sink. Then she got another spoon and started stirring again. Finally, after a deep breath, she said, "My mom has cancer. Breast cancer."

He'd never felt such a bolt of fear, not even facing an Iraqi fighter at twenty thousand feet. "Celia, I'm sorry. Is she very sick?"

"No. She says they caught it early. The doctor is encouraging. He thinks everything will be okay." Her tears dripped into the pot.

Mack took the spoon and set it down on the stovetop, then pulled her into his arms. "That sounds better."

Celia pounded a fist against his shoulder. "Women die of breast cancer, Mack. They die all the time."

He didn't know enough to say anything useful. "Your dad will take care of her."

"He's more scared than she is. I have to go up there."

"Well, sure. I've put in for some leave—"

She stepped back to look in his face. "I have to go now."

"Thanksgiving is two weeks—"

"No, I've already made a reservation to fly out tomorrow afternoon."

Mack backed into a chair at the table and watched her drain the boiling spaghetti into the sink. "With the kids?" That would be at least a thousand dollars worth of plane tickets.

"No, the kids are in school."

"But…" He rubbed a hand over his face. "Who's going to be here with Jake?"

"Kathy said she would keep him during the day. He

won't get his lessons, but she'll talk to him, take him places."

"What about after school? Will M.J., Courtney and Ella go to her house, too?"

"That's too much to ask." A bowl of spaghetti clanked onto the table, followed by the sauce. A plate of garlic bread and a salad joined them. "You'll have to get home by three, three-thirty at the latest. Kids, come to dinner," she called. "Wash your hands first."

"How long," Mack managed to say before the kids came in, "do you think you'll be gone?"

"I have no idea."

Dinner wasn't the time to talk, of course, and then came cleanup, baths, stories, bedtime. Waiting for Celia to take her bath, Mack fell asleep in the recliner while watching the news. He woke up near midnight and went to the bedroom.

She'd left a lamp on, but her side of the bed was dark. Still, it didn't feel as if she was asleep.

He sat down next to her pillow. "We need to talk, babe."

She didn't immediately roll over. "About…?"

"Well, this trip of yours. There are some problems, don't you think?"

"Nothing you can't handle."

Mack put a hand on her shoulder. "Celia, I might get orders to fly to California when I arrive at work tomorrow morning. How can I take care of the kids after school?"

"You can apply for emergency leave."

"If you were the one who was sick, yeah. But not

for my mother-in-law, who has a husband to look after her. Especially not when a third of the squadron is already on leave after deployment. You know that's not the way it works."

"I know I've never asked anything from the Navy in over ten years. Don't you think they owe me some consideration?"

"The military doesn't think in individual terms, Celia. And the needs of the Navy always come first." He hesitated, then said what was on his mind. "And I think the needs of this family ought to come first for you."

She turned over and sat up in one jerky move. "You're accusing me of being selfish?"

"I think you're panicking."

"And why not? This is really serious." When she threw the covers off and stood up, he saw that last night's sexy green gown had been replaced by well-worn flannel pajamas. Not exactly the same message.

He took a deep breath. "I know this is really serious. I remember the feeling of helplessness, the fear. Given time, you get past that."

"You want me to just stay home and let my mother and dad go through this by themselves?"

"They're adults, Celia. They've managed most of their lives without you. Our kids aren't ready to do the same. I'm not ready to manage without you."

"Well, I wouldn't want to inconvenience *you*." She stalked into the bathroom and shut the door with a snap.

Mack swore under his breath and waited for her to come out again. After ten minutes, he walked over and spoke through the panel. "Are you sleeping in the tub, Celia? We need to talk about this."

"What is there to talk about? I'm at your beck and call and that's all there is to it."

"I simply said—"

"You said you didn't want me to go." Without warning, she stepped out of the bathroom, stomped over to the bed and crawled in between the covers again.

After a frustrated minute, Mack turned off the light and stretched out carefully, near the edge, on his side of the bed. "Of course I don't want you to go. You're my wife and I like having you here."

"I'm your housekeeper, babysitter and cook, you mean."

He rolled to face her and punched the mattress with his fist. "Where the hell did that come from? I've never treated you like an employee."

"No, I don't get paid."

"Well, you've been spending money around here like you do. New furniture, closets, now a plane ticket…"

"You resent that I spent money on a plane ticket to see my mother who might be dying?"

"No. Go see your mom for the weekend—we'll manage somehow. But I can't spare you for weeks and weeks, Celia. Life goes on, even when somebody you love dies. And I know that for a fact, if you'll remember."

In the next moment, he heard her sobbing in the dark. "Aw, Celia." He rolled over and pulled her against him. It's okay, honey. It'll be okay."

"I'm…so…scared." After more sobs and hiccups, she said, "This means I might…and the girls…"

He'd already thought about that. "All we can do is live our lives and try to be happy now." Smoothing her hair away from her hot face, he said, "You make me very happy."

The sobs died away, her body relaxed against his and then, without warning, he knew she'd gone to sleep. Bunching the pillow under his head, Mack closed his eyes and started adding by sevens in his head. On the ship, he usually drifted off somewhere around the twenty thousand mark.

Tonight, he was still wide-awake at a million.

Celia arrived at the Jacksonville airport around seven Sunday evening, traipsed through the November darkness to the parking space where she'd left Mack's Camry, and made the forty-five minute drive back to the west side of town without thinking about much of anything. She'd slept on the plane from Maryland, but didn't feel any less tired.

The house was a welcome sight as she pulled into the driveway. Lamps shone in windows of the living room and the girls' bedroom. The porch light glowed by the front door.

Just inside, her children mobbed her with delight.

"You're home! You're home!"

Celia laughed and tried to hug them all at once. "I'm home!"

Mack stood in the doorway to the dining room, leaning against the wall with his arms crossed over his chest, grinning.

"Supper's ready, Mommy." Ella tugged at her shirt. "Let's eat."

"Yeah, let's eat." M.J. jumped over the coffee table and sprinted toward the kitchen, only to be brought up short when Mack caught his T-shirt tail. "This isn't a hurdles race. Walk through the house." He glanced at the girls. "All of you."

Courtney and Ella giggled at each other and tiptoed past him with their hands out as if they held up long skirts.

Jake still stood with his head buried against Celia's waist. "Oh, Jakey, I missed you, too." She picked him up and headed toward the kitchen.

"Looks like you have everything under control," she told Mack. "Not one phone call for help all weekend?"

He cupped her cheek in his hand and leaned down for a kiss, quick but soft. "We did okay. A few minor disasters, but we made a good recovery. Right, Jakester?"

Jake peeked at him from her shoulder and nodded.

"If you've got Jake's approval, you did more than okay." All during her trip, she'd worried about Jake and his routine. Would Mack understand the instructions she'd written down? Would he be patient with Jake's demands? Father and younger son hadn't spent much time together, thanks to the Navy. How would they get along?

Judging from the tales told during dinner, she might as well have stayed four weeks, instead of four days.

"Dad made blueberry pancakes for breakfast Saturday." M.J. attacked the chicken Mack had grilled for dinner. "Then we went to St. Augustine to see the fort. Man, was that cool."

"Friday night we went to the movies," Ella said. "We saw the pirate movie, Mommy. It was so funny, even Jake laughed."

"After church today, we skated on the basketball court at the park and had hot chocolate Daddy made without a mix." Courtney wiped her milk mustache off with her napkin—a point of etiquette Celia had been trying to elicit for months. "And then you came back."

"Sounds like a good time. Did you get your homework done in this whirlwind of fun?"

M.J. waved off the question. "Dad said we had to have our work done and our rooms neat on Friday or we couldn't do anything else this weekend."

"I'll clean up," Mack told her as she started to take her empty plate to the sink. "I know the kids would like your undivided attention for a while."

"Oh. Well…sure. Thanks." Feeling completely re-placeable, Celia went to start the bathwater…in a bathroom so clean she could see herself in the sink.

The kids restored some of her confidence with their story and song requests—the oldest stories, the sweetest songs she'd been using since they were all babies. They still wanted her, even if they didn't exactly need her.

After she'd flicked the night-lights on, she went to find Mack. He was lying stretched out on their bed, wearing a T-shirt and flannel pj bottoms, looking for all the world as if he was asleep.

Too tired for a bath, she pulled on her own flannel

pajamas, brushed her teeth and her hair, then turned off the lamps and got into bed.

Immediately, Mack rolled toward her and slipped his fingers in between hers. "Welcome home." He lifted their joined hands and kissed her knuckles, savoring the coolness of her skin. "How's your mom?"

He heard Celia sigh into the darkness. "Pretty good, actually. She says her doctor is really optimistic, and she doesn't want me to worry. I think she might not even have told me, except for the fact that she's starting chemotherapy and radiation and they can't come here for Christmas."

"We could go up there."

"Probably not. Mom's thinking she might not be feeling so good at that point. But she and Dad have everything planned, practically down to the menus for each week. They don't need my help." Her sniff sounded pitiful. "Neither do you."

"That's bull." Mack shifted on the mattress, trying to find a comfortable position for his tired body. "I'm trashed, after this weekend. Completely trashed."

Now Celia rolled to face him. "What do you mean?"

Confession time. "I mean I managed about three hours of sleep each night, just trying to keep up with the laundry, get the kitchen cleaned up before breakfast, and make some kind of decent lunch for the kids."

"You did?" She sounded pleased.

"The only way I could be sure the house stayed neat was to take them someplace else."

"That does help." She scooted close to his side, resting

her head on his shoulder, her knee on his thigh. "So I'm not dispensable?"

"Hell, no." He tucked her even closer and his left hand found its accustomed place on the curve of her hip. "We survived without you, but just barely. Given a few more days, though…"

Her even breathing told him she wasn't listening anymore. In the space between one breath and the next, Mack realized, Celia had fallen asleep. No wonder… She had to be tired from the emotional stress of the last few days.

As for him, he'd gone way beyond tired four days ago. But he'd surprised himself—and the kids, too, he thought—with his ability to cope. Not just cope, in fact, but succeed. They'd had a good time while Celia was gone. Not as good as if she'd been able to share their adventures, of course. Having Mom around always made things easier.

Still, he'd kept his temper, his patience and his sense of humor. The children had squabbled, but not too much or too often. They'd enjoyed his bedtime stories, and if he didn't have a good singing voice like Celia's, well, there was nothing wrong with a little laughter before you fell asleep.

Smiling, Mack closed his eyes and, for the first time in five days, relaxed completely. He'd done okay, flying solo as the parent-in-charge.

That didn't mean he wasn't damn glad to be turning the job back over to the resident expert!

★ ★ ★

Mack and Celia
at the Williamsburg Inn
for our 13th anniversary
May 22, 1998
Still as elegant, as beautiful as when we were here on our
honeymoon! Williamsburg has expanded, and it's so busy
now—tourists everywhere and all the restaurants full at din-
nertime. But we did have a lovely weekend all by ourselves.

"Two wonderful things about moving back to Norfolk." Celia sighed as she buckled her seat belt.

"What are they?" Mack glanced over with a smile.

"Being closer to my parents." She gestured at the scenery outside the car. "And being close to Williamsburg. It's been such a lovely weekend."

"Yeah. Now back to the real world."

After a silence, she said, "You're sailing in two weeks."

"'Fraid so."

"Once school ends and M.J. passes math and science, can I let him join the swim team again?"

"You're assuming he will pass math and science."

"I've been keeping track of his grades. He's doing okay."

"If you call C's okay. He's smarter than that, Celia. He should be working to his full potential."

"He doesn't like school."

"That's not an excuse. He can't expect to support himself by swimming for a living."

Celia laughed. "I doubt that M.J. looks further ahead

than next week, Mack. He's certainly not thinking about earning a living."

"He's thirteen. He should be. You never know what will happen." Before Celia could answer, Mack continued. "I also think you ought to look into getting Jake into a special-needs school."

She realized she'd clenched her hands into fists, and deliberately relaxed them. "Jake is doing fine at home with me. I think we'll be able to mainstream him in another year or so."

Mack put his palm over hers. "I think you might be too optimistic on that idea, honey."

"Well, then, I can homeschool him. There are programs available for homeschooling kids with special needs. I don't want Jake put into an—an institution."

"That's not what I'm suggesting. There are public and private schools with resources that you'll never have."

"Jake hates being away from home. Being away from me."

"That's another reason to consider a school. Don't you want him to be independent someday? Make his own life?"

She turned her face toward the side window, hiding the tears summoned by that idea. "I'm just trying to get him ready for elementary school. He's not seven yet."

Mack gripped the steering wheel with both hands. He didn't say anything until they reached the Hampton Roads Tunnel. "At least the girls don't make trouble."

"Unless you listen to Courtney and her friends talk about boys constantly, and they're only eleven! They want to dress like they're eighteen, which is even worse. Ella worries me because she's so determined not to gain an ounce. I think she's as driven about a dance career as you were about the Navy."

"Maybe she just doesn't need much food."

"Lettuce for dinner is a little extreme, don't you think? That's the kind of trick an anorexic pulls."

He threw Celia an angry glance. "You think she's anorexic? Why didn't you say something before now?"

"I don't think she's anorexic yet. I've asked her dance teacher to talk to her about good nutrition. I didn't say anything to you because there's never enough time to deal with everything."

"Some things are too important to ignore."

"Well, maybe you should write me in on your appointment calendar at the office, Commander, and we could discuss all the issues with the children."

"Maybe so."

The rest of the trip home passed in silence. When he'd suggested getting away, Mack had hoped a weekend alone together would bring them close enough to talk over some of the problems they'd left behind in Norfolk. Obviously, he'd been wrong.

"I do the best I can," he said quietly, as he turned into their neighborhood. "I'm not gone because I want to be."

Celia didn't answer until he stopped the car in their driveway. Then she gazed at him for a long moment.

"I'm not sure of that," she said finally, with her hand on the door latch. "I'm not sure of that at all."

★ ★ ★

Ella as Clara in
The Nutcracker *Ballet*
December 1999
She was so beautiful—slender like a fairy, so expressive
with her dark eyes and hair, her gorgeous long arms. And
her dancing was flawless. Mack brought flowers for
opening night and we all applauded loudly, including
Grandmother and Granddad Monroe.

Long years of rising early to get the kids ready for
school had broken Celia of the ability to sleep late.
Saturday morning, just like every other day, she was out
of bed by six and in the kitchen. At least now she had
an automatic coffeemaker, which she could set the night
before, so she didn't have to sit at the table, half-awake,
waiting for the coffee to brew.

Today, Mack hadn't even stirred when she left the bed.
He was getting the squadron ready for a new commander, because he would be going to Rhode Island
again, for the advanced program at the Naval War
College. They hadn't told the kids or anyone else yet. Why
spoil the holidays with news of an impending move?

As she stood at the sink, sipping coffee and watching
the redbirds flock to her sunflower seed feeder, Celia
heard a step on the tile floor.

"Morning, Mrs. Butler." Her dad put an arm around
her shoulders and kissed her on the cheek.

"Good morning. Can I pour you some coffee?"

"I'll get it myself. You've got a lot of hungry birds out there. Good thing you don't have a cat."

"No cats. Just one old dog who doesn't care if the birds get fed, as long as he does, too." In his bed in the corner, Pilot cocked an ear and thumped his tail, then went back to sleep.

Celia pulled the remains of yesterday's coffee cake out of the pantry and set it on the table. "We can munch for a while, then I'll start breakfast. Everyone seems to be sleeping in today."

"That was some dance performance last night. Ella makes me real proud."

"She's wonderful, isn't she?"

He nodded. "Reminds me of your mother when she was young. All that grace and elegance."

"I can see that. I'll have to tell Ella—she'll be happy to know she resembles Grandmother Monroe."

Her dad held his mug in both hands and sipped for a few minutes without saying anything. Finally, he set his coffee down and placed his hands flat on the table.

"I have to tell you something, sweetheart."

A bolt of fear struck her chest. "What's wrong?"

"Your mother…" He squeezed his eyes shut for a second. "The cancer has come back."

"Oh, Daddy." Tears rained down Celia's cheeks. She stumbled to the counter for a paper towel. "When?"

"She had her tests in November, and the scans showed tumors in her lungs and bones."

"Oh, my God. What's going to happen?"

"More chemo. Maybe radiation. But sweetheart, I

have to tell you—" Though he cleared his throat, his voice still came out hoarse. "This happened fast. The cancer is very aggressive. The doctors aren't sure…"

Celia dropped her head on her arms and sobbed. After a second, her dad pulled his chair over and put his arms around her. "I'm sorry, Celia. I'm so sorry."

"No, I'm the one who is sorry." She turned and wrapped her arms around his neck. "I should have been there more, should have helped."

"Nobody could change what's happened." He rubbed her back. "We just have to go on and hope for the best. If we're lucky, the chemo will work and life will go back to normal."

They hugged for a long time, then Celia pulled back and wiped her face with the paper towel. "Do you want to tell everybody now?"

Dan Monroe shook his head. "Let's wait until after the holiday. There will be plenty of time."

Celia nodded, and set about making breakfast. She put on a brave front for Mack and the kids, and greeted her mother with a kiss on the cheek, suppressing the urge to cling. Life would go on as usual.

Late that night, though, as she was getting ready for bed, the truth hit her in the face and she gasped.

"Man, am I tired." Mack slid into bed with a groan. "What's wrong? What did you think of?"

Celia turned from her dressing table to face him. She'd told him about her mom's recurrence earlier in the day. "I just remembered…you're going to Rhode Island in February."

"That's right."

"I can't go with you."

Mack sat up in bed. "What are you talking about?"

"I have to stay here, in Virginia. To be with my mom."

He rubbed his face with his fingers. "I understand how you feel. But it's a two-hour trip by plane. If your mom needs you, you can be over here in an afternoon."

"It was bad enough that we had to move the kids in the middle of school last year. Now M.J. has finally settled down and started studying. Courtney is in with a good group of girls. And Ella would be devastated to leave her dance teacher."

"I understand we'll have to deal with all of that. We've done it before."

"Now my mother is sick. Seriously ill, Mack. She might not survive this time."

"Celia—"

"There is no way I can move so far away." She took a deep breath and turned to the mirror, meeting Mack's gaze in the glass.

"The kids and I will come when we can," she said quietly. "But for now, you'll have to go to Rhode Island alone. Because we are staying here."

Chapter 13

*Jake and Celia
in front of their garden
Norfolk, Virginia
Summer 2000
Do we remind you of* American Gothic *with our pitch-
forks?*

*Jake and I planted a full vegetable garden in May—
tomatoes, corn, okra, beans, zucchini, squash, cantaloupe
and watermelon, four different kinds of peppers, eggplants
and cucumbers.*

*Jake did all the weeding and was careful to water when
we went through dry spells, which happened frequently
this summer.*

*We learned to love ratatouille (eggplant stew), watermelon
sherbet and gazpacho.*

Grace Monroe fought hard and lasted much longer than the doctors predicted. Mack made trips back to Norfolk every six weeks or so, to see his family and visit his in-laws.

Early in January of 2001, though, he traveled back for Grace's funeral. The kids were sad, but Celia was resigned.

"She was so tired. I'm glad she doesn't have to struggle anymore."

Dan Monroe seemed like a man lost in a fog. Mack tried to offer help, but Dan shook his head. "I don't know what I'm going to do without Grace. She was everything to me."

Celia closed up the Monroe house in Maryland and moved her father into the guest bedroom in Norfolk. Everybody seemed to accept the situation as permanent. Everybody but Mack.

"I could start looking for a house when I go back to school," he said, a few days after the funeral. "You could be up there by the end of the month."

Celia gazed at him in surprise. "I don't think we can leave in the middle of the school year."

"We have before."

"But the kids are older now. M.J. is on the swim team, and that's the peak of the season. Ella's working on a solo dance for the spring recital—she can't leave before then and start at a new studio. Courtney is committed to the student government, the Junior Honor Society and the Spanish Club."

"Celia—"

"And Dad's not ready to move anywhere. He's going

to need time to adjust before he leaves the life he shared with Mom."

"I didn't think he would come with you. He's got friends of his own. He should stay with them."

"All alone?"

"Well, it's him or me, I guess. The Bachelor Officers' Quarters isn't exactly home sweet home."

"You haven't lost the most important person in your life."

"Just my entire family, Celia. Do you think it doesn't matter whether you and the kids are with me? Do you believe I'm satisfied being alone?"

She gazed at him in silence for a long time. "I'd like to think we matter," she said at last. "But sometimes your needs can't come first, Mack. My dad has asked me to stay around for a while. The children want to finish the school year. We'll join you in the summer."

And so Mack returned to Rhode Island alone. He flew back to Norfolk for Ella's recital and for the swim meet where M.J. got the Most Valuable Swimmer award.

In June, Mack's appointment as commanding officer of a guided missile cruiser came through.

If you're interested, he e-mailed Celia, meet me in Bremerton, Washington. I'll be there for the next couple of years.

The Butler Institute for Advanced Study
Bremerton, Washington
March 2003
I snapped this picture one evening when I walked by the

living room and saw the whole crew buried in books. Mack with his policy manuals, M.J. working on physics, Courtney writing an English paper and Ella struggling with geometry. Even Jake had homework to do for class the next day. Me? I curled up on my bed with Bea's latest book and sailed away to a desert island with a mysterious pirate. We can't all be geniuses!

"No way. No frigging way." M.J. pounded his fist on the kitchen table, scraped back his chair and stood up. "I am not leaving this school the summer before my senior year."

Mack folded his arms over his chest. "I have orders to leave Bremerton and a new assignment in San Diego. The family will be moving. Can you support yourself?"

"I can stay with Tim at his house. His parents won't mind."

"That is an option," Celia said. "We could pay board."

"And miss our son's senior year of high school? I don't think so."

"So instead, *I* miss my senior year. That's a great solution."

"You will have a senior year. You still have friends in San Diego, and you can connect with them again."

"I'm not captain of the swim team in San Diego. And I haven't seen those guys for years. I don't remember them and they don't give a f—a damn about me."

Celia would have scolded her son on his language, but the tension was too high already.

M.J. offered his dad one chance to negotiate. "Can we at least get another dog?" Pilot had died peacefully in his sleep just before they left Virginia. Their Washington landlord adamantly refused to allow pets.

Mack shook his head wearily. "Not a good idea, son. Do you know how many houses we couldn't rent over the years because the owners wouldn't allow dogs? I don't want to go into the San Diego market with that kind of handicap."

"Oh, yeah, right. That's so important."

"We all make sacrifices," Mack began.

"Except you," M.J. retorted. "You get what you want. We go whenever, wherever you get a promotion, and if it tears up our lives, well, that's just too frigging bad. And I'm not doing it anymore. This is my life and I won't let you mess it up one more time." He went outside, slamming the kitchen door behind him. The motor on the Toyota growled and a squeal of tires announced that M.J. had left the premises.

Mack set his elbows on the table and buried his face in his hands. "I guess that's an example of how the other kids will react."

"Courtney has a new boyfriend. Ella's supposed to dance the part of the Sugar Plum Fairy in the *Nutcracker* next Christmas. Jake really likes his school and his teachers." Celia sighed. "They're growing up, Mack. They have their own lives and don't want them interrupted."

He got up and walked to the window, staring out at the rain. "I'm in line to be captain. I'm taking over as executive officer on the *Nimitz*, and 2007 will see me the commanding officer of a carrier. After twenty-two years, I will reach my goal." Turning, he held her gaze across the kitchen. "Am I supposed to give up? Say, 'Aw, forget it. I didn't want it that bad.'? Let the one thing I've worked for my entire life pass by because my kids will be unhappy for a couple of months?"

"The kids have made many moves without complaining, Mack. As I said, they are older now, more protective of their personal choices. You know M.J. was just mad. He'll settle down."

"I'm getting tired of fighting this battle. First, you refuse to accompany me to Rhode Island—"

"There was a good reason, and you know it."

"Then we had an argument over moving to Bremerton, and now another one about San Diego." He started to go outside, but turned back in the doorway. "I am not going to leave my son here alone, like an orphan in someone else's house, just so he can live out some fantasy that the reality won't measure up to, anyway." Mack didn't slam the door quite as hard as M.J. had.

Celia folded her arms on the table and closed her eyes. Mack didn't have the first clue about what being tired really meant. He hadn't tried to keep peace for the last six years, since M.J. became a teenager. He hadn't talked himself hoarse explaining the incomprehensible needs of the Navy to kids who just wanted a predictable, stable life.

A series of rhythmic footsteps and the sound of a jeté announced Ella's arrival. "What's up, Mom?" She performed a series of *pas de chat* hops to the refrigerator, where she pulled out a diet soda.

"You could drink regular soda," Celia said automatically. "You need the calories."

"Don't think so." Ella straddled the chair next to her and sat down by way of a deep plié. "Why are you frazzled?"

"Orders."

Her daughter stared at her for a second. "Another move?" Celia nodded. "Shit." Ella downed half her soda in disgust.

"Ella, don't use that language."

"Sorry. Do we have to move?"

Celia was tempted to soften the blow. But instead, she said, "Yes. Your dad is going to San Diego and we will all go with him."

Ella finished off her drink. "Well, you know, I kinda hate all the rain here, anyway. I'll just audition for the *Nutcracker* in every production between Los Angeles and Mexico." Getting up from her chair, she performed an arabesque to throw her drink bottle in the garbage, and another to kiss Celia on the cheek. "It'll be okay, Mom. We know we have to go, so we don't get too settled, or let the friendships get too deep."

Which was the saddest rationalization Celia had ever heard.

1539 Bougainvillea Drive
Then and Now
Just for fun, we drove through that first neighborhood, up near Miramar, to see if the old house looked the same as when we'd lived there. I don't think it had been painted in the sixteen years between 1989 and 2005—still the same robin's-egg blue, now faded and dirty. Of course, our family has changed radically since those days. Jake hadn't

even been born. M.J., Courtney and Ella were little kids—now they're adults. Mack's getting ready to make captain—is that really silver streaking his hair? As for me, I think I've gained and lost that same twenty pounds at least ten times over the years!

Mack departed on May 9 for his first Pacific cruise as an executive officer, aboard the *Nimitz*.

M.J. moved out of the house on May 10.

"I don't understand," Celia said, as her oldest son toted a duffel bag of clothes and his stereo speakers out to a friend's van. "Why are you doing this?"

"Because it's time. I'm almost twenty years old."

"Yesterday wasn't the time? Tomorrow isn't the time? What's so special about today?"

"Yesterday Dad left. I wasn't going to argue with him about this."

Celia stood on the front step. "That's very brave of you."

M.J. rolled his eyes and threw his duffel into the back of the van. The speakers he placed gently in the back seat.

"What exactly are you planning to do after you move out?"

"Surf. Swim. Live." He passed her on his way back in.

"Eat? Are you planning to do that? Because it takes money, M.J. Do you have a trust fund I don't know about?"

"Hah. That's funny." Emerging from his bedroom, he carried his sound system components. "I got a job, Mom. I'm getting paid."

"What kind of job?"

"I work as a lifeguard and swimming instructor at the

Bay Point Club, up in Mission Beach. I can surf in the morning, work in the afternoons and evenings."

"Six hours of minimum wage is not going to buy much food. What about rent? What about gas and car insurance?"

"I'll work it out, Mom. I won't always be just a lifeguard."

"Considering that you refused to go to college, just what will you be?"

M.J. didn't bother to answer. He turned around at the far end of the sidewalk from where she stood. "I'll give you a call, Mom. And I'll be careful. 'Bye."

Then her son got in the van and was driven away.

Celia remained in shock all day. She couldn't cry, she was so stunned, and she couldn't decide how much to tell Mack in an e-mail. Should she say anything at all? He couldn't—wouldn't—come back to shore. Why upset him with news he could do nothing about?

She did tell her dad, on the phone, and Dan Monroe came charging across the country to "talk some sense into that boy."

"You're supposed to be the man around the house," he said the night M.J. came to dinner. "You're responsible for your mother and sisters, and your brother."

"Come on, Granddad, give it a rest." M.J. looked like a surfer—sun-streaked hair, dark tan and a faraway expression in his eyes. Celia wondered if he was using drugs. "I've heard that since I was in diapers. Nobody here needs me to take care of them. I gotta take care of myself."

Her dad's face flushed, his hands clenched. "What happened to you, son? Where's your sense of family?"

"I grew up. I looked at the life I was living and decided I was tired of getting jerked around. So now I do what I want." M.J. stood, grabbed the last roll out of the basket and kissed Celia's cheek with his mouth full of bread. "See you, Mom. Thanks for dinner. 'Bye, Granddad."

Celia had heard his reasoning before, and wasn't as shocked as her father. She began clearing the table.

"I've never seen anything like it," Dan Monroe said. "You'd think he'd been abused, instead of being given just about anything he could ask for."

"Except roots," Celia said. "I guess he's protecting himself this time. If he's not part of the household, he doesn't have to leave his friends if we move on."

"He'd rather lose his family than his friends?"

"Um…yes. I think so."

Dan Monroe shook his head. "I think I'm glad your mother didn't live to see this day."

Celia lay alone in her big bed that night and thought, *Sometimes I wish I hadn't, either.*

Her dad had no reason to hurry back to the East Coast, and as long as M.J.'s room was empty, Celia was glad he wanted to stay. In September, she left the kids in his care and drove north for a long-postponed visit with Bea Fiedler. Taking the scenic route along the coast, Celia relished the golden hills on her right and the rocky cliffs on her left. She spent the night in Morro Bay, where the big stones stood on the soft sand beach like sentinels waiting for a ship to come in. The sea wind blew through her open window all night long.

In the morning she drove to San Jose, in the heart of Silicon Valley. She knew how much money had been made there—over the years, her family had certainly contributed their fair share to the incomes of computer geeks.

Somehow, though, she hadn't been prepared for the Fiedlers' portion of that wealth. Her friends lived in a huge house made of glass and cedar, overlooking the south end of the valley. The three boys, all as smart as their dad, attended Stanford University.

"Adam and Aaron went into computers, like Jerry." Bea had oil paintings of each boy hanging in her library. "Zachary is headed for medical school, but he hopes to work with computers and surgery, something like that." Pulling Celia to sit down on the leather couch, she kept hold of her hands. "You wear a size two, right?"

Celia laughed. "I wish. I usually wear an eight."

"I can't believe it! What are you doing to stay so thin? You can tell by looking at me, sitting behind a computer all day does not make for skinny hips."

"Nothing special." Celia shrugged. "I tend to exercise when Mack's at sea. Being the one in charge keeps me so busy, I forget to eat."

Bea tilted her head and studied Celia's face. "On the other hand, you don't look happy. What's going on, hon? Why are you sad?"

"Things have been…unsettled. As soon as Mack left, M.J. moved out to share a place with his surfer friends.

He's working, but not making much money. I think Courtney's been taking cash from my wallet to give him."

"I can see why you're worried."

"I don't know if he's doing drugs or not. I ask, he says no. But the lifestyle…" She drew a deep breath. "Courtney just started her freshman year at the University of California, San Diego. She wants to major in business and go to cooking school, so she can open a restaurant." Bea made a funny face, and Celia laughed. "I don't know where it comes from, either. In the meantime, she's taken up with a crowd that wears black clothes and heavy makeup and listens to harsh music about death and depression. She dyed her gorgeous blond hair a dead black color. I hate it. When Mack sees it, he'll have a fit."

"I hate the thought of it, too. She always had beautiful blond curls, like yours."

"Ella admitted to me last week she's been making herself throw up so she won't gain weight. Her dance teacher is always pushing the girls to stay light. I've got an appointment for her with a counselor next week. I will not let her ruin her health, if I have to stick by her every minute of the day."

By now, Bea had leaned closer and put an arm around her shoulders. "How about Jake? How's he doing?"

That's when Celia burst into tears. "Poor Jake. He loved his school in Washington so much, and he just hates the one in San Diego. He was sick to his stomach in the mornings, thinking about going. So I've withdrawn him from the school. He's never going to master math or science, never get to college. But he reads at a sixth-grade level and he understands every word, so I give him books about gardening, about animals, about the kinds of planes his dad flies and how mountains get made. He's completely happy at home, tending the yard and reading books. I don't know what else to do."

Bea let Celia cry herself out. Then she said, "Doesn't Mack have any advice about these issues? He could talk to the kids by e-mail."

Celia started crying again. "That's the biggest problem of them all. I haven't told him any of this yet!"

Celia and Bea at Spa Fiedler
Bea spoiled me to death—gourmet meals, long bubble baths in her gorgeous whirlpool tub, sauna sessions and late afternoon naps by the pool, with a margarita to wake me up for dinner. Her masseuse visited the house…I nearly died from the pleasure. A beauty advisor came over to do manicures and pedicures, and then gave both of us makeup tips. Do I have to go home?

Over the weekend, Bea helped Celia compose an e-mail to Mack explaining what was happening at home. Sunday afternoon they hit Send, then closed the program, turned off the computer and left the room.

"I'll come your way next time." Bea walked with Celia to her Suburban, parked in the six-car garage. "I've got a January deadline and then I'll head south."

"I like the sound of that." Celia gave her friend a hug. "Thanks so much for letting me whine. I really needed someone to listen."

"Anytime. But, Celia, you ought to tell Mack how you feel. He needs to know. You've let him go his own way for twenty years—how's he supposed to change if you don't say what *you* want?"

Without answering, Celia started the engine, waved goodbye and left her friend behind. She stayed in Morro Bay again, and spent a long time on the beach, staring out to sea with the sentinel stones.

She'd reached Los Angeles the next morning when her cell phone rang. "Hi, Ella. What are you up to this morning? It's nine-thirty. You should be in school."

"Mom, are you almost home? We need you to come home, Mom."

"Calm down, honey. Tell me what's wrong."

"M.J. showed up at the house early this morning. He and Granddad had a huge argument. Then Granddad started having trouble breathing. Courtney is driving us to the hospital. He says his chest hurts.

"Mom, I think Granddad's having a heart attack."

After dinner in the officers' wardroom, Mack sat at the desk in his stateroom and turned on his computer. Three months at sea, three to go. He'd really started looking forward to e-mails from Celia and the kids. The girls wrote quite often, and sent pictures of themselves and their activities. Jake sent book reports and garden news. M.J. hadn't written in a couple of months. Whenever Mack asked Celia about that, she always promised in her reply to remind M.J. to e-mail his dad.

Tonight, though…tonight Mack was discovering the

truth. M.J. had left home. Ella had an eating disorder. Courtney had taken up with a bad crowd. Celia had removed Jake from his special school.

A second note added catastrophe to disaster—Celia's dad was in the hospital for tests. The doctors thought he might have had a heart attack. Celia would write again when she knew something definite.

"Terrific. Just great." Mack knocked his head against the bulkhead behind him. "My family is falling apart, and I'm in the middle of the frigging Persian Gulf. Again."

During the last couple of deployments, he'd begun to question whether the rewards of his career were worth the personal price.

He'd convinced himself before. He could again. First, he would write to Celia.

Sorry to hear about your dad—will be hoping he's okay. Try to keep him in CA until I get back. I like the idea of having him there with you.
M.J. made his decision, now he has to live with it. Don't give him extra money. I'll talk to him when I get home. I hope Ella can get some help from the counselor. Maybe she should stop dancing for a while?
Courtney's friends are always temporary. She'll get a new group in a month or two. Try not to worry.
Am sending Jake attached files with pictures of a pod of whales we kept company with for a couple of days in the Pacific. Amazing creatures.
Hope you are taking care of yourself—you tend to forget that when everything else goes crazy. Make sure you eat, get some rest. Wish I could be there to

hold you and see you through. Look at the ring and remember I love you. Mack

With the message sent, he stretched out on his rack and tried to get some sleep. He would have control of the ship tomorrow—and he couldn't afford to be anything less than his sharpest. A moment's distraction could cost lives, end careers.

And Mack simply refused to make a mistake when he'd come within sighting distance of his goal.

Chapter 14

The Butlers Plus Granddad Monroe
Christmas 2005
I decided we should have a formal family portrait done
for the first time ever. The girls and I had fun shopping
for red dresses—even Courtney enjoyed wearing some-
thing besides black for a change. Mack wore his dinner
dress blue formal uniform. Dad and Jake rented tuxes.
Mack, Jr. showed up looking good in his black shirt, tie
and slacks. So here we are, all decked out in our finery
for the holidays.

Only Celia and her dad waited on the pier for the *Nimitz* to arrive in December. Courtney had offered to host Jake and Ella in her dorm room for the day and take them to a concert that night. M.J. probably didn't even know when the ship would be in.

Though Celia regretted her children's absence, her father provided her with details she'd never known about the way the ship prepared for docking, the importance of the tugboats and the skills of the pilot who guided the carrier into San Diego Bay and then the berth at North Island Naval Station.

"They still need real people on the bridge," he said, as the *Nimitz* grew larger on the horizon. "Computers can't do it all. Somewhere there has to be human brains at work."

As usual, Mack appeared after the crowd had thinned. He came toward them with his swinging stride, looking every inch the superior officer in his dress blue uniform. Every two or three feet, he returned yet another salute, from officers and sailors alike. When he reached them, he gave Celia a hard, swift hug, then turned to shake hands with his father-in-law.

"I'm glad to see you looking so well, sir."

Dan Monroe waved the issue away. "A little chest pain, nothing to get excited about. If it hadn't been for the girls, I probably would have gone to bed and forgotten about it."

Celia remembered the anxiety in her dad's eyes while he'd been confined to the hospital, but she didn't mention it. "At least now you're on a cardiologist's patient list, and we can keep you monitored." She hugged his arm against her side. "I can't afford to lose you for a good long time."

Once they got home, about three o'clock, her dad

showed an unexpected sensitivity. "I'm going to lie down for a while. I'll be up again before dinner."

As Dan shut his bedroom door, Mack grinned at Celia. "He obviously remembers what homecomings are about."

She surveyed him from across the living room. "You're looking very trim and fit. You must have spent a lot of time in the weight room."

He walked slowly toward her. "I'm one of the old guys now. I have to work harder so the young ones don't show me up." He leaned down to nuzzle her neck. "Besides, I need to keep in shape for my gorgeous wife, or one of the lieutenants might steal her away."

She leaned back to look up at him. "Are you kidding? I wouldn't settle for anything less than an admiral to replace you."

"Good to hear." He took his time kissing his way across her cheek to her mouth. "I know for a fact all those admirals are too old to do this." Before she could blink, Mack swept her off her feet. Holding her high in his arms, he carried her up to their second-floor bedroom and kicked the door shut.

If Dan Monroe got up for dinner, he cooked and ate by himself.

The papers came across Mack's desk on his first day back at work after the holidays. He took one look at the top sheet and groaned. "No. Please, spare me this."

Commander Peyton Abbott had transferred into the engineering department of the *Nimitz*.

"Sir?" His aide stuck his head through the door. "Did you need something, sir?"

"No, that's okay, Lieutenant. Just talking to myself like old guys do."

The lieutenant grinned. "Yes, sir."

A read-through of Peyton's service record gave Mack no encouragement. The commander had been passed over once for promotion and was coming up for approval a second time. He would be filling out her fitness report aboard the *Nimitz*. If she didn't get promoted to captain, she'd blame him.

Cursing wouldn't change the facts. Mack resolved to be fair, impartial, friendly but distant. There would be no meetings off the ship, no possible spark to ignite gossip. His own promotion was in the pipeline. He would command a carrier within eighteen months. He didn't need any trouble with a woman on the ship.

And Celia didn't deserve to go through that torture again.

Early in February, Mack attended a Hail and Farewell dinner for his squadron at the Miramar Officers Club. He left early, to get some sleep before he went back to the ship at seven.

And, of course, the one person he didn't want to talk to was waiting in the lobby of the club. "Well, if it isn't Captain Butler." Peyton Abbott lounged in a chair in the corner, nearly hidden by a potted plant. "It's been a long time, Mack. How are you?"

She wore her uniform, but her appearance was sloppy, unbefitting an officer and totally unlike the woman he'd known fifteen years ago. Her blond hair revealed a brown line at the part, and her makeup was overdone.

Mack stopped but didn't sit down. "I'm okay. How are you?"

"Good. I'm good." She'd brought her drink with her, and she took a sip. "I guess you've heard—I'm reporting to the *Nimitz*."

"I did hear that."

"We'll be working together again. Only you'll be the XO and I'll be just another wires officer."

"I'm sure you'll do a good job." He turned toward the door.

Peyton followed him outside. "How about a drink, Mack? For old times' sake?"

"We didn't have any old times."

"So let's make some to remember."

In the parking lot, he stopped and faced her. "There's no chance of that, Peyton. You'll be one of my officers on the *Nimitz* and I intend to treat you with the same respect I use with every other officer. That's all there is to it."

She didn't say anything as he walked away, and he thought he'd finally gotten free.

Then he heard heels clicking on the pavement. "You're going back to that corn-fed wife of yours, aren't you? What did she ever do for you that I couldn't? We could have had a spectacular life, Mack Butler—all the way to the Pentagon for both of us. But you wouldn't leave your *Celia*." She made the name sound like vulgar slang.

They were alone in the dark, thank God. And she really did look pathetic, yelling at him across the parking lot with a half-empty glass in her hand and mascara streaks on her cheeks.

Mack swung back around. "As your superior officer, Commander Abbott, I'm notifying you that you are way out of line. Your uniform is disgraceful and your behavior inappropriate. I suggest you go home, sober up and report to work tomorrow morning looking like the professional you are supposed to be. Do you understand?"

"Think you're so high and mighty, don't you?"

"Do you understand me, Commander Abbott?" He stared her down, forcing her to meet his gaze and slowly come to attention.

"Yes, sir."

He nodded once. "Carry on." Peyton saluted, and they went their separate ways.

As far as he was concerned, that settled the issue. He'd laid down the boundaries. Peyton would be a fool to persist in her efforts to entangle him. With any luck, they could both live and work on a ship with five thousand other people and never see each other again.

The letters began arriving about a week later. Computer generated business envelopes addressed to Captain M.C. Butler were layered in with the other correspondence directed to Mack's attention. Inside, a couple of paragraphs from Peyton Abbott, at first casual and friendly, then increasingly more explicit about the relationship she imagined between them.

Out of embarrassment and disgust, out of a desire to make Peyton and her sickness disappear, Mack committed the major mistake of his military career.

He shredded the letters. After a while, he shredded the envelopes without opening them. In April of the next year, he turned over his office on the *Nimitz* to his successor without a single flake of the trash he'd received left for anyone to find.

Change of Command Ceremony
USS Jefferson
May 2007
"Captain Mackenzie Butler accepts command of the aircraft carrier USS Thomas Jefferson *from the retiring commanding officer, Captain T. Chester Maris. Captain Butler graduated from USNA in 1985, earned his Wings of Gold in 1986 and trained as an F/A-18 Hornet pilot. He has logged over 3300 flight hours and 780 carrier landings. His decorations include a Joint Meritorious Service Medal, two Meritorious Service Medals, two Strike Flight Air Medals, two Navy and Marine Corps Commendation Medals and two Navy and Marine Corps Achievement Medals."*
Navy News, *May 1, 2007*

The ceremony passed in a blur. A stiff wind off the water blew into Celia's face, bringing tears to her eyes…as if she'd needed any help. Watching Mack achieve the goal he'd worked for as long as she'd known him left her breathless and dizzy, more terrified than she'd ever been in her whole life. Where would he go from here?

She and the kids posed beside Mack for an endless

stream of photographers, and she had to be proud of the way her children rose to the occasion. No pouts, no sulks, no rolled eyes, even when asked stupid questions. M.J. had worn a suit without argument, Courtney had settled for discreet makeup and Ella had consented to keep her midriff covered at all times. Jake managed not to fidget his tie off until most of the pictures had been taken.

During the reception, she found herself cornered by a reporter from the *Military Times*, who introduced herself as Deb Mason. "So, Mrs. Butler, how does it feel to have your husband take over one of the premier carriers in the U.S. fleet?"

"I'm delighted that Mack has the opportunity to serve the Navy and the country in this new capacity. He's worked long and hard for the honor, and I know he'll be equal to the responsibilities he's taking on."

"What's the secret of the military marriage, Mrs. Butler? How do you cope with absentee spouses, long separations and the ever-present threat of violent death?"

Celia drew upon words she'd rehearsed many times over the years. "You accept your husband or wife's choices because you love them. You make their goals your own. Husband and wife are not separate individuals but a team dedicated to their military commitment and the life that commitment requires."

"Yes, but—"

"I'm sorry." Celia pulled up her best smile. "I'm being signaled by one of my children. Please excuse me." Eyes stretched wide to keep the tears from falling, she walked past the reporter without waiting to be released, and kept walking until she was outside the ballroom in the quiet hall of the O Club.

She needed to get her emotions under control. How could such a great day leave her so unsettled?

"Mom?" Courtney came toward her down the hallway. "Can we leave yet? This is really boring." She wore a sky-blue silk dress with a finesse that even the black hair couldn't diminish. She'd inherited her father's slender build and height, and moved like a model.

"You're so beautiful," Celia said. "And, yes, we need to get home. There's still a lot to do before the party tonight. Corral your brothers and sister. I'll tell your dad we're leaving."

Back in the ballroom, Mack was still talking with the three admirals who'd attended the ceremony. Celia stepped up to his elbow and waited for a break in the conversation…quite a long wait, as it turned out.

Finally, she touched Mack's arm. "The children and I are going home," she said quietly. "The party begins at six, so we'll plan to see you before then?"

He gave her a quick, distracted smile. "Without fail, I'll be home by five." Leaning over, he kissed her cheek. She thought he might say some private word, but he only straightened up and let her go.

Five o'clock turned into five-thirty. "Not too bad," Mack said as he rushed through the kitchen. "I've been later. I'll take a shower, lose the uniform and we'll get this party going."

Celia calmly finished slicing the fruit for drinks, then turned to the oven to remove pans of cocktail meatballs.

As she transferred the balls to a chafing dish, the front doorbell rang. "M.J., can you answer the door?" The big event was under way.

By seven the house was filled with almost everyone they'd ever met in southern California. A live band played out on the pool deck, bartenders served drinks in the living room, the game room and by the pool, and there were food tables in every downstairs room. Mack stood out on the deck, the center of a large group of guys telling tall tales. Many of their wives stayed in the house, examining all the treasures Mack had brought back from his deployments—silk rugs from the Middle East, jade, porcelain and rosewood from Japan, inlaid screens and elaborate kimonos from China, African carvings and masks, Venetian glass, European knickknacks. Celia had spent time typing up cards to identify their treasures so she wouldn't have to act as tour guide, but she still got trapped several times during the evening when someone begged her to explain how Mack had managed to collect such exquisite souvenirs.

Bea and Jerry arrived about eight-thirty. M.J. took their boys down to the game room, Jerry wandered out to find Mack, and Celia led Bea upstairs for a few minutes of private conversation.

"That's quite a crowd," Bea said, as Celia shut the master bedroom door between them and the noise. "I hate to think what your house will look like tomorrow."

"I know." Celia sat sideways on the chair at her dressing table. "I expect we'll just replace the carpet—this one is already worn."

Bea sat on the end of the bed. "So, how's it going? Are you okay?"

Bracing her elbows on the back of the chair, Celia propped her head on her hands. "Do I have a choice?"

"You and Mack aren't doing so good?"

"Oh, we're okay. Just too busy to really connect, these days. Mack's at the ship almost all the time now. He shows up when it's absolutely imperative—high-school graduations, that kind of thing. He's furious with M.J. because he's not in college. He's mad at Courtney because he doesn't like this boy she's dating."

"I saw them together downstairs. He's a little creepy."

"I know. Ella and I call him Terrible Trevor. He plays in a band, really awful music. Ella's grades aren't too good, and all she wants to do is dance, which Mack sees as a waste of time. And Jake…well, his hopes for Jake have never been very high."

"What about you?"

"I…keep doing what needs to be done." Celia watched the light reflecting off her diamond ring. "And I try to remember that we've had plenty of good times. We'll have plenty more. When Mack's not so preoccupied."

Bea nodded. "Jerry says he usually feels like an item on Mack's to-do list these days, something to be checked off and filed away."

"You can't argue with success, though. Mack's dedication has taken him straight to the destination he wanted. He's the first carrier CO in his class."

"Sacrificing other people for your own success isn't anything to be proud of." Bea came over and put her hands on Celia's shoulders. "You and the kids deserve to be first, at least part of the time."

"Maybe when he retires." With an effort, Celia stood up and straightened her dress. A glance in the mirror showed a need for new makeup. "Why don't you go on? I'll fix my face and be down in a couple of minutes."

"Sure, sweetie." Bea slipped out and Celia sat down again to powder and blush and lipstick. She ran a comb through her hair, which loosened the careful layers the salon had created early this morning, but seemed to ease her headache. Once she'd swallowed three aspirin and a glass of water, she felt ready to face the party again.

As she walked to the stairs, she heard someone bouncing on one of the beds. She'd made sure the kids understood the upstairs was off-limits to everyone, even them. Maybe Jake had wanted to escape the noise in his room for a little while. She might cut him some slack.

But she found Jake's room empty, along with M.J.'s and Ella's. Courtney's room was closest to the stairs. As Celia approached, she realized the noise came from there. Without knocking, she twisted the knob and stepped through the doorway.

Inside, on the rumpled pink sheets of her canopy bed, a naked Courtney straddled Terrible Trevor.

"Oh, my God." Waves of heat washed over Celia, followed by cold chills. She thought she would throw up. Or pass out where she stood.

Courtney gasped. "Mom!" She dived for cover.

Trevor swore and jerked the sheet over his nakedness.

Celia stood silent, panting, while her mind screamed.

Mack would kill the boy. He might kill Courtney. He couldn't be allowed to discover this disaster. Not tonight.

"Get out," she told Trevor. "Get out of this house and don't ever come back."

"Mom!"

"If I hear you've been anywhere near Courtney, I'll let my husband come after you."

Trevor's eyes got round. "Yes, ma'am."

"Trevor!"

Courtney reached for him, but he jerked away and sidled out of bed, taking the black clothes on the floor with him into the bathroom Courtney shared with Ella. In less than a minute, Ella's bedroom door shut and Trevor rushed behind Celia down the stairs.

Celia looked at her daughter. "Quite a champion you picked for yourself."

Courtney turned her face away. "Leave me alone."

"Is this the first time?" When Courtney didn't say anything, Celia closed her eyes. "Of course not." The party downstairs sounded like someone else's life, or a TV program in another room. "Get yourself dressed and come downstairs. This is your dad's party and I won't have you spoil it."

Her daughter hunched one shoulder. "Like he cares."

Celia swallowed the impulse to laugh. "Oh, he cares. You'll find out just how much when I tell him what's happened."

Courtney rushed across the room to grab her arm. "You don't have to tell him, Mom. It's just sex."

She looked at her daughter. "Just?"

"Everybody does it. You don't have to tell Daddy."

"Not tonight. Beyond that, I'm making no promises." Turning away from the woman her daughter had become, Celia straightened her shoulders and went downstairs to do her duty…and deceive her husband.

Mack didn't get time to appreciate his accomplishment. The *Jefferson* would deploy on August 3, heading for the Persian Gulf. He had the responsibility of making sure every department, every squadron, was ready. Stabilizing the Middle East had become a never-ending task for the U.S. Navy.

He arrived on the ship each morning around 6:00 a.m., needing an hour of quiet time to organize his agenda for the day. He stayed in his office from seven to seven most days, to give his staff ample access to ask questions or discuss problems. Several evenings a week, he attended meetings with the Pacific Fleet command staff and sometimes, given the situation in the Middle East, the Pentagon. Most nights, he fell asleep as soon as his head hit the pillow.

Tonight, though, he was taking a break. He'd managed to leave the ship at 6:00 p.m. and, short of a terrorist attack, he wasn't going to think about work until six tomorrow morning.

May 22. His twenty-second wedding anniversary. He'd missed so many during deployments, he made a point of celebrating whenever he could. Celia deserved that much.

He'd sent flowers earlier, a big bouquet of roses, lilies and other blooms in yellow and white. Celia had said she didn't want to go out, so they would grill steaks by the pool. He had two bottles of Dom Perignon in the refrigerator and a box on the seat beside him containing her favorite raspberry cheesecake from a restaurant in Coronado Village. He liked having staff he could detail to run errands like that for him, though he tried not to abuse the privilege too often.

The town home they now rented on the south end of the island meant they never crossed the Coronado Bridge unless they needed to go to the hospital in San Diego. Thanks to his flight pay, they had four bedrooms and a house that could host a great party like the one Celia had arranged for his change of command ceremony three weeks ago. Who needed a big lawn to mow, anyway?

He pressed the button on the garage door control and drove into the free space next to Celia's Suburban. M.J.'s Jetta was gone, but Courtney's pink VW Beetle sat out front. Privacy with Celia would have to wait. Nothing new there.

As he set the cheesecake in the refrigerator, the house seemed quieter than normal. The flowers he'd sent were arranged on the dining room table, which was set for two with china, crystal and silver. Celia intended to celebrate, too. Maybe Courtney had gone out in someone else's car.

But when he reached the top of the stairs, he found her bedroom door open. Courtney sat on the bed, a pillow clutched to her chest. It took a moment to realize she looked strange because she wasn't wearing the heavy eye makeup she'd used for the last year, ever since she'd started dating the music guy.

Celia sat on the chair at Courtney's desk, her hands gripped together in her lap. Those white knuckles warned him of trouble.

"What's wrong?" He looked from wife to daughter. "Are you having a fight, or solving a problem?"

"Neither." Celia sounded as if she had a sore throat. She stared at Courtney without saying anything else. Courtney put her face down on the end of the pillow.

After a minute, Mack said, "I'm not good at guessing games. Somebody tell me what's going on here."

Celia said nothing.

Mack walked up to the bed. "Spit it out, Courtney. I'm losing my patience."

She spoke into the pillow.

"No good. Look me in the face and give me the news. Whatever it is, I can take it."

His little girl jerked her head up and skewered him with her gaze. "I'm pregnant, Daddy, okay? I'm going to have a baby!"

Chapter 15

He'd lied. He couldn't take it. No man could bear hearing such words from his nineteen-year-old unmarried daughter.

Mack looked at Celia and found her gaze on him. "Tell me this isn't true."

"Courtney says it is."

Liquid boiled in his belly, spurting fire into his throat and mouth. His heart pounded like a hammer against his ribs. "The father?"

"Trevor," Courtney said.

"Where is he?"

"I don't know."

He took her cell phone off the bedside table and tossed it in front of her. "Call him. Get him over here."

Tears ran down her cheeks. "I tried. I can't find him. His number doesn't work and his friends won't tell me where he is."

"Does he know?"

She nodded, still crying.

Mack turned back to Celia. "Have you tried his parents?"

She shook her head. "I just found out."

"Get me the number. I'll call."

Courtney rose to her knees. "What are you going to say?"

"I'm going to find out if they know what irresponsible scum they have for a son. I'm going to find out where he is. Then I'm going to have him picked up by the police." Turning on his heel, he started out of the room.

"You can't have him arrested," Courtney cried. "He didn't do anything wrong."

Mack stopped in the doorway. "He didn't rape you?" he said, voicing his only hope.

"N-no."

He clenched his fist. "This…it happened more than once?"

"Yes." Celia's voice.

Mack slammed his fist against the door. Once. Twice. Then he went down the steps and walked straight out the front door.

Celia jumped as Mack's punch rammed the door against the wall. The second time, the knob broke through the drywall and stayed stuck in the hole.

Courtney gave a wordless cry and buried her face in the pillow as her father stalked away. All the windows in the house rattled when he slammed the front door. After a second of silence, glass shattered on a tile floor somewhere downstairs.

Celia sat for a few minutes more, gathering her strength. She'd been fearing this announcement since the party, so she hadn't been surprised. Angry, maybe. God could have spared them this particular tragedy. They'd lost two grandmothers and dealt with a learning-disabled son. Wasn't that enough?

Taking a deep breath, she got to her feet and walked to the bed where Courtney lay sobbing. She clicked on the little lamp by her pillow and propped a hip on the edge of the mattress.

"Calm down, honey. Don't make yourself sick." She stroked the slender shoulders, the lithe spine. "We'll get through this, I promise. Just relax, baby. You'll be fine." She petted and soothed until Courtney lay back, sniffling and hiccupping, to have her face wiped with a towel. "You haven't ruined your life, or ours. Be patient and we'll work it out together."

Leaning forward, Celia kissed the dyed-black hair. "I love you." As she left, she jerked the door—pulling the knob out of the wall—and closed it behind her.

Mack came back long after the sun had set. Celia still held the cup of tea she'd made, which had grown cold as she huddled in the living room, waiting for him to return.

"Sorry," he said. "I had to take a walk." He dropped

into the armchair and put his head back. They sat for a long time in silence.

"How could this happen?" he said finally. "Why?"

"She's an adult, Mack. She makes her own choices."

"We taught her to respect herself. Not just to go to bed with any slob she hangs around with."

"I don't think she did that. I think she believes she loves him."

Mack threw her an incredulous, horrified look.

Celia shrugged. "Maybe we don't know him."

"I know he won't take her phone calls. He won't let his friends tell her where he is. Did you get his parents' number?"

When she shook her head, he frowned. "I told you to—"

"I'm not your aide, Mack, and I'm not part of your crew. I'm also not sure calling his parents will be very helpful."

"Why?"

"I've never seen any evidence that they care about Courtney, or their son, for that matter. I invited them to the party, but they didn't attend, or call with regrets. Trevor seems to me to be pretty much on his own."

"Has she been to the doctor?"

"No. She just did a home test."

"Don't those give false positives?"

"She hasn't had a period for two months." Which meant she'd been pregnant at the party. The knowledge didn't do much to assuage Celia's guilt.

"Then there's still time for an abortion."

Once her ears stopped buzzing, she said, "I beg your pardon?"

Across the room, Mack sat up, propped his elbows on his knees and clasped his hands. "I think that's the best option."

"Really?"

He shrugged. "She's too young to be a mother. She's in the middle of college, for God's sake. She made a mistake—she can put it behind her and get on with her life."

"I don't believe what I'm hearing. We're talking about your grandchild."

"We're talking about an accident, not a baby conceived in love and welcomed into the family."

"What about adoption?"

"Then we do have a grandchild…given away to strangers who may or may not be decent parents. Do you want to think of your grandson being abused by his adoptive parents? Your granddaughter working her way through the foster care system?"

"That's not typical."

"Oh, I'm afraid it's all too typical. I think the baby is better off never being born than being brought into a cruel, cold world."

Despite Celia's best intentions, the words slipped out. "You didn't think that about our baby."

"I was a lot younger then. A lot more naive."

The conclusion was inescapable. "You think M.J. was a mistake." Mack didn't answer immediately, and she knew the truth. "You wish I'd…aborted…M.J."

"No. God, no." Mack covered his face with his hands.

"But I don't want my child trapped into marriage, forced to fail when she doesn't deserve to. Is that so wrong?"

When Celia didn't reply, Mack looked over. She sat straight in the chair, knees and ankles pressed together, feet flat on the floor. Her hands cradled the mug in her lap.

"No," she said, barely above a whisper. "Of course not."

That blind gaze scared him. "Look, Celia, I didn't mean anything about you. About us." She got to her feet, and he followed as she went to the kitchen. "I loved you and wanted a life with you. This is about Courtney. Her situation is completely different. The guy doesn't love her."

Celia nodded. "I understand." He put a hand on her arm and she jerked away.

Mack blew out a sharp breath. "You don't understand anything."

"Evidently." She put her mug in the dishwasher and went up the stairs, with him following. In the upper hallway, she opened Courtney's door a crack. Mack could see his daughter curled on her side, sleeping with her cheek pillowed on her hand like the baby she was.

"Where's Ella?" he asked quietly when the door closed. "And Jake?"

"They went to friends' houses for the night." Celia walked to their bedroom and looked back at Mack over her shoulder. "I think you should do the same." Then she shut the door in his face.

Mack returned to the ship and slept in his quarters there. The irony wasn't lost on him—like his father before him, he'd just walked out on his family.

Sure, Celia had told him to go. But the fact was he'd been an absentee husband and father over the years, as surely as his own dad had. Mack had spent his whole career leaving home, expecting his wife and kids to fend for themselves. Why be surprised that all of them had ended up in trouble of one kind or another? Judging by outcomes—and that was the only way he knew to evaluate his performance—he'd failed as a husband and father.

Unlike his old man, however, Mack tried to make amends. Every minute he could steal from preparations for the cruise, he spent at home, watching TV with Jake and Ella, talking to them over jigsaw puzzles or board games. Occasionally M.J. blew through. Courtney stayed in her room almost all the time.

And Celia continued to avoid him. If he arrived in time for supper, she disappeared as soon as the kitchen was cleaned up. Inevitably, he would find her locked inside their bedroom. He wasn't going to try talking to her through a barrier.

But this couldn't go on—they had to work through the situation. He would be leaving with the ship for a two-week training exercise on June 4. At that point, Courtney would be into her fourth month of pregnancy—too far along to have an abortion.

He called Celia from work on the Friday before they sailed. "Don't hang up," he said when she answered. "We have to talk."

She didn't say anything, but he didn't hear a dial tone, either.

"I think you and Courtney and I need to sit down

and figure out where to go from here. She's got to make some decisions. *We* have to make some decisions."

"We'll be here tonight," Celia said. Then the line went dead.

He left work undone and got home before six. M.J. had agreed to take Ella and Jake to the movies.

"They'll be home about nine-thirty." Celia set a platter of sandwiches and a bowl of chips on the kitchen table. "What did you want to say?"

Mack pulled out his usual chair and sat down. "I want to hear what Courtney has to say." He looked at his daughter with the black hair and shadowed brown eyes. "Have you made plans? What are you going to do?"

She shrugged, twisting her hands together. "I don't know."

He met Celia's eyes with his own. "Haven't you talked to her at all?"

"Of course not." She gave him an exasperated look. "You're the only one who knows how to take care of the problems in this family."

He put his hands up in surrender. "Okay, sorry. Courtney, you have to make some choices. You can't just drift along waiting for the situation to resolve itself."

"Like what?"

"Are you going to have the baby? Or do you want an abortion?"

She threw Celia a terrified glance. "Kill the baby?"

"You know it's one of the options," Celia said, her voice low and strained.

"It's not a baby yet," Mack said. "It's a very tiny collection of cells. You wouldn't be destroying a person." He'd researched all the arguments on the Internet, though if he thought about it too closely, the prospect made him sick.

"I can't—" Courtney put her hand to her mouth. "Excuse me."

She made it to the hall bathroom, and they could hear her retching.

"She's sick most of the time." Celia got up and poured a glass of ginger ale. "She spends her days in bed."

He nodded. "Another reason to end the pregnancy. She doesn't have to suffer like this."

Courtney returned and sat down. "Sorry." Her thin fingers played with a sheet of tissue.

Mack put his hand over hers. "You don't have to continue the pregnancy, sweetheart. I know it will be hard, and sad. But sometimes the hardest decision is the right one."

Courtney looked at her mother. "What do you think, Mom?"

Celia took the girl's other hand. "I don't believe abortion is right, Courtney. I couldn't do that in your place. But," she said firmly, when Mack made a protesting noise, "you can make your own decision and I will do my best to accept whatever that is. I will love you regardless of your choice. I'll help you any way I can." Tears welled in her eyes, ran down her cheeks.

Courtney looked at her mother, and at Mack. She closed her eyes and took a deep breath. "I'm sorry, Daddy. I can't end my baby's life. I just can't."

Mack dropped back in his chair, covering his face with his hands. A part of him was relieved. But his greatest emotion was dread.

"Are you going to keep the baby, then?" He dropped his hands to stare at his daughter. "Raise it as a single mother? Or will you marry the worthless bastard who got you pregnant? Given his current attitude, and that of his parents, what kind of father do you think he'll be?"

Now it was Courtney who hid behind her hands. "I don't know."

"Being a parent is tough enough when you're an adult, Courtney, when you know where you're going in life. Do you have any idea what you're getting yourself into, planning to raise a child?"

With her face still shielded, Courtney shook her head.

Mack nodded. "I'm not surprised to see how badly I've screwed up—I had no concept of what it meant to be a good father. But your mother knew what she was doing, and she put all her effort into the job of raising you kids. If she can fail—"

"Daddy!"

He saw Courtney's horrified stare. He heard Celia's gasp, but the pressure of words inside him was too great to be restrained. "If your mother can fail at the most important job in the world, what possible hope do you have of succeeding?"

The USS *Jefferson* left for the training exercise without the CO's wife on the dock to see her off. Ella drove Jake to the pier and they waved to their dad before he went into the control room to get the ship under way.

Celia sat in her bedroom behind a locked door and cried, as she had every day and night since May 22. After all these years, all the troubles she and Mack had weathered together, her marriage had fallen completely apart. And she had no confidence that the pieces could be put back together. Sadly, she took off her diamond ring and locked it in her jewelry box.

Later in the morning, she took Courtney to an obstetrician outside the Navy system. Everything seemed fine, the doctor assured them. Mild exercise would be better for morning sickness than a whole day in bed. Vitamins and a good diet were essential. She talked about adoption options, touched on abortion and said she was glad Courtney had decided against it.

"So many people want babies," she said. "There will be a safe and loving home for yours, if that's what you decide to do."

Celia had tried to contact Trevor's parents, but they were as unconcerned as she'd feared they would be. A friend of Courtney's heard that Trevor had moved up to Los Angeles to pursue a music career. Courtney cried for a few days and then announced that she intended to forget the jerk. As a first step, she invited her girlfriends from high school for a pizza and movie night. Celia stayed in her room, but she could hear the laughter downstairs. Courtney would be okay.

Celia wasn't sure she could say the same. Mack felt that she'd trapped him into marriage. And he blamed her for their problems with Courtney and M.J. and Ella. He'd expected to fail as a parent, he'd said, but he'd also expected her to succeed. From his perspective, she'd failed him as well as their children. How could she stay with a man who was convinced she'd let him down?

Should she leave him? The kids were practically grown; they didn't need their parents living together anymore. These days, half the officers in the fleet seemed to be divorced. What difference would it make if the Butlers followed the trend?

Where would she go? Back East, to live with her dad? She hadn't yet brought herself to tell him what had happened. Was she ready to admit his early doubts about Mack had been justified?

She could settle somewhere totally new, instead, somewhere inland with grass in the yard and tall trees and snow, spring bulbs and fall leaves. The kids could come visit, or maybe Jake would choose to live with her. He wasn't as fond of the beach as the rest.

Wandering through the empty days and the empty house, she knew she ought to find someone to talk to—a therapist, or maybe a lawyer. Bea called, and Celia told her about Courtney. Her friend pretty much guessed the rest.

"You can come to us," she said. "We'll take care of you."

"Maybe," Celia replied, not meaning it. "Maybe I'll do that."

The worst time was late at night, when she normally would have sat down to write Mack a letter. She asked Courtney's doctor for some of the new nonaddictive sleeping medicines, blaming the stress of Mack's absence for her inability to rest. The pills helped her sleep instead of writing letters begging him to forgive her, promising she'd be waiting when he got home.

Assuming, of course, that he cared one way or the other.

She woke up early on the second Sunday of the cruise because no one else in the house, apparently, could hear the phone ring. She rolled over, grumbling. "I'm the only one who can answer the damn phone? Hello? Hello?"

"Hi, Celia. It's Mack."

Suddenly, there wasn't enough air in the room. "Hi."

"I wanted to see how things were going. Everybody okay?"

"Sure. Sure. Fine."

"Good." After a pause, he cleared his throat. "How's Courtney? Did she go to the doctor?"

"Yes. Everything seems fine. She's taking walks, which helps with the sickness."

"Good to hear. She's eating better?"

"Yes, she is."

"Still going to have the baby?"

"Yes, Mack. The doctor says there will be plenty of good parents to adopt."

He didn't answer, but Celia heard his sigh.

Making a major effort, she said, "How's the cruise going?"

"Great. No problems."

"Is it what you imagined, when you thought about being a CO?"

A long minute passed in silence. "I thought I'd be happy," he said. "How funny is that?"

★ ★ ★

The training exercise went flawlessly. The *Jefferson* and crew performed with precision, the pilots knew their stuff and Mack felt comfortable giving his orders to the COs of the other ships. Maybe some of them were older, had been in service longer. He was every bit as good, though. He'd worked his whole life for this job.

They returned to San Diego on a cloudy afternoon, in weather that felt more like March than June, sliding without effort or bumps into the berth at North Island. None of his family appeared on the dock to greet the ship. Not that Mack had expected them. He worked until seven, and was shrugging into his jacket to go for something to eat when his desk phone rang.

The fleet commander asked him if the training cruise had gone well.

"Yes, sir, Admiral Estes, like clockwork. We're ready for the Persian Gulf right now."

The admiral cracked a joke, and Mack laughed. "Yes, sir. We'll wait till you send us in August."

Five minutes later, Mack wasn't laughing. "That's bullshit, sir. I never… I haven't… Can I ask the name of the person making the complaint? I believe I have the right to know my accuser, sir." The answer knocked the breath out of his chest. "Yes, sir, I'll report to the legal department. Thank you, sir. Good night."

Mack set the receiver carefully in the cradle, and only moved when he realized that minutes had passed and he was still staring at his hand on the phone, his mind a total blank.

He didn't consciously decide what to do or where to go. There wasn't really a choice. He had only one refuge, one hope. One place to hide.

Celia opened the door and stared at him in surprise. "Mack! Did you…I mean, I didn't realize you'd be back today."

Standing on the front step with his cap in his hands, Mack gazed past her at the warm lamplight in the living room. He heard Jake's laughter tumble down the stairs, breathed in the scent of *home* and the light fragrance of Celia's perfume. Then he looked up at his beautiful, desirable, indispensable wife.

"Mack?" She put her hand on his arm. "Are you all right?"

He shook his head. "I'm in trouble, Celia. A complaint has been filed…there's an investigation under way. If I lose—and maybe even if I win—that's the end. My career will be over."

Chapter 16

She stared at him as if he spoke a foreign language. "I don't understand. What kind of complaint?"

"Sexual harassment."

Her eyes went round and her jaw dropped in shock. "What did you say?"

Mack looked over his shoulder at a couple walking their dog on the sidewalk thirty feet away. "Can I come in?"

With a quick jerk of her head, Celia stepped back and then closed the door behind them. Mack waited to be invited to sit down.

"Don't be ridiculous. Sit." She waved him into the recliner. "Who would make up something so bizarre?"

His heart warmed, hearing her assume the best of him. "Peyton Abbott."

Celia looked as stunned as he felt. "How could she possibly accuse you of harassment? Have you seen her even once in the last decade?"

"She served in the engineering department of the *Nimitz* while I was XO."

"Oh." Celia wilted back against the sofa cushion. "I see."

"No, dammit, you don't." Mack moved from the recliner to sit on the coffee table right in front of her, clasping his hands between his knees because he wasn't sure she would let him hold hers. "I had nothing to do with the transfer. I made sure she knew I wasn't playing her game. I saw her once or twice on the ship, but we never talked."

"Then how could she have any evidence that a sane person would believe?"

"I don't know."

"Is this some kind of sick revenge fantasy? Because you didn't take her offer?"

"Peyton is more pragmatic than that. Her fitness report came across my desk. Reading her division head's report, and going by his recommendation, I did not approve her for promotion. She'd already been passed over once."

"So she's finished in the Navy? She won't go any higher?"

"Right."

Celia got to her feet and moved to the fireplace, staring down at the empty hearth. "Even if this is revenge on her part, she still needs evidence. Once the Navy sees that there is none, she'll slink away. And you can take off on your carrier with a clean conscience."

"Except for the whole 'appearance of impropriety' issue."

She looked over at him. "What's that?"

Mack scrubbed his face with his hands. "Not only should an officer *avoid* impropriety, but even the *appearance* of impropriety can be damaging."

"Damned if you do or if you don't?"

"More or less. Taking charge of a ship means more than just understanding how the engines work and where the heads are. The crew's confidence is the biggest factor in a successful command. If my crew doesn't believe in me…" He drew a deep breath and let it out again. "I've got five hundred women on the *Jefferson*. Every one of them will now be looking for evidence of harassment. Going into a battle situation with that kind of division in the crew is going to cause trouble."

Celia gazed at him with a troubled expression. "What do you have to do to make this go away?"

"I'm supposed to report to the legal offices tomorrow morning at ten."

"Well, I wish you good luck, Mack. I hope you escape with no damage."

He got slowly to his feet. "That's it? Good luck, have a nice life?"

She crossed her arms and lifted her chin. "What else?"

"You're my wife, Celia. You're supposed to be on my side."

"I have been on your side every day of the last twenty-one years."

"So what's the problem?" When she didn't answer

right away, he pushed. "Celia? Why have you kicked me out of the house?"

For another long moment she stared at him. "As long as we've been married, Mack, you've twisted and turned this family in whatever direction you felt would benefit your career most. You asked us over and over again to sacrifice our friends, our home, our lives for you." She took a deep breath. "I did my best to support you, and the kids followed. But now...now you're blaming me for whatever's gone wrong."

"I said I knew—"

She held up a hand—her left hand. He saw with a pang that the diamond ring wasn't there.

"That's right," she continued. "You said it's not your fault because you were never going to be a good dad in the first place. You can't be responsible for what's happened because you never had a father to learn from."

He tried to focus, to marshal his arguments. "Yeah, well..."

"But it's just an excuse, Mack, another way of blaming your dad for your mistakes. You're the one who's been here, or not, who's lived this life. Your choices, your words, your actions and reactions, shaped the world for Courtney, M.J., Ella, Jake and me. You're the commander of an aircraft carrier. You lead people into battle, sometimes at the cost of their lives. And you've led this family for twenty years. For better or worse, remember?"

A headache pounded behind his eyes all of a sudden.

"If you can't accept that responsibility," Celia continued in a calm, sad voice, "if you can't acknowledge your role in our family's destiny, then I don't see how we can continue to *be* a family any longer."

His temples throbbed and his throat ached. He couldn't think, couldn't begin to process or accept what he'd heard.

"Got it," he said, finally. "Thanks." He stood up and headed for the door. "I'll be on the *Jefferson* if you need me. You can e-mail or call. Tell the kids I'd like to hear from them when they get a chance."

He hoped she might follow him, might ask him to stay. But Celia stood on the other side of the room and didn't say a word.

Mack shut the door behind him and went back to his ship.

The next morning, he walked into the Navy Services Legal Office ten minutes before his appointment. Peyton Abbott sat in a chair in the waiting room.

Hit by the urge to punch a wall—or lose the coffee that was all he'd managed for breakfast—Mack went to the other side of the room and stared out the window at the rear of the building next door, turning his back to Peyton. He thought he might grind his teeth down to nubs before the JAG officer called his name.

"Captain Butler? Commander Abbott? This way, please."

He followed Peyton and the short, thin man ahead of her to a tiny conference room almost filled by a table and chairs. Mack wasn't sure he could share such a tight space with Peyton and maintain his composure.

The JAG officer sat down in front of a file folder.

"Please, take a seat." He rifled through the papers, adjusted his glasses and then looked up. "I'm Lieutenant Commander Petry. This is a preliminary meeting on a complaint filed by Commander Abbott alleging sexual harassment by Captain Butler, who until April 2007 was her superior officer aboard the USS *Nimitz*. Is that correct?"

"Yes." Peyton had pulled herself together for this circus—blond hair pulled smoothly into a knot, her uniform shirt and skirt knife-edge crisp, her makeup flawless.

"Captain?"

"That's what I'm told," Mack said. "I don't have much of a clue about what's going on."

"You have seen Commander Peyton's complaint, correct?"

"No."

Petry looked confused. "I have here a copy of a letter to you from Commander Abbott, recording the complaint."

A knot formed in Mack's belly. "I don't know what you're talking about."

Petry passed a paper across the table. "This copy, sir."

Mack recognized the format—just like all the trashy notes he'd shredded. "I never received that letter."

Petry looked across the table. "Commander?"

She shrugged. "You have the copy," she told the officer. "I made sure I got a signature on delivery—you have the receipt there."

"Yes. Though it's not the captain's signature."

"His aide, Lieutenant Creech, signed for it."

"So, back to you, Captain. You've never seen this letter?"

"I said so."

"Will you read it now?"

Mack skimmed the contents. "Now I've read it."

"Is this your version of events?"

"There are no events." He let his hand drop heavily on the table. "Commander Abbott received a poor fitness report from her superior in the engineering department. I concurred with his assessment and supported his recommendation against promotion. I never spoke to the commander during the time I was stationed on the *Nimitz*."

"Well, actually…" Peyton leaned forward. "We did meet at the club."

"Accidentally and for maybe five minutes, during which *you* harassed *me*."

Petry held up a hand. "It's already apparent that this meeting will not be productive. I had hoped we could negotiate redress for the complaint and let the matter drop. As it is—"

"I can't redress something I didn't do, something I didn't even know about."

"That does appear to be part of the problem." Petry pushed his glasses up on his nose and then closed his file. "I'm going to forward this issue to my superior, who will initiate further investigation and notify you when ready to proceed."

"Proceed?" Mack surged to his feet. "We don't need to proceed. We need to have Commander Peyton—"

"Captain Butler." For such a small guy, Petry could generate a surprisingly big sound. "I suggest you say as little as possible. Speak to the sailor at the desk about securing an attorney to represent you." He nodded without really looking at Mack or Peyton. "Have a good day."

Before Mack could move, he heard Peyton chuckle. "You should have listened, Captain Butler. You should have done what I asked."

"Go to hell," Mack told her, and went out to get himself a lawyer.

On Mack's orders, the *Jefferson* crew was preparing to host an Independence Day celebration, inviting their families aboard for a party and a short evening cruise. Celia had helped him develop the idea before the change of command ceremony, had chosen the invitations and planned the activities for kids and adults alike.

She left her copy of the invitation lying on the kitchen counter, trying to decide whether to throw it away or choose an outfit to wear. Mack had his command—he didn't need her anymore. The facade of a happy family could fall away.

Ella picked up the red-white-and-blue card at dinnertime one night. "Sounds like fun. Have you told M.J.?"

At precisely that moment, Mack, Jr. came through the back door. "Told M.J. what?" His sister handed him the invitation. "I've never been on a carrier. Sounds cool."

Celia stared at them. "Are you serious?"

"Sure." M.J. grabbed a tuna salad sandwich she'd just made. "I'll watch TV until dinner."

Courtney came downstairs when Celia called. It was still a shock to see her belly rounding out. Celia often had to remind herself that she was going to be a grand-mother. Almost as shocking was Courtney's hair; cut severely short, the strands were half blond, half black. With the next trim, the black would disappear.

"Are you going to this party?" Courtney asked, studying the invitation.

"We are," Ella announced as Mack, Jr. and Jake sat down at the table.

"I'm not sure," Celia confessed. "Do you want to go?"

Eyes downcast, Courtney took her chair. "I don't think so."

"It'll be fun, Courtney." Jake poked her in the arm. "We get to ride Daddy's carrier out into the ocean."

She flinched away from him. "I know, Jake. I know." He kept poking, thinking he was being funny. "Leave me alone," she said loudly.

Pouting, Jake turned his shoulder to his sister. "Me and M.J. will go, won't we?"

"You bet, dude."

Celia signaled for silence. "I'll call your dad and let him know you'll be there. But you have to dress well, M.J. No showing up in a wrinkled T-shirt and shorts hanging from your hips."

"Got it."

"No bare stomach," Ella said before Celia could. "Skirt preferred."

"That's right. There will probably be guests aboard, officers your dad needs to impress. You want him to be proud of you."

"We know," the three said, in unison.

After dinner, Celia went up to Courtney's room. "Can we talk?"

Courtney set aside the book she was reading for a summer accounting course. "What's up?"

"You sounded like you wanted to go on the cruise, but felt you couldn't. I'm wondering what you're thinking."

She shrugged, but didn't respond for a minute. "I guess…I'm pretty sure Dad wouldn't want me there."

"You think he's ashamed of you?" Sitting on the side of the bed, Celia took her daughter's hand in both of hers.

"I think he's just plain mad. I'm the reason you two aren't living together, after all."

Celia took a sharp breath. "That's not true, honey. The…distance…between your dad and me has nothing to do with you."

"You were fine until I got pregnant."

Even after two months, Celia found herself fumbling for an explanation. "Our relationship, your dad's and mine, has been like the story of the princess and the pea. Do you remember?"

"A fairy tale, you mean. And I spoiled it."

"No. In our life together, there's always been one pea—very small—in the big picture, something we could hardly see most of the time. All these years, we kept putting mattresses on top of it, layer after layer, and pretending the pea didn't matter."

"What's the pea?"

"Not something you need to worry about. What's happened, though, is that we can't sleep on all those mattresses anymore. The pea is there and we feel it every time we move. To solve the problem, we have to take all the padding off and remove the source of the problem."

"You mean, like marital counseling or something?"

"Maybe. Or maybe just time to get our thoughts together, figure out where to go from here." Celia leaned over to give her daughter a hug. "But whatever happens, you're not the reason. You are not that pea."

Courtney laughed, then sobered. "Still, he wouldn't want his whole crew to know his daughter's knocked up. I just can't go."

Celia was afraid she was right. "Your dad loves you, Courtney." She kissed the smooth cheek. "Me, too."

Mack was still pushing paper around his desk when the phone rang late in the evening. "Captain Butler, USS *Jefferson*. May I help you?"

"You must love answering the phone." It was the last voice he'd expected.

"Celia?" A fist of need and hurt and joy punched him in the gut. "What's wrong?"

"Nothing. Are you busy?"

"No, of course not." He didn't know what to say to his wife, who had called him. Who had called *him*. "What's going on?"

"The kids wanted me to let you know that they would like to attend the Independence Day party and cruise. M.J., Ella and Jake, that is."

"What about Courtney?"

He heard her sigh. "Well, there's a problem with

Courtney. She believes you wouldn't want her to show up pregnant."

"Oh." He thought about that. "It's not my first choice."

"That's not an answer, Mack."

"I know." He leaned back in his chair, rubbing his tired eyes with one hand. "Courtney is my daughter. She's a smart, beautiful girl who made a mistake. Anybody who wants to criticize her is going to answer to me."

"I don't know if she'll believe that coming from me. She may think I coerced you into agreeing."

"I'll handle it." He made a note on his calendar: Lunch with Courtney.

"Well, then. That's good." Now she sounded uneasy. "Um…how's the whole harassment thing going?"

"There's going to be a hearing, lawyers on both sides, her evidence, which is nil, and mine, which is also nil." He blew out a frustrated breath. "Hard to believe you can spend your whole life trying to do the right thing and still get screwed."

"Yes, it is." The reserve in her tone reminded him of all the issues they had yet to resolve.

"So, I'll make sure you and the kids are on the guest list for July Fourth."

She hesitated, then said, "I…um, I haven't decided whether or not I can be there."

A wall could have fallen on top of him, and he'd have been less stunned. "I see." He cleared his throat. "Well, let me know. Last minute will be fine. It's late now. I'd better let you go."

"Okay."

"Take care, Celia."

"You, too."

He started to take the phone from his ear, but heard her say, "Wait. Mack? Are you still there? Wait!"

He slammed the receiver against his ear. "I'm here."

"I changed my mind. I'll be there." She sounded breathless. "For the cruise…and the party. If you don't mind."

He pumped his fist in the air. "I don't mind, honey. I don't mind at all."

Chapter 17

At 5:00 a.m. on Sunday, Mack parked in a public lot at the north end of Ocean Beach. Three other cars had already claimed spots next to the walkway over the dunes. Offshore, he could see dark heads bobbing next to pale surfboards.

A stiff breeze made him hunch into his jacket and wish he'd worn slacks instead of shorts. Only crazy people came to the beach before dawn. Crazy people and surfers.

He didn't know if M.J. had arrived. Hell, his son might not even be here today. Ella had said she thought this would be the best time and place to find him. Ella could be wrong.

Leaving his shoes in the car, Mack crossed to the beach and stood near the waterline. A wave loomed dark over the surfers, with a threatening curl of white on the edge. Two of the three boards upended as the water crashed down. One of them sailed through the tube and toward the shore, its rider balanced and sure. As he got closer, Mack recognized his son.

And M.J. recognized him. Rather than turn around and paddle out to catch another wave, M.J. picked up his board and came to where Mack stood. His dark hair, spiked with saltwater, was surprisingly short. A wet suit covered him from chin to ankles, but his face was lean and tan, his eyes rimmed with the pale ghosts of sunglasses.

"Hey." His gaze wasn't apologetic or embarrassed. "What's going on?" Two dogs raced toward them across the sand, and Mack prepared to be jumped on. But when the mutts arrived, they sat immediately at M.J.'s feet and simply gazed at him, panting in adoration.

"That's a good trick." Mack nodded at the dogs. "Yours?"

"Yeah, Curly's the one with short black hair. Moe is the one with the blond shag."

"Right." He looked out to sea, then back at M.J. "I, uh, thought I'd come out this morning, see what you're up to."

"Just catching a few. Have to go to work in a couple of hours."

"Still lifeguarding?"

M.J. shook his head. "That didn't pay enough. I'm working at North Island, actually, doing maintenance. I work mostly in the buildings used by the SEAL school."

Mack choked back his reaction to the idea of his son

working as a janitor on the naval base. "I suppose next you'll tell me you're applying to the school."

"Not yet. I have to go to college, get a degree. I'm starting at UCSD in the fall."

"Does your mother know?"

"Nah. I just got it all worked out in the last week."

"Were you going to tell us?"

"Well, sure. When I got a chance." Head tilted, he studied Mack's face. "What are you so pissed about?"

After a deep breath, Mack said, "I'm not used to being an afterthought in your life."

"I wouldn't put it that way." He looked over his shoulder. "I've got coffee and bagels in my bag. Let's get something to eat."

The dogs followed as M.J. led the way down the beach. Mack sat on the sand with his son, drinking lukewarm coffee from a plastic cup and eating a cold bagel, watching surfers challenge the sea. There were at least ten boards out there now, though none of their riders seemed to be having much success.

"You're the only one who's gotten a good run so far," Mack said.

"It's tricky," M.J. admitted. "But those guys will get the hang of it. I surf here a lot."

"So, I hear you'll be on board the *Jefferson* on July Fourth."

"Yeah. Sounds like a good time. Okay if I bring a date?"

"Sure." He had to ask. "Somebody special?"

M.J. grinned at him. "Maybe."

"Your mom will be thrilled."

He rolled his eyes, but his grin faded fast. "This thing with you living on the ship, though. It makes her unhappy."

"Me, too. I only left because that's what she wanted."

M.J. drew a stick figure in the sand by his feet. "I know you argued over what's happened with Court. Maybe I had something to do with your fight, as well?" For the first time that morning, Mack caught a glimpse of the little boy he used to know.

"Only indirectly, as part of the family. I've made…more than my share of mistakes, as a husband, as a dad. Your mother is a generous woman, and she's made everything work out right for me, for you kids, all our lives."

"No shit." Mack frowned, and M.J. said, "Sorry."

"This spring, I finally went too far. With all the stresses and responsibilities coming down on her, your mother had to jettison some of the load. That was me."

"Is this permanent? Are you getting…a divorce?"

A question Mack had asked himself a thousand times. "I hope not. Nothing would make me happier than to spend the rest of my days making up to your mom for my mistakes. Maybe we can work it out before the *Jefferson* deploys."

"That gives you—what?—a whole month?"

Mack nodded at the dubious look on his son's face, and felt his own doubts rise to the surface. "You're right. Not too likely, is it?"

As the sun popped over the mountains to the east, M.J. and his dogs walked Mack to his car. "It'll start getting hot now. And the waves will flatten with the heat."

"Sorry. I didn't mean to spoil your morning."

"You didn't. There's always another day."

"Listen, M.J., I—"

His son took a backward step, hands held up in front of him. "You're not going to do the reconciliation thing, are you?"

"I think I owe you an apology, yes."

"Well, consider it said." He clapped Mack on the shoulder. "I needed to grow up, get out on my own. I picked a stupid way to do it, which meant I wasn't as grown up as I thought."

Mack stared at his suddenly adult son.

"Oh, and about those mistakes, Dad? The ones you say you made?" Mack nodded and M.J. shrugged. "You're human, man. You did okay with all of us. Really. So let it go." He walked back to the wooden dune bridge, got to the top, then turned and waved. "I'll see you on the fourth!"

Mack raised his hand, but waited until M.J. disappeared before he wiped his eyes. He was luckier than he deserved.

Please God it wasn't too late to make amends. To his family—and especially to his wife.

Mack picked Courtney up at the UCSD campus on Friday at noon. He had no trouble finding her—she was the only nineteen-year-old who looked pregnant. Cute, in her lime tank top and bright floral skirt. But pregnant.

"Hey, beautiful," he said as she slid into the passenger seat. "I like what you've done with your hair."

She checked the vanity mirror and then stuck her tongue out at him. "Okay, so I look better as a blonde. Eat your hearts out, brunettes."

They chatted about her classes, the weather and the Padres as he drove back toward Coronado Island. When they reached the top of the bridge, Courtney looked around. "Where are we going to eat?"

"It's a surprise," Mack said. A good one, he hoped.

She got quieter as he drove toward the naval piers…and the USS *Jefferson*. When he stopped the car, she didn't get out. Mack walked around and opened the passenger door. "I asked the kitchen staff for something special today. I thought you might like to dine in the officers' wardroom."

She stared at him with wide, frightened eyes. "I don't want to do this, Daddy."

"Are your table manners that bad? I could swear your mother—"

Courtney shook her head. Tear drops flew off her lashes. "It's not funny. You'll be embarrassed. I'll be embarrassed."

"I will not be embarrassed." He crouched down to look up into her face. "You are my smart, lovely daughter. You're going to make a big splash in the restaurant business one day. You made a mistake, and you got caught. It happens to the best of us. Believe me," Mack said, lifting her chin with his fingertips, "I know."

Straightening up, he took her hand and tugged gently. "So, I'd like to take a smart young woman who has recently learned some valuable life lessons into my ship's dining room for lunch. Are you game?"

Her smile was almost as wonderful as her mother's. "I guess I am."

The atmosphere in the wardroom was cordial—his

officers were a great bunch of people, most with daughters of their own. No one brought up the pregnancy, but they asked about Courtney's classes, her plans, her free time activities, and shared their own. Only a few minutes into the meal, Mack knew he could relax.

Once they'd reached the coffee stage, he excused himself for a few minutes to compliment the kitchen staff on the wonderful meal—grilled chicken, potatoes au gratin, spinach salad and strawberry shortcake. Courtney had disappeared when he returned, but he found her in his office, looking at the photos on his desk.

"You can hardly work here for all the pictures." She walked to the bulkhead, where he'd mounted maybe twenty different frames showing the Butler family's progress—individual pictures of all the kids, shots of Celia and kids or himself and kids, or just four kids and a dog.

Courtney grinned at him. "You like us. You really like us."

Her imitation of the Sally Fields quote made him laugh. "Yes, I do." He joined her at the wall. "I wouldn't trade my time with all of you for anything in the world." Taking a risk, he put his arms around her slender shoulders. They hadn't hugged for a long, long time.

He felt her deep sigh. "I won't have pictures of…my baby."

Mack squeezed his eyes shut. "No."

"I won't know where he is or what he's done."

"I'm afraid not."

"I can't stand it, Daddy. I can't."

All at once, she was crying against his chest. His aide

came to the office door with a questioning look. Mack shook his head slightly, and the aide closed the door.

When the sobs quieted, Mack reached to his desk for a tissue. "Do you want to keep the baby, Courtney? If you do, we'll support you, in whatever way we can."

She blew her nose, pulled another tissue for herself and did it again. Then she shook her head. "No. I think he—or she—will be better off with two parents who are ready to take on a baby." A weak smile broke through the tears. "I'm not nearly as mature as you and Mom were when M.J. was born."

One of us, anyway. "You'll know when you're ready. There will be this great guy who knocks you off your feet—"

"Not just knocks me up?" Courtney said, with a rueful laugh.

Mack frowned at her. "And the two of you will start out on this great adventure together. When the time is right, you'll add kids."

"I hope so."

"I know so. Now, I'd better get you home so I can get some work done."

"The captain has to work?"

"That's the theory."

They passed officers and sailors on their way off the ship, and in every case were greeted with respect and good manners.

As he pulled up in front of the house to let her off, he said, "So, do you think you might show up for the party, after all? Your mom said she would come."

"She did?" Courtney's face brightened. "Then, yeah, I think I'll be okay." She got out, closed the door and leaned in the window. "So does this mean you two are working things out?"

Mack held up his crossed fingers. "I'm going to do my best."

She gave him two thumbs-up. "You go, Dad."

The preliminary hearing on Peyton's complaint was set for 4:00 p.m. on Friday, July 1.

The hearing room wasn't fancy—folding chairs and tables, a metal desk at the front for the judge. As Mack settled beside his attorney, he heard the door open. Peyton entered, accompanied by a woman with iron-gray hair, light eyes behind steel-rimmed glasses and no warmth in her expression. Mack's lawyer glanced at her once, smiled, and continued shuffling papers.

The next time the door squeaked, Mack didn't look back. The judge emerged at the same time from a door behind the desk, and took his seat. Mack felt his intestines cramp. What if Peyton bamboozled them all?

"So, we have a charge of sexual harassment, made against Captain Butler, formerly executive officer of the *Nimitz,* now commanding officer of the *Jefferson.*" The judge's voice was slow and deep. "The complainant is Commander Abbott, a member of the engineering department on the *Nimitz.*" He looked over his glasses. "This is correct?"

The lawyers nodded. "Yes, sir."

Elbows propped on the desk, the judge fixed his eyes

on Peyton. "Talk to me, Commander Abbott. What is this harassment you allege?"

She recited the whole insane story, her voice controlled, respectful. Her lawyer made notes, as did Mack's. The judge listened without changing expression.

Mack sat with every muscle in his body clenched, his jaw locked, his face burning. To remain silent, while hearing such lies about himself, required almost more control that he could muster.

"When I joined the *Nimitz,* I told him I didn't want to resume our affair," Peyton said. "He kept pushing, waiting for me in passageways, demanding I come to his office. I continued to refuse, but I was scared."

Mack made a noise, half choke, half laugh. Everyone looked his way. As long as he had their attention…

A hand came to rest on his shoulder, firm but not heavy. He glanced back, into Celia's beautiful brown eyes. She shook her head slightly and gave him a smile. A flash of light caught his eye, and he realized she was wearing the diamond again. *Their* diamond.

Talk about reinforcements. Taking a deep breath, Mack turned back to face the judge. Celia was here, and Peyton's lies couldn't touch him. Celia believed in him. He might lose the command, he might lose the career he'd worked for his whole life. But as long as Celia saw the truth, the Navy—the whole world, for that matter— could go to hell.

After Peyton stopped, the judge made a few notes. Then he turned to Mack.

"Captain Butler, let me hear your side."

Mack got to his feet. "My side is simple, sir. I have never, at any time, treated Commander Abbott with anything but the respect due a fellow officer. I did not contact her in any way while serving on the *Nimitz,* or since. That's all, sir." His lawyer looked up at him in surprise. They had planned a longer statement. But Mack sat down again, satisfied. He'd told the important truth.

The judge wrote again, shuffled papers, flipped through a notebook. At the other table, Peyton conferred with her lawyer. Mack glanced over his shoulder and received another of Celia's smiles.

"Very well." The judge cleared his throat. "I've reviewed the evidence presented by Commander Abbott—a photocopy of her letter notifying the captain of her complaint, statements from *witnesses,*" he emphasized the word in a dubious tone, "and the fitness report in question. I've reviewed Captain Butler's service record, in which no other such complaints have been noted, and talked to the engineering department head on the *Nimitz* during the time period in question. Is there any other evidence offered?"

When no one spoke, he nodded. "Right. Commander Abbott, I have to tell you that this is the most pernicious bundle of nonsense it's been my misfortune to hear. I find no substance in your allegation. Your witnesses based their reports on gossip and hearsay. The only person who has seen or heard any of the events you describe is yourself, which leads me to believe that it all happened in your head."

Peyton's attorney started to rise. "Your Honor, I—"

"I'm speaking." He looked at her over the top of his glasses. "On the other hand, Captain Butler has a spotless reputation and an unblemished record. The officers he's served with, men and women, and the crews who have worked under him have nothing but praise for his integrity.

"In conclusion, I find the allegation of harassment against Captain Butler to be malicious nonsense. I absolve him of any hint of blame and declare him fully fit to command."

Peyton burst into tears.

The judge nodded at Mack. "This hearing is adjourned."

A cheer went up from the back of the room. Mack turned around to see his kids in the back row, whistling and applauding. He blinked hard and turned to offer his thanks to his attorney.

"I didn't do anything. Easiest case I ever handled." He shook Mack's hand and walked away whistling.

Mack turned to Celia. "Thank God."

She gave him her glowing smile. "I never had a moment's doubt."

Then the kids were on top of him, celebrating, teasing, laughing. The six of them moved outside into the sharp afternoon sunlight.

"I think this calls for a celebration," he said to Celia as they walked to the parking lot.

"The hearing?"

He shook his head. "Our family."

They traveled in three different cars to one of the family's favorite restaurants, where the Mexican food was always delicious and they could eat outside. A strolling band played traditional music, accompanied by the splash of a fountain. Mack and Celia ordered margaritas, the kids all had virgin margaritas and their party was the most festive of the afternoon.

As they all walked to the parking lot afterward, carrying several boxes of leftovers home for lunch tomorrow, Celia saw M.J. jog to catch up with his dad. As she unlocked the driver's door of the Suburban, Courtney called from her VW on the opposite side.

"Mom, we're going to a movie."

"It's been a long day," Celia protested. "Why don't we all just go home and relax. You can see a movie tomorrow night." She saw Mack approaching. M.J., on the other hand, had vanished.

"But it's Friday night and they're showing horror flicks, two for ten dollars. Please?"

Celia sent a resigned glance toward the heavens. "If you must. Please be careful. And let me know when you get home."

"Sure thing." Courtney, Jake and Ella piled into the pink VW and puttered off.

"Well." Celia looked around, then at Mack. "Where's your car?"

He leaned one hip against the bumper of the Suburban. "M.J. has a date."

"Oh." Mack looked so good in his white uniform, with the captain's bars on his shoulder boards and the "scrambled eggs"—gold decoration—on the black brim of his cap. After a second, she said, "Well, then, I guess we'll take this car. Do you want to drive?"

"Not necessarily."

She got in the driver's side and started the engine while Mack swung into the passenger seat. He took up quite a bit of room, even in such a big vehicle. He used a lot of the air, too, because she was having trouble breathing. "Do you think we've been set up?"

"Probably."

"Right." When she turned to look over her shoulder while backing up, his arm was there to bump into. "Sorry."

"No problem." He didn't move, and her shoulder rubbed against him as she negotiated the big car out of the parking space.

Distracted by Mack's presence, Celia found herself driving through wooded hills on a long, winding lane that ended in a maze of tile-roofed minimansions.

"My next car will have GPS," she muttered, backing out of a cul-de-sac. "Don't sit there laughing."

"I'm not. After all these years, though, I can't imagine GPS would help that much. You don't usually get lost."

"Actually, I get lost all the time. It's how I learn my way around." Back at the entrance to the neighborhood, she started down the hilly approach road once again.

"Slow down," Mack said. "I saw a pull-off on the side somewhere. Yeah…right there."

The small parking area was actually marked Scenic Overlook. And it certainly was. The entire city lay at their feet glazed with gold by the setting sun. Behind the glowing landscape lay the sapphire velvet of the sea.

"Spectacular." Celia took a deep breath. "And this is the first time I've been here."

"There are always surprises," Mack said. "Like turning around to see you in that hearing today. You made the difference."

She couldn't think of what to say, so she simply enjoyed the view. After a few minutes, she realized Mack wasn't looking at the scenery. He was gazing at her.

Her heart fluttered. "What?"

"Don't you think this is a really good place and time to talk about us?"

Before she could speak, Mack said, "I'm sorry, Celia. So sorry for all the hurt I caused you."

That stopped whatever words she might have found.

"When I married you, I knew you would be a good wife, a great mother. And I was right. You haven't failed, not in any way. I want you to know that. I was…upset…that day."

"I know. It's okay."

He took a deep breath. "And I intended to be a good husband."

"You have been."

"I haven't done enough." He shrugged and looked away. "I haven't acknowledged often enough your strength, your wisdom, your courage. I haven't said how much I depend on you to make the world turn the right way. How grateful I am you've been there for our children when I chose not to be."

"Mack, that's not fair." She put her hand on his cheek and brought his gaze back to hers. "You've balanced career and family as well as any naval officer I've known. Well," she said, smiling, "except for my dad. But he only went as far as commander."

Mack laughed, and she joined him. They laughed until tears ran down their cheeks, then laughed some more.

"You were right." He sighed. "All these years, I used my dad as an excuse to think of myself, my career, first."

"You should have trusted yourself more." Celia looked down at their joined hands. "We've done just fine, working together. Your career gave me the chance to develop my own independence. I wasn't always comfortable doing it, or happy. But I do know that I can handle anything that comes my way, and survive."

Mack stroked two fingers down her cheek. "I wish I could say I'd planned it that way."

"That would be condescending. You needed my help. It's taken me twenty years to realize that. I made things better for you."

"You did. And I should have said thank-you every day."

"We were busy, Mack. Four kids, jets, ships, moves, parents…that's a lot to do. It's enough that we both understand it now."

"I love you, Celia."

"I know. I love you, too."

There wasn't much to say, after all. They rolled down the windows and listened to the night music around them. Traffic sounds came up the hill, but crickets fiddled in the trees around them, muting the noise. The air was warm, the breeze cool.

Mack lifted their joined fingers and kissed each of her knuckles. Then he turned toward her and slipped his free hand into her hair. "You want to make out in the back seat?"

He took her mouth with his, and Celia nearly whimpered at the touch she'd missed so much. Her first impulse was to crawl across the console into his lap. To hell with the back seat…

She drew away. "I think what I'd like most is to go home and lie down together in our marriage bed. What do you think?"

Mack gave her his sexy, devilish grin. "A woman after my own heart."

He paused, then added gently, "The woman of my heart."

Aircraft Carrier USS Jefferson
Independence Day Family Cruise
July 4, 2007
Mack drove the ship out to sea about twenty-five miles while the crew and their families enjoyed a barbecue with all the fixings, plus games, tours, movies and talent shows. As you see, the Butler clan came out in force, wearing red-white-and-blue and looking nearly as happy as I believe we all are right now. The ammunition department set off a fireworks display as we headed home, while the band kept up a concert of patriotic tunes.
We sailed into San Diego singing "God Bless America." And God bless our men and women in the military, wherever they serve.

"Wow." Avery sighed as she closed the scrapbook. "That's a wonderful collection. So many great memories of your parents' life together. And all the good times your family has had."

"Yeah, we've been pretty lucky." Jake put his fingers under Avery's chin and tilted her face up to his. "Maybe you and I can be lucky, too?"

Her eyes sparkled, and she nodded at him. Jake touched his mouth to hers, to kiss her sweet smile.

"Jake? Hey, Jakester?" His brother stood at the top of the stairs, yelling for him. "Come on, man. We're having the official pictures taken."

Rolling his eyes, Jake got to his feet. Avery put the scrapbook on the coffee table and followed him to the living room, where the rest of the family had gathered.

"Come stand beside your sister, Jake." His dad indicated the empty spot between him and Ella, who always posed as if she was taking a bow on stage after a ballet performance. She did a lot of that, performing with a professional dance group up in San Francisco.

Jake stepped into place, keeping Avery in front of him with his hands on her shoulders for moral support. She glanced nervously up at his dad, who grinned at her and nodded. He might be an admiral, but he was still a good guy.

A thump on his head had Jake turning around to look at his brother. "Hey, what's that for?"

"General principles," M.J. said. He wore a Navy uniform, with lots of ribbons on his chest and the SEAL insignia he'd earned a few years ago. They didn't see much of M.J. these days—he was usually in some far-off place on a secret mission. He always brought back some kind of souvenir for Jake, everything from a nugget of African gold to a jar of sand from the Sahara desert.

Beside M.J., Courtney's husband Quinn was holding up their son, two-year-old Danny. Courtney stood in the front row, on the other side of their dad, with her new baby, Maeve, in her arms. The little boy Courtney had given up for adoption lived in Michigan with parents who loved him dearly. That was all the family knew about him, and Courtney believed it was for the best. After working in restaurants for a few years, she and Quinn owned a catering business which was beginning to be a real success. Thanks to today's party, where so many people were tasting the great food they'd provided, they would probably have more business than they could handle.

"Now, if your mother would join us…" his dad murmured to Jake.

Just at that second, she came in from the back of the house. She was still so pretty, laughing at something Aunt Bea had said, with her hair still gold, her skin smooth. When she caught sight of the group of them waiting for her, though, she stopped and clasped her hands in front of her lips. Even from a distance, Jake saw the tears spring to her eyes.

"Oh, my goodness." She blinked hard. "Don't I have the most beautiful family in the world? I am so proud of all of you. And now my makeup will be ruined." Taking the tissue Aunt Bea offered, she dabbed at her eyes. "Let's take this picture before I completely fall apart."

Their dad held out his hand, and she came to him, turning to stand inside the circle of his arm. The photographer took lots of shots, but Jake's favorite always remained the one that caught his mom and dad gazing straight into each other's eyes, the true love between them shining for anyone to see.

Mack's Retirement Party
June 30, 2015
If a picture is worth a thousand words, then this one describes the joys in my life, and my gratitude for all the ways we've been blessed.

★ ★ ★ ★ ★

THE ROYAL HOUSE OF NIROLI
Always passionate, always proud

The richest royal family in the world—united by
blood and passion, torn apart by deceit and desire

Nestled in the azure blue of the Mediterranean Sea, the
majestic island of Niroli has prospered for centuries. The
Fierezza men have worn the crown with passion and
pride since ancient times. But now, as the king's health
declines, and his two sons have been tragically killed, the
crown is in jeopardy.

The clock is ticking—a new heir must be found
before the king is forced to abdicate. By royal decree the
internationally scattered members of the Fierezza family
are summoned to claim their destiny. But any person
who takes the throne must do so according to The Rules
of the Royal House of Niroli. Soon secrets and rivalries
emerge as the descendents of this ancient royal line vie
for position and power. Only a true Fierezza can become
ruler—a person dedicated to their country, their
people…and their eternal love!

Each month starting in July 2007,
Harlequin Presents is delighted to bring you
an exciting installment from
THE ROYAL HOUSE OF NIROLI,
in which you can follow the epic search
for the true Nirolian king.
Eight heirs, eight romances, eight fantastic stories!

Here's your chance to enjoy a sneak preview of the
first book delivered to you by royal decree…

Five minutes later she was standing immobile in front of the study's window, her original purpose of coming in forgotten, as she stared in shocked horror at the envelope she was holding. Waves of heat followed by icy chill surged through her body. She could hardly see the address now through her blurred vision, but the crest on its left-hand front corner stood out, its royal crest, followed by the address: HRH Prince Marco of Niroli...

She didn't hear Marco's key in the apartment door, she didn't even hear him calling out her name. Her shock was so great that nothing could penetrate it. It encased her in a kind of bubble, which only concentrated the torment of what she was suffering and branded it on her brain so that it could never be forgotten. It was only finally pierced by the sudden opening of the study door as Marco walked in.

"Welcome home, *Your Highness*. I suppose I ought to curtsy." She waited, praying that he would laugh and tell her that she had got it all wrong, that the envelope she was holding, addressing him as Prince Marco of Niroli, was some silly mistake. But like a tiny candle flame shivering vulnerably in the dark, her hope trembled fearfully. And then the look in Marco's eyes extinguished it as cruelly as a hand placed callously over a dying person's face to stem their last breath.

"Give that to me," he demanded, taking the envelope from her.

"It's too late, Marco," Emily told him brokenly. "I know the truth now…." She dug her teeth in her lower lip to try to force back her own pain.

"You had no right to go through my desk," Marco shot back at her furiously, full of loathing at being caught off-guard and forced into a position in which he was in the wrong, making him determined to find something he could accuse Emily of. "I trusted you…."

Emily could hardly believe what she was hearing. "No, you didn't trust me, Marco, and you didn't trust me because you knew that I couldn't trust you. And you knew that because you're a liar, and liars don't trust people because they know that they themselves cannot be trusted." She not only felt sick, she also felt as though she could hardly breathe. "You are Prince Marco of Niroli…. How could you not tell me who you are and still live with me as intimately as we have lived together?" she demanded brokenly.

"Stop being so ridiculously dramatic," Marco demanded fiercely. "You are making too much of the situation."

"*Too much?*" Emily almost screamed the words at him. "When were you going to tell me, Marco? Perhaps you just planned to walk away without telling me anything? After all, what do my feelings matter to you?"

"Of course they matter." Marco stopped her sharply. "And it was in part to protect them, and you, that I decided not to inform you when my grandfather first announced that he intended to step down from the throne and hand it on to me."

"To protect me?" Emily nearly choked on her fury. "Hand on the throne? No wonder you told me when you first took me to bed that all you wanted was sex. You *knew* that was the only kind of relationship there could ever be between us! You *knew* that one day you would be Niroli's king. No doubt you are expected to marry a princess. Is she picked out for you already, your *royal* bride?"

Look for
**THE FUTURE KING'S
PREGNANT MISTRESS**
*by Penny Jordan
in July 2007, from Harlequin Presents,
available wherever books are sold.*